SOLDIER

THE GUARDIANS OF TIME · BOOK THREE

SOLDIER

THE GUARDIANS OF TIME · BOOK THREE

VIVIENNE LEE FRASER

www.viviennelfraser.com.au

Copyright © 2021 Vivienne Lee Fraser
All rights reserved.

First published in Australia 2021 by Vivienne Lee Fraser

The right of Vivienne Lee Fraser to be identified as the author of this work has been asserted by her under the *Copyright Amendment (Moral Rights) Act 2000.*

This is a work of fiction. Names, characters, businesses, places, events and incidents are either the products of the author's imagination or used in a fictitious manner. Any resemblance to actual persons living or dead, or actual events, is purely coincidental.

This work is copyright. Apart from any use as permitted under the *Copyright Act 1968,* no part of this publication may be reproduced, stored in a retrieval system, recorded or transmitted in any form or by any means, electronic, mechanical, photocopying, recording or otherwise, without the prior written permission of the publisher.

Vivienne Lee Fraser
www.viviennelfraser.com.au

Cataloguing-in-Publication details are available
from the National Library of Australia
www.trove.nla.gov.au
ISBN: 978-0-6488860-4-4

Formatting and cover design by KILA Designs
www.kiladesigns.com.au

I wrote this book for Stan.
He has appeared along with my dad in all the
Time Guardian Books, but this one really is for him.

It is also for Sandy (and not just because she always checks my work for me) and Margot. They are the only two people who read my first ever book, and they may enjoy the elements that made it into this story.

PROLOGUE
GUARDIAN CITY
TO THE RIGHT OF HISTORY

Beta entered the room using a door out of respect for the inhabitants. Time Wreckers—oops, World Fixers—didn't lose their corporeal body when they ascended out of time, so just popping into the room would be rude. Alpha, however, had no such qualms. He appeared beside Beta.

'What are they doing?' Alpha whispered.

Beta moved a little further into the room before he spoke. 'I don't know. Why don't we ask them?' He raised his voice a little before he added, 'Good Morning, Gerald, Cynthia. Welcome to Guardian City.'

The man and the woman seated at the conference table both raised their heads almost as one. Beta noted that they might not have given up their bodies, but they had used their magical powers to smooth away any signs of ageing.

For the benefit of their guests, he had taken on the form of the man he was when he joined the Time Guardians. Their guests would see a middle-aged man with a full beard and sparkling blue eyes. He tried to hide his slightly rounded figure with loose chinos and a polo shirt. Alpha, forever the showman, had ascended when he was well into his eighties, but today he was a slim, dapper twenty-year-old dressed in jeans and a T-shirt.

Cynthia flicked her auburn hair aside, revealing cat-green eyes, and she smiled. Gerald, who would not have been out of place at a sixties poetry reading, ignored them and lower ed his head back to whatever they were studying, his floppy black fringe hiding his pale thin face.

'Thank you for having us here. This is an... unusual situation, but I am sure we can work on this little project together for a short time without too much stress,' Cynthia said.

Her smile warmed what was left of Beta's heart and he responded with, 'I hope your accommodation is suitable, and I will show you our other amenities a little later. I am just waiting for coffee and tea to arrive, then we shall begin.'

While Beta played the part of the host, Alpha took a seat across from Gerald and glared at the World Fixer, emanating dislike from every pore.

'What are you doing?' Alpha demanded.

Beta bristled at his colleague's tone, but it didn't seem to bother Gerald, who responded by ignoring the question.

As Beta took a seat at a right angle to Alpha, carefully avoiding a seating arrangement that might appear confrontational, Cynthia began speaking.

'Gerald is doing what we all do every day, trying to stop the end of time.'

'How, specifically?' Beta asked.

'By studying events leading up to the last world war, trying to identify for the millionth time if we could change anything to prevent the utter devastation that followed,' Cynthia responded.

Alpha grunted his displeasure, but Beta spoke before the other being was able to say anything too insulting. 'We can't help with anything along those lines as it goes against our philosophy.'

Cynthia nodded as if this was no more than she expected. 'We understand, but the point is moot since we didn't find anything that would help. We thought a review might start us thinking of ways to support our operatives on the ground. Have you managed to make contact yet?'

'We spoke with Theta yesterday their time when she managed to slip out of the underground city for a while. Their cover is all set, and it seems they will be taking part in the search for the boy causing the blip in the time map,' Beta said before waving at a screen, which flickered a little before showing their timeline monitoring room. About thirty operatives sat around a screen watching coloured lines.

'What are they searching for?' Cynthia asked.

'A red blip.' Beta answered. 'When something deviates from history, a red blip appears and we send someone to investigate. If further action is required, we send down a team.'

'BETA!' Alpha's voice rumbled. He had stopped glaring

at Gerald for long enough to listen to what was being said.

'It is not like I've given away any secrets, Alpha,' Beta said, attempting to hide his exasperation. 'Cynthia already knows we monitor history and the timeline, just as they do. I haven't revealed how the system was built, or how it actually identifies deviations.'

Alpha frowned, and Beta knew he was ready to begin a full-blown battle in front of their guests. He had not wanted the World Fixers anywhere near their home in the first place, and he was not even mollified by the fact a Guardian team was at this very moment working at their base.

Not for the first time Beta wondered whether Alpha had been at this game for too long and had lost his perspective. After all, they were all working towards the same goal here. Perhaps it was time for Alpha to retire. That was not a problem for the present though.

Beta turned to Cynthia. Hoping to change the subject, he asked, 'Have you made contact with your chief operative?'

She shook her head. 'He contacted us before entering the city, but nothing since then. I hope he managed to make it to the rendezvous point. At least Isolde and Sigma were travelling together. And... ah... who is this other person with them?'

Beta shrugged, not sure how to answer. He had argued against the boy being sent along, but he had been overruled. 'You mean Lee. We've been watching him for many lifetimes. Under normal circumstances we would not send someone like him on such a perilous mission. However, our analysts ran multiple scenarios, and it seems our best chances of saving history and time occur when he is included in the team.'

'Why is that?' Cynthia leaned forward and placed her chin on her hand.

Again, Beta was not sure what to say or, more to the point, what he should say. 'There is a team of future Time Guardians who appear together in many historical periods, and we think... well, we're guessing... that his friends might be close by... and that they can—'

Gerald glanced up from the tablet he had been intently studying, and asked, 'Can do what? Save the world?' The contempt in his voice set Beta's teeth on edge.

'Help with whatever needs to be done when we find out what that is.' Alpha almost snarled his answer.

'Gerald, did you find anything?' Cynthia asked, perhaps to divert her partner's attention.

'No, I just reached the beginning of the war, and I can't find anyone or anything that might influence a change. I told you it would be a waste of time.' Gerald did not even lift his gaze from the screen as he answered.

Ignoring her colleague's rudeness, Cynthia swung around on her chair. 'Our system runs through history and identifies points where we might be able to intervene to alter small events to save the world from what happened.'

Alpha ignored Cynthia, but Beta was interested in this insight into how their oldest foes operated.

'Gerald has been running through time to see if he can identify anything, but clearly he was not able to. Perhaps you'd like to watch the rest with us.'

She nodded at Gerald and he scowled back.

'It might help us all to revisit what happened,' she insisted.

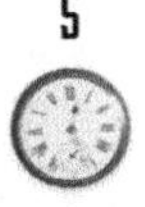

'Fine.' His fingers tapped on the tablet, and in the next moment an image flashed on the main screen. He tapped once and the image began moving as the distinctive plume of a bomb mushrooming up came into focus.

'Television footage of the New York bomb,' Cynthia explained, although she didn't need to, as Beta had lived through the war itself.

He still remembered watching in horror as the event was played live on the news. The commentators likened it to when planes crashed into the Twin Towers in the early twenty-first century. In hindsight this image was much more sinister; it was this bomb that had tumbled the house of cards. Its effects rippled out around the rest of the world, ending civilisations on many continents.

Beta watched as the screen flicked through more news coverage of people retreating from major cities. Many were caught by foreign missiles directed at motorways, and still more were caught in the streets as bombs fell. There were more nuclear attacks, mostly directed towards Asia and America. So many it would take years for the fallout to clear from the atmosphere.

The screen went blank. At this point most technology stopped working and news stories stopped being transmitted. Magic all but disappeared, so time travel to the era was not possible. Although the strongest Guardians had tried, they simply couldn't open the portal on the other side. Even now they didn't know if enough local magical energy could be harnessed for their agents' return.

'History shows that even before the bombs began falling, many people in the United Kingdom retreated to underground towns. In more rural areas many realised what was coming and set themselves up to ride out the storm,' Cynthia said.

'Yes, we modelled the scenarios too. In addition to the people in the underground city of Portsdown, there are likely survivors dotted around the area we sent our team into.' Beta was pleased to finally be working with someone who shared his excitement about the opportunities this mission provided.

'Mm, even so, we have no idea what our operatives are likely to find in twenty-second century Hampshire.' Cynthia drummed her fingers on the table, as if trying to decide what to do next. 'Well, there's not much we can do here today. I suggest we all get some rest and meet back here tomorrow.'

Alpha blanched as the World Fixer effectively dismissed them, and Gerald smirked at his reaction.

'I'm happy with that. We weren't getting anything done anyway,' Gerald said as he packed up his things.

'I'll call someone to show you to your quarters,' Beta responded smoothly, a little disappointed Cynthia had ended the meeting so abruptly. Was Alpha right, had they only come here because they believed they could learn something to their advantage from the Time Guardians? He mentally shook his head. No, he would not fall into that trap.

'That would be lovely,' Cynthia said as Alpha blinked out of the room without a by-your-leave.

'I will send someone in,' Beta said as he left by more traditional means.

CHAPTER ONE
WHEN AM I?

Lee stepped into the void. Izzy followed, pushed him in the small of the back, and he stumbled forward on uncertain feet. Not only was it dark, but the air around him was wet and clammy. No, it was heavier than clammy—it was like what he imagined walking through mercury would feel like. He quickly pushed that thought from his mind as claustrophobia began to press on him.

Moments later the tension under his foot changed and he pushed himself forward, relieved to finally be able to gulp down some fresh air. Stumbling forward, he was only prevented from tumbling down the slope by Izzy grabbing hold of his shirt.

Leaning over, hands on knees, he took in lungfuls of fresh air until his body was reassured its supply was not going to be cut off again. Eventually he stood and surveyed his surroundings while he waited for his heart rate to return to normal.

The first thing that hit him was the eerie silence. Few places he had ever visited were this silent. Even in the Australian bush there were always sounds: animals moving, water flowing, or leaves moving in the breeze. Here there was nothing.

In the pre-dawn darkness, he could just make out the sun beginning to peek over the horizon as the moon still shimmered on the water. As his eyes adjusted, he could make out deserted buildings on the edge of a lake, or was it the ocean?

'Where are we?' he asked.

'Quick, inside. It's not safe out here.'

He glanced around. 'Where's Trouble?'

'I said inside. Come on.' Once again Izzy pushed him in the small of his back, urging him towards a cave entrance to their left. 'I'll tell you everything once we're safe.'

He hoisted his backpack more firmly onto his shoulder and did as Izzy asked, if only to avoid another sharp dig in his back. When he agreed to join her and Trouble on a journey to the future, he hadn't thought to ask where and when they were going. Now he was regretting that.

As his eyes adjusted to the darkness of the cave, he thought he caught sight of a faint glimmer of light ahead.

'That way?' he asked.

'I guess so,' she said, and his stomach knotted as he heard a note of uncertainty in her voice.

Where *was* Trouble? He would feel a little less nervous if the Time Guardian was with them. He looked around for a cute spoodle, Trouble's current form. He found

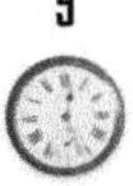

nothing, not even a place where Trouble might be hiding.

The sound of voices drifted out, and Izzy put a restraining hand on his arm, pulling him back a little. He followed her gaze downwards. An enormous German Shepard stared up at him.

Turning back to Izzy, she placed a finger to her lips, urging him to be silent.

Let's find out what's going on before we announce our presence, she spoke into his mind.

Yes, we don't want to upset any plans by blundering in, another voice added.

Trouble? Lee asked. He had only just got his mind around the fact the curly haired spoodle was a Time Guardian, and it still threw him off when the dog spoke. *Where are you?* His eyes dropped to the dog at his feet. *Look, if you're worried about the big dog, Izzy and I will protect you.*

The dog snorted and raised his head to stare at Lee, almost as if he too understood mindspeak.

I am the big dog. Trouble's tone was amused as he made the declaration.

Time Guardian Sigma likes to take an animal form suited to the time and situation he is in. He obviously thinks this task requires him to change into this brute, Izzy explained as she bent down to ruffle the dog's fur.

Lee felt like he had lost a friend. The animal in front of him did not project the same warm, reassuring presence as the cuddly spoodle.

I can't be called Trouble while we're here. It doesn't suit my new body, the Time Guardian said, rolling over so Izzy could rub his tummy, his right back leg shuddering as she found the right spot.

How about Brutus? Izzy offered, not quite suppressing a grin.

The dog raised his eyebrows in disdain and turned pleading eyes to Lee, whose mind went blank. *Not Brutus, that's too... um, brutish.* He frowned, thinking, then he remembered the large stuffed teddy bear he spent many an hour wrestling as a child—Big Bruno Bear. Just the right mix of scary to soft. *How about Bruno?*

Bruno.... Mmm.... The Time Guardian considered the name and the dog nodded once. Bruno he would be. *Now we have dealt with the essential things, my colleague, Theta, is inside talking to someone. I don't think they're from the city, but I don't recognise the voice.*

Both Izzy and Lee listened for a moment.

'I brought outdoor gear for your Sigma as well as for Isolde. Though if they don't get here soon, there won't be any time for them to change before the others arrive. I've no idea how we will explain their lack of military clothing when they do turn up.'

Lee would describe the male's voice as posh English with an underlying whine. As the unidentified male spoke, Izzy's lips curled in distaste.

That's Jason. Her tone was bitter. *My new minder, and one of the most incompetent fools I have ever had the displeasure to work with,* she added.

Well, this is going to be fun, Lee thought as Theta's voice drifted down the cave entrance. 'As I told you earlier, Sigma won't be needing a uniform. What are we going to do with it now? It will look odd having an extra set of clothes and travel gear.'

Before Jason could answer, Izzy took step forward as she said, 'Actually, we have one extra with us, so that won't be a problem.'

Lee and Bruno joined her, and the three of them walked into the cavern together: the lanky fair-haired boy with the huge dog beside him, and the diminutive dark-haired girl on the far side.

'Isolde, nice of you to join us.' The owner of the whiney voice sent Izzy a smarmy smile as he spoke.

He was just as Lee imagined. Built like a rugby player, he was good looking in the blond, weak-chinned English aristocratic style. If Lee had been a dog his hackles would have risen, as Jason oozed entitlement and condescension from every pore.

'Won't you introduce us to your friend.' Jason's tone suggested this was not a request.

'The name is Izzy, and this is Lee and Bruno. Guys, this is Jason.' Izzy forced the introductions through gritted teeth, not even trying to hide her distaste of Jason and the fact that he could order her about.

'Lovely Isolde, and this is Theta, or Thea as she has been asked to be called on this mission. We are just waiting for the other Time Guardians to turn up. I have a uniform for you, don't know what we'll do about your one extra though.'

Izzy stiffened and Theta—Thea—sighed. 'How many times must I tell you— ' they both said together then stopped and glared at each other. It was as if some silent message passed between them, but Lee did not feel the tell-tale tingling of mindspeak.

Whatever happened between them, they both turned

their backs on Jason, and Izzy held out her hand. 'I'm Izzy,'

Thea shook the offered hand tentatively. 'Thea. Do you two want to take your uniforms and packs and get changed? You can put your current clothes inside, along with anything else you want to take with you.' She pointed at Lee's backpack.

Lee held up the all-black uniform Isolde passed to him and frowned. How would he ever fit into that?

'The fabric is self-adjusting. There are also boots in the pack,' Thea told them. 'And please hurry, as the Captain leading this expedition should be here any minute.'

Lee glanced down at Bruno. 'Don't worry, Lee. He and I are old friends. We'll be fine together,' Thea assured him.

'He's just a dog. He doesn't need a babysitter,' Jason said, attempting to regain control of the situation.

As you dress, I'll bring you up to speed. Thea's voice entered his head, causing Lee to misstep. *I've managed to assign us to a troop on a special mission to find a citizen who's headed out into the wasteland. The critical changes in time appear to be clustered around the boy, so our first task is to find him.*

Should be piece of cake if you follow my lead, Jason added.

Or perhaps we should follow the Captain of this troop's lead so we don't stand out too much, Thea said, not bothering to hide the annoyance in her voice.

Best to assess the lay of the land, as you always taught me, Jason, Izzy added, attempting to smooth things between the two.

Right, yes, of course, Jason blustered.

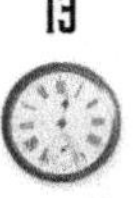

Our team was supposed to consist of the Captain, a medic, two grunts, and a dog handler-tracker. I altered the records so that our names are assigned. The Captain, Kiandra, and Corporal Rodgers, our medic, are still to arrive, Thea said.

Who is doing what? Izzy asked before Lee was able.

Thea answered, *Jason and I are enlisted soldiers. The Captain has met us in the city and sent us here to start preparations. Izzy, you were meant to be the tracker with dog handling skills, but I suggest you tell the Captain Lee and his dog have been assigned to you to train. Sigma, I'm assuming you are able to access all the dog's... um... faculties?*

Yes, Bruno said, his tone abrupt and business-like.

'You mean Sigma is the dog?' Jason gasped.

'Bruno,' they all said together.

'So the dog is called Bruno, and who are each of you?' A new voice entered the conversation.

As the others greeted the Captain and her companion in the room next door, Lee undressed and picked up his suit. The texture was a cross between rubber and cotton, and rather unpleasant to touch. Holding it up, he shook his head. He was never going to be able to fit into it.

He opened the front zip and began pulling it over each of his legs in turn, and audibly gasped as the suit expanded, then contracted around his body. As it settled into shape,

it formed what felt like a hard shell on the outside while still feeling soft on the inside.

After finishing the job, he pulled the zip up and did a few squats before twirling his arms. 'Cool', he said as the suit moved with him almost like a second skin.

'Are you done yet, Lee?' Izzy called.

Realising he was taking longer than expected, he squished his clothes and trainers into the bottom of his new backpack, moving the packs of freezedried rations to make room for them. Pulling some food bars and a book from his own bag, he added them to the load, making sure they were out of sight should anyone else look inside.

He hid his own bag behind a rock, then picked up his boots and the army backpack and walked barefoot back into the cavern. Everyone was crowded round an athletic woman whose height was accentuated by the mass of black braids wound around her head under her army issue cap. Beside her stood a rather stocky man with the stoic appearance of a career soldier found in armies the world over.

Dropping his bag to the ground, Lee watched the water bottle in the side pocket slip out. As he bent to tighten the strap, he heard a strange female voice say, 'So this is the dog handler?'

Lee raised his eyes to find Captain Kiandra giving him the once over.

'Yes, ma'am,' Izzy said.

The woman raised an eyebrow, and Lee's military training took over. Standing to attention he said, 'Yes, sir.'

The woman smiled. 'Better. I am Captain Kiandra, and I am in charge of this little foray into the outside.

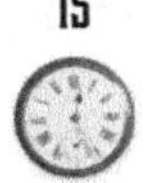

Although we will be a little less formal on this mission, I need you to appreciate that the chain of command still applies. That means when I say jump, you jump.'

Lee "Yes, sired" along with the others.

'When I am not around, you will listen to Sergeant Thea, my second.'

Biting back as smile as he watched it dawn on Jason that he was just a foot soldier on this mission, Lee said, 'Yes, Sir.' again.

'This gentleman, and I use that term loosely, is our medic, Corporal Rodgers. He may not look like much, but let me assure you, if we're forced into a fight you'll be pleased he's with us. There's very little he can't patch up on the run.'

The grim-faced man's expression did not alter as the Captain spoke, and Lee sneaked a few glances at him, trying to get the measure of the man. He gave very little away.

'Right, make sure your packs contain all the necessary personal items. Everything else we need is there.' She nodded towards the crate on a trolley beside her. 'Corporal Rodgers, if you would make sure they're all kitted out while I contact base and tell them we're heading out.'

Lee joined the team, noticing Izzy had managed to make it into her black uniform and her boots. As they gathered around the crate, the change in lighting highlighted purple piping on the seams of Thea's suit. The Captain's piping was silver, and the Corporal's red. The military was so predictable; rank must always be shown in some form or other.

Dropping to the floor as the others received their gear,

Lee hauled on the "boots" from his pack. Unfortunately, there was nothing remotely boot-like about them. The thick, rough terrain soles had strange ridges down the side, and were almost shoe-like. The top, though, was similar to a thick cotton sock.

As he put his foot inside, he frowned. The fabric stretched, but the sole was going to be too short by at least the length of his toes. He wriggled his toes, and found he was right, they hung over the edge. To his amazement, the boot sole flexed by itself and adjusted to his size before the top section hardened around his foot and ankle. His eyes widened as he stared at the second boot, which now looked nothing like the one on his foot.

A soft wet nose touched his face, then Bruno sat beside him. *A while ago the military found it was easier to produce clothing that adjusted to fit the person rather than producing different sizes. The suit is a special weave that can expand or contract as required, and will keep you warm in the cold and cool in the sun. The boots have some sort of nano technology built in allowing them to adjust as needed.*

Lee found it hard to say anything. *So this is how Alain felt coming to our time?*

A few weeks ago, Bruno had introduced him to Alain, a time traveller from medieval Britain who had joined him to solve a mystery in the New Forest in 2017. He and Alain become firm friends when Lee took it upon himself to help the other boy adjust to life in modern times. In fact, it was Alain who suggest he read the book he now carried in his pack.

I would imagine so, Bruno said.

Lee put on his other boot and stood.

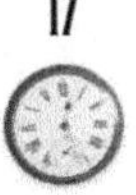

Could you please make sure you bring some decent food for me? I can't bear that freeze dried stuff. Hurry now, or you'll miss the briefing.

Lee sighed as Corporal Rodgers said, 'Righto boy, here's your equipment jacket. Check your blaster's charged when we're outside. Sleeping roll—oh, you have one already. All right, take the helmet, sunglasses, gloves. Oh yes, and this.' He handed Lee a smaller backpack type thing. 'This is for the dog. He's a big 'un, but you should be able to adjust it to fit.'

Lee took the contraption and almost laughed out loud. It was a backpack filled with dog biscuits and had a water bottle attached to the side. It appeared military dogs looked after themselves, because it was designed to be carried by an animal.

I'm not wearing that, Bruno informed him.

You will if you want to eat. The interruption came from Sergeant Thea, who frowned severely at Bruno. *Your unique form does not mean you don't need to blend in. Military dogs here either pull their weight or... well, let's just say that a society on the edge of extinction cannot afford to carry dead weight.*

Society on the edge of what? Lee asked in alarm. *What is going on here?*

'Right, now you've stowed your gear, let's get the briefing over and done with. We need to move out at first light.'

Lee gazed around, a little uncertain in this strange environment. The others all had their jackets on, and their sleeping rolls were attached to their backpacks, which were all lined against the wall along with their sleek black helmets that were upside down with sunglasses and gloves inside.

Corporal Rodgers slipped in beside him. 'Your first mission outside, lad?'

Lee nodded.

'You can put your jacket on and sort the dog while you listen. If you miss anything, we can pick it up later.'

'Thank you,' Lee said, grateful for the help.

Rodgers clapped him on the shoulder. 'We all had a first time outside. It's a little scary, but you'll be all right.'

As Lee shrugged into the jacket, he asked, *Bruno, where have you brought me?*

The future, just as I said.

Lee grunted his frustration, realised Corporal Rodgers was watching him, and feigned trouble with a zipper to cover his outburst. In the jacket pockets, he found some sort of gun, a couple of different types of knives, something that looked like string but felt like plastic, a spray bottle of some kind, a lighter, and an extra water bottle. Everything the outdoor soldier might need.

What sort of a future and what are we doing here? he asked Bruno as he put everything back where he found it.

Shh, the Captain is starting, and I want to hear what she has to say.

'The information in your mission notification stated a member of Citizens for Change managed to make it outside using the very exit we came through.' Captain Kiandra turned and gestured to the wall behind.

Lee couldn't see a door, and was impressed with whatever technology was hiding it from view.

'No one knows how they knew about this place. That isn't our worry though, so we'll leave it to the interior guards.'

Citizens for Change? Lee looked down at Bruno.

Shh, I'll update you later.

'The interior guards are also compiling details about the escapee and will send them through when we next make contact. All we currently know is that it is a young male, and that he left the city early yesterday morning,' the Captain continued.

In frustration Lee busied himself sorting Bruno's pack, much to the Guardians' disgust. He couldn't do anything about it though, not if he wanted to hear what the Captain was saying.

'A platoon chased him down the old motorway for some time before losing him in the car forest.'

Lee stopped himself asking what on earth a car forest was, realising he wouldn't prise anything out of Bruno until the Captain finished speaking.

'One of the soldiers believed he winged the boy with a blaster shot, so he's unlikely to be too far from here. Yes, Rodgers?' The Captain paused to let the Corporal speak.

'If he's injured, sir, isn't this a wasted effort? The zombies will—'

'RODGERS!'

'Sorry, sir, but surely some of the Fallout Affected will... well, you know what they do to our kind. Or the scavengers will have picked him over for his belongings and left him to die.'

Lee was not sure he had heard correctly and had to

stop himself from speaking out loud. *Fallout Affected! Bleeding hell, Bruno, what have you dragged me into?*

The dog shuffled uneasily as Lee tightened the straps of his backpack.

Too tight, need to breathe.

Taking pity on the dog in spite of his growing anger, Lee loosened the contraption and sat on the ground down beside Bruno.

'You might be right, Rodgers, but our orders are to make certain he is no longer a threat. I don't need to remind you all of the consequences should he tell any outsiders how he escaped. Or, even worse, what will happen if he manages to get back inside without being detected and starts talking about what he's seen,' Captain Kiandra responded.

Lee's stomach churned and he worried he might lose his last meal in front of everyone. *Bruno, I want you to tell me what I've walked into here.*

Calm down, Lee. We're in no immediate danger.

Then why are we here? Something must be going on. Time Guardians don't just drop into somewhere if things are going well... and there are two of you here, so it's likely to be something beyond bad, Lee insisted.

Well—

Lee ignored Bruno and carried on. *And it must be even worse, because you're working with Izzy, and she's a Time Wrecker. Aren't you guys like sworn enemies?*

I wouldn't—

And there are two of them, because that prat Jason is with her! Lee was winding himself up into a rant now.

Lee!

Bruno's voice did nothing to slow his outburst. *This is big, isn't it? What is big enough for a Time Guardian/ Time Wrecker Collaboration?*

We are World Fixers, Izzy's voice interrupted. *And we're here to ensure time continues. Now can you shut up so we can listen? We might need to know some of this if we are to survive the next few days.*

How did you—I thought I was just talking to Bruno. Lee coloured.

Neither of you bothered to shield your conversation, so we all heard. Well, maybe not the Captain and Corporal as I doubt anyone from this world has magical abilities, Izzy answered. *Now, shhh!*

Lee shut up just in time to hear the last of the safety briefing. 'For those of you who haven't been above ground before, please ensure you wear your helmet at all times, and your gloves. Although we live with simulated sunlight, we filter out the more harmful rays. If your face or hands are exposed for any reason, there is sunblock in your jackets, I strongly suggest you use it.'

Lee half heard the rest of Captain Kiandra's safety tips, but he took very little in. The very fact that Izzy was worried about her survival raised his anxiety levels, and his foot started tapping of its own accord, as it tended to when he was stressed.

His head was spinning as he tried to put together the fact that he was now in a world where people lived underground and nuclear fallout was a real issue.

He focussed back on the Captain. She was showing them how the inside of their helmets came down to create a mask over their faces, and then tucked into the top of their uniform. 'This is standard issue external patrol gear and is designed to filter radiation. You have your safety strip, which will monitor total exposure and give you a warning when you're getting close to overexposure levels.'

Lee glanced down at his jacket to find his monitor, and was relieved to see it showed no radiation exposure.

Captain Kiandra continued, 'There are water filtration tablets in your packs. Do not, I repeat do not, drink the local water without waiting ten minutes for the tablets to work. And also in your packs are ten days' worth of prescribed anti-radiation measures: take them daily.'

As the Captain wound up with, 'In line with patrol guidelines, this is a five day out, five day return mission to ensure our exposure to the lethal atmosphere is limited,' a worrying thought suddenly hit Lee.

Izzy, we were outside when we arrived. Will we get sick?

Not if you take the tablets. They probably contain potassium iodine and something to help your white blood cells regenerate. That should combat any radiation in the atmosphere for the short time we were outside.

Lee raised an eyebrow. *Are you sure?*

Not completely, I know very little about this time period. But I did try to get you inside when you insisted on fluffing.

Lee stared at Izzy, trying to assess whether she would actually tell him if his insides were already melting. He wanted to take his tablet right now! Was there time?

No use worrying. What he needed was more information. He hated being in new situations, especially ones he hadn't been able to investigate thoroughly in advance. If only Trouble—Bruno—had warned him he would face nuclear fallout, he could have at least been prepared.

Oh no, *Bruno.*

Bruno, won't you need protection?

The German Shepard turned to look at him. *Dogs are expendable here, so they don't protect them in the same way they do humans. I should be all right, though. I can't actually die and, unless the radiation levels are extremely high, we should be gone before the body I am wearing dies.*

'Right, sun should be rising soon. Cover up and let's get going,' Captain Kiandra ordered.

Everyone stood as one and began pulling on their outdoor gear. Sunglasses first, followed by helmet. The face covering was then pulled down and tucked into the collar of the uniform. Lee adjusted his hood and breathed; it wasn't too bad.

Captain Kiandra checked everyone before donning her own gear. 'Just breathe normally. Nanites in the material will filter out any alien particles,' she advised.

The thought alone caused Lee to begin to hyperventilate. Breathe, he told himself, and slowly calmed down. He pulled on his gloves and slung his pack over his back.

'Lights off,' the Captain said, and the cavern plunged into darkness.

A torch built in to Lee's helmet turned on automatically. He and Bruno headed out after the others, with Izzy walking in behind them. The Captain stopped in the entranceway. The sun was not quite yet up and she seemed reluctant to leave the safety of the cave until it was.

She is not used to working outside in the dark, but the locals are. She will wait until our high-tech gear tips the advantage our way, Thea told them.

Finally, they stepped into the sunlight. In the distance Lee could see a town partially submerged by a rising sea. It had the appearance of a city abandoned for centuries; some of the buildings were crumbling into piles of rubble, while others stood intact and seemingly abandoned. It reminded him of a post-apocalyptic movie set.

Almost immediately below them, he got his first glimpse of the motorway forest. The A3 he travelled along to his Aunt's place only a few weeks ago in his time was covered with a forest of green entwining hundreds of abandoned vehicles. There was no tarmac to be seen.

That wreckage is Portsmouth, he said in amazement.

Yes, Bruno confirmed.

How long ago did the nuclear war happen? Lee asked.

About eighteen years.

Lee froze, hardly able to believe that in less than twenty years such a heavily populated area could be reduced to almost nothing.

'Roll Out!' Captain Kiandra ordered, and his legs obeyed without thinking.

CHAPTER TWO
A NEW WORLD ORDER

The Captain took the lead down the slopes of the Portsdown Hill towards the A3. 'Just until we reach the spot the patrol last saw the escapee. Then we'll let the dog take over,' she informed them.

All right, Bruno, spill, Lee said as he and the dog hung back behind the others.

Give me a minute to shield our conversation, the dog answered.

Lee tried to wait patiently. *Bruno?*

Sorry, the magic here is weak, but we are good to go. As you have already guessed, we are just outside Portsmouth—

What year? Lee interrupted.

That's not important, because after the last world war they started counting again. It is the year NW19.

NW? Lee could not immediately think of what those

initials might mean.

New World Order, Bruno provided.

Lee laughed. *Sounds like something out of 1984 or Star Wars.*

I guess in some places the world is a little like that.

'What are you two doing?'

Lee looked up to find Izzy had joined them.

'Bruno is getting me up to speed on the mission. From what I've heard and seen so far, there's a lot I need to learn.' He swept his hand around, indicating the scenery.

'I think I'll stay and listen, if I may?' she asked Bruno, and the dog nodded, indicating he would include her.

'Good. I would hate for you only to hear the Time Guardian's side of the mission. After all, we're supposed to be working together.'

Bruno waited for Izzy to stop talking before continuing. *So, a brief history lesson up to NWO. Not long after your time, a pandemic swept the world, during which the United Kingdom finally ceded from the European Union. For a couple of years, things carried on as normal until a second pandemic hit. Countries around the world ping-ponged from lockdowns to periods of relative freedom while scientists rushed to find a cure, or at least a vaccine.*

It was chaos, Izzy continued. *Everyone thought a vaccine would be produced in a year like during the last pandemic, but this time it was different. As the number of deaths grew daily, countries locked their borders, airlines stop flying, and each government focussed only on protecting their own people.*

So all this devastation happened because of a pandemic? Lee asked.

Izzy laughed. *No, that was just the beginning of the end.*

Bruno took over the lesson. *During the end of the pandemic, an ultra-Conservative leader was elected Prime Minster in the United Kingdom and began isolating what he began to call Great Briton from the rest of Europe. Tempers flared and things escalated; war appeared inevitable.*

Hold on, Lee said. *Surely the United Nations intervened to stop it.*

Normally they would have, but they had their hands full trying to stop a war between superpowers after the United States had accused China of causing both pandemics. When mass riots broke out in the US after a presidential election, China saw an opportunity to hit back, Bruno said.

That doesn't sound too much different to now, Lee interrupted. *I don't see how it caused this.*

What... what are we calling you this time, Sigma? Was it Bruno? Izzy chuckled. *What Bruno hasn't told you is that during the pandemics the world became a cleaner space. Fewer emissions, rivers clearing up, people returning to producing their own food. After the first pandemic ran its course, many governments latched on to the social changes. Some countries didn't want to open their borders and they moved towards a more sustainable way of life. The rest of the world called them crackpots.*

Still not seeing how this had an impact. Lee wondered why were they bothering with this history lesson? All he wanted to find out was why the world went to war.

Patience, Lee, Bruno counselled. *Just a little more. Carry on, Isolde.*

Izzy wrinkled her nose at the use of her full name and Lee could have sworn Bruno smiled.

Izzy picked up the story, *Global warming was soon back at disaster levels, and, with escalating political divisions, no one was interested in a global solution. Eventually, some countries found they didn't have enough food or water to sustain their population. Those countries that were better off either didn't have enough to share, or relationships had deteriorated so much they didn't want to help anyone else out. In the end the world went to war over food.*

You're kidding me. Lee could not imagine a world where countries were so insular.

Unfortunately, she isn't. For all of humankind's technological advancements, it was the struggle for basic human needs that let them down, Bruno confirmed.

Lee frowned, unable to understand how a lack of food would lead to a nuclear war. Surely such actions would only make food shortages worse. *I'm finding it difficult to make the leap here, guys.*

Izzy sighed. *In a world where countries are focussed inwards, it doesn't take much to set things off. When the United States hijacked a food shipment from New Zealand destined for China, it was the straw that broke the camel's back.*

Okay, I get it. *So, what's left now?* Lee asked

Bear in mind our last solid update was in the first few weeks of the apocalypse, so it may not be so accurate now. China, Asia, and America were decimated in those first few weeks, Bruno said. *There are pockets of survivors in the United States, and in the wilds of Canada and Alaska—mostly living way off-grid.*

Izzy took over. *South America and Africa managed to*

keep to themselves during the war but were worst hit with nuclear fallout. They didn't have the resources to cope with the ensuing medical emergencies. I believe if anyone is still alive, they will have reverted back to tribalism.

What about my home? And Europe? Lee asked.

Australia and New Zealand had isolated themselves somewhat before the war. They fared the best out of all of this, but their societies quickly moved away from technology and are now most likely agricultural—think nineteenth-century rural, Bruno said.

Nice the whole world didn't go to hell in a handbasket. Lee's comment was laced with sarcasm.

Izzy carried on. *Europe fared much the same as the United States, or actually, perhaps a little worse. Once the nuclear bombs began falling and the world order crumbled, many old hurts between countries flared up, and they continued fighting for years using traditional weaponry. Our last reports described a continent controlled by military units and living in a continuous state of war.*

What about here? Lee asked.

With England already isolated from Europe, after the first few bombs decimated London, Manchester, and Edinburgh, they were left alone. Infighting in Europe meant everyone was kept too busy to invade, said Bruno

From what scientists tell us, Izzy said, *a few small communities will have survived on the surface. The bulk of people likely still live underground and intend to stay there until the world and the atmosphere settle.*

How many of these underground cities are there? Lee asked.

We believe about a hundred dotted around. They are

all completely self-sufficient, with a governing council whose leader holds a seat on the National Council, which operates much like the House of Lords in your time, Bruno answered.

And the other communities—Lee started.

Would be pretty much lawless, I think, Izzy finished.

They walked in silence for a while as Lee digested the fate of the human race. The thought that this was what they were reduced to made him sick. As they recached the flattish terrain of the old motorway, Lee voiced the something that had been niggling in the back of his head for a while. 'Couldn't you guys have prevented this?'

'Them or us?' asked Izzy.

'Both. Either.'

The Time Guardian's job is to ensure time flows as it always has, Bruno said, *and this was how the human race chose to evolve.*

'We tried to change things, tried to make people more aware of their impact on other people and on the world they lived in, but we were thwarted as often as we were successful.' Izzy's tone was accusatory, and Bruno hung his head.

The Time Guardians and World Fixers both wove in and out of time, doing their best to help humanity, but they were often at odds with each other. It was unusual for them to work together. That thought made Lee stop and think—what was so bad their two Councils would allow them to be here now?

Bruno, Izzy, what are you here to do? I mean, what are you here to make sure happens?

Nothing, Bruno answered. *I am not here to ensure*

anything happens.

Okay, then what are you guys planning to do that Bruno must stop? he asked Izzy.

You have this wrong, Lee. None of us are here to do anything in particular, Izzy said.

Lee looked from one to the other in confusion. *Then why are we all here?*

To prevent time from ending, Izzy and Bruno said together.

'What?' Lee stumbled over some overgrown car part.

As far as the Guardians are concerned, they cannot plot human history past the next few days, Bruno said.

Nor can my Council, Izzy admitted.

Lee could not believe what he was hearing. *But surely you have both sent someone here to find out what happens.*

It's not that easy. Bruno's head hung down as he trotted alongside Lee. *We need a certain amount of magic to do what we do. Unfortunately, World War Three dispelled the little magic left in the world—until now.*

So we have been sent here to find out what we can. The hope is that our teams will work together to ensure there is a future for us to fight over, Izzy finished.

Lee frowned and he rubbed his thumb over his middle finger, an outward sign of the worry building inside. In fact, it was more than worry. His anxiety levels were shooting off the charts.

Bruno had promised to take him back to his time before anyone would miss him. Now he was saying there was very little magic here for him to work with, and he had no idea what would happen over the next few days.

Will I be able to go home? The thought entered Lee's head and came straight out of his mouth.

We have all agreed that you are the first priority to be returned, Izzy said.

Jason agreed to that? He hoped the joke would cover the turmoil within.

Izzy grinned. *No, but he was the only one who didn't agree, so he was outvoted.*

Changing the subject so as not to dwell on what was really worrying him, Lee asked, *How much factual information do you have about NW time?*

Umm, let me see. Theta arrived here three days ago, and what little intel she gathered I have shared with you, Bruno said.

Which is not much, Lee said wryly.

Not much more than we knew already, I agree. She did have to arrange our covers and for us to be assigned to this expedition. It was a busy few days for her.

Another thought occurred to Lee. *From what you have said, the whole world is in disarray, so how can something happening in this small corner of England cause time to stop?*

We have no idea. All we know is that it does. Bruno's tone was sharp in Lee's head, and he realised the Guardian must be as frustrated over the lack of information as he was.

NW time has always been a blur, and no one could travel

here. Then a week ago a blip showed up on both time radars. It was so unusual our Councils got together to discuss what it meant and… well, here we are, Izzy said.

So what has changed? Why now? Lee's finger was still rubbing, and he took a couple of deep breaths in an attempt to calm himself down.

From what our people can make out, the boy leaving Portsdown triggered something, Izzy said.

So, are we supposed to help find him and bring him back? Or help him stay free? Lee stopped, almost banging into Izzy who had come to a halt.

We're not sure, Bruno said as he came to a stop beside him. *We're playing it pretty much by ear. The Councils have people watching the time stream to advise us when they can. They hope that while we're here, a little more will be revealed and we can come up with a proper plan.*

Captain Kiandra was talking over top of Bruno, and Lee strained to hear her.

'… this is where the patrol last saw the escaped citizen.' She reached into her pack and pulled out a strip of fabric. 'The earlier patrol picked this up. It belonged to the boy. Bring up that dog and let him have a sniff.'

Bruno followed Lee to where the Captain stood. Lee took the garment and held it out for Bruno to plant his nose in.

Can you really do this tracking thing? Lee asked the dog once Bruno had removed his nose.

I could distinguish scents when I was Trouble, so I believe I can do this. I think all I have to do is match a scent to this one. How hard can that be?

Lee grimaced and stood to find the Captain staring

at him as if she expected something else. Lee looked around and realised she was waiting on him. He took the fabric away and said with as much command as he could muster, 'Find, boy.'

Bruno stuck his muzzle in the air and sniffed, then began wandering around the abandoned vehicles, nose to the ground.

'This may take a while,' Lee informed them with more confidence than he felt.

'Break time,' the Captain said, and they all dropped their packs to the ground. Some opened their water bottles, loosened the front of their masks, and took sips through the straw.

It was Lee's first chance for a good look around. It was eerily quiet on the motorway, and he felt more like he was on a movie set than in the real world in the future. His shoulders tensed and the hair on the back of his neck stood on end. He turned around slowly. Something moved. Someone was watching them.

Bruno paused and sniffed the air again. 'I feel it too, boy,' Lee said.

Two, over in the trees. They smell of fear, and... something else... like death, Bruno sent.

'Captain, I think we have company,' Lee said, jerking his head towards the bushes Bruno had indicated.

'Yes, soldier. We picked them up on our descent. They're probably FAs and won't trouble us too much.' After a moment she added, 'Fallout Affected... people whose bodies have some form of radiation sickness. They'll be weakened by whatever disease they have and won't attack an armed troop.'

'Why would they be out here so far away from other people?' Lee asked.

'You really are a newbie.' Rodgers leaned around the Captain to answer Lee. 'Out here they're treated like pariahs. They're a reminder of what will happen to everyone outside... eventually.'

'Don't they have drugs for treatment?' Lee asked, remembering the briefing this morning.

'Not out here, I wouldn't imagine. Not anymore.' Rodgers returned to sipping his water.

'Europe attacked Portsmouth with conventional warheads, decimating the military infrastructure. Luckily, most civilian leaders were already underground. A few people survived the attack, but they were not organised, so I doubt anyone thought to gather and distribute medication,' the Captain explained, then frowned at him. 'Didn't you learn all of this in school? I thought local history was a mandatory subject.'

'Pardon, Captain, but our dog trainer is a recent transfer from a London community. He won't have been taught our local history,' Thea interrupted.

'Of course, I forgot. It must be quite different in the old capitol.'

'Yes.' Lee confirmed, mostly because some sort of an answer was expected.

You need to be smarter. Ask less questions of the locals, otherwise we will all be found out.

The voice in his head was new, and he started when he realised it was coming from Thea.

Bruno, keep him in line. This is not a mission for newbies. I don't understand why the Council let you bring him, Thea added.

They insisted I ask him along. Apparently, his presence is essential to our success.

'Soldier, what is that dog doing lolling around? Get him moving. I want to be well on the way to catching up with this boy before midday.'

Lee shook his head to clear his thoughts before searching out Bruno. He found the dog lying on the ground, his head resting on outstretched paws.

I was waiting for you to all finish. I have the scent. Almost before Bruno had finished speaking, figures emerged from the forest, from behind cars, and seemingly from out of the vegetation covering the road. They were armed and none too friendly looking as they circled the small troop.

Lee froze, his hand on his blaster. Captain Kiandra put out a hand and said, 'Stand down.'

Lee relaxed a little, but he didn't remove his hand, as the people surrounding wore quasi-military clothing and carried their weapons like soldiers. Nothing in their faces indicated their intentions were friendly.

Captain Kiandra took a step forward, as did one of their people.

'I am Captain Kiandra of the Portsdown Regiment. We are in neutral territory.'

'Your information is out of date. The City of Portsmouth

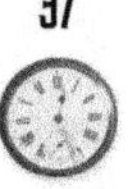

and the Portsmouth Militia now claim the A3 as our territory. We notified your commanders over a month ago and warned them not to use the motorway.' The other woman's voice was brittle in its attempt to sound commanding. 'You will come with us.'

'We must have been given old maps. If you can show us the new boundary, we will keep to our side of it until we are out of your territory.' Captain Kiandra made as if to leave.

'Halt.' The Portsmouth Militia cocked their rifles.

'You are the second group in as many days to violate our boundaries. You must be made an example of. You have a choice— come with us, or make a stand.'

The leader of the militia stood with a hand on her weapon. She was only young, and Lee had met her type before. Promoted quickly, she likely substituted aggression for leadership.

'Can't we—' Captain Kiandra started.

'Corporal, over there. The zombie kids we were chasing.' One of the militia closest to Lee pointed to the bushes where he and Bruno had detected movement moments before.

The Corporal froze, undecided on which target would bring her the most kudos. Lee had no such qualms. He feigned a trip and fell into the person who had noticed the kids. Bruno, taking his lead, started barking and leaping at two armed men beside him.

As Lee regained his feet, he looked towards the bushes and shouted, "Run!" His team took it as if he was speaking to them and started off down the road-jungle, slipping in between the cars and heading towards Southampton.

Movement in the bushes told Lee the children also

took the warning. Ducking behind the closest vehicle, he jumped as a bullet clipped the metal beside his head—too close for comfort. Bruno scooted to a halt beside him.

Dropping to his knees, Lee stared around the side of the car. The militia had split into two groups. The first was heading after the children, and the rest were making their way in his direction.

Which way is the escapee? he asked Bruno.

The dog nodded towards their left.

Of course, towards Portsmouth.

No, I think whoever is carrying the boy headed off more towards Southampton, Bruno said.

'Come on, you two,' Thea yelled from about a hundred meters ahead, and Lee realised if they didn't move soon, they would be stranded without support.

Theta, go more right. I have a trail heading that way. We'll meet up with you later, Bruno sent.

What did you do that for? Lee was aghast. *You just sent away our cover.*

Come, this way. Bruno padded away from him, weaving in-between automotive debris following a scent only he could smell. Keeping to a crouch, Lee had no option but to follow, making sure he kept something in between him and his pursuers at all times.

When one of the Portsmouth militia yelled out, "Over by the roadside," Lee froze, then realised they had seen the others leaving the cover of the motorway. He used the diversion to pop his head above the Mini he hid behind.

Lee dropped back to the ground. A boy about his own age was standing on the other side watching the rest of Lee's team run across open ground. His heart pounded and his hands shook, and he tried to control his breathing, hoping all the while the militia man hadn't heard him.

He's gone, Bruno said. *Follow me.* A German Shepard head peeked around the side of a rolled BMW near the edge of the road. Lee crawled over to him.

Let's wait here until the militia are far enough ahead they won't look back, Bruno instructed.

Lee sunk to the ground and leaned against the car. Bruno stayed standing beside him, occasionally sniffing the air or cocking his head to the side to listen.

What just happened? Lee asked.

From what I can gather, the Portsdown and Portsmouth communities have been in consultation often enough to agree, or at least communicate, localised boundaries.

That means there are groups of people out here organising, Lee said, turning this new information over in his head, then added, *And, if I'm supposed to be on loan from London, then it sounds like the underground cities still have a structure that governs them all.*

Yes. Where are you going with this? Bruno asked.

Lee chewed the information over, trying to put the kernel of fear in his mind into words. *Local militias and a single large government—*

Ah, and if that government sees itself as the natural successor to the pre-war government.... Bruno stared at Lee. *I see where you're going with this. The local situation might be more unstable than we first thought.*

Lee listened to the sounds around him. *Is he gone?*

Yes, let's go. I will feel better when we catch up with the others, and I want to talk to Thea about this new development.

They made their way through the edge of the cars on the motorway, using a few vehicles that had tumbled down the embankment as cover to make their way towards a copse of trees. The militia was still ahead of them searching for the others, but so far hadn't thought to look behind.

Every now and then Bruno sniffed the ground or put his nose to the air, occasionally correcting their path. Lee concentrated on staying out of sight until a hand grabbed the back of his suit and he lost his footing. Suppressing a yelp, he turned to find himself face-to-face with Captain Kiandra.

'Phew, I thought you were the militia,' he whispered.

Captain Kiandra loomed in closer until their noses were almost touching, 'You might wish I was one of them by the time I've finished with you.'

Lee gulped.

'What the hell did you think you were doing back there?' she asked, her voice a low rumble.

'Sa... s... saving the children in the bushes,' Lee said as Bruno growled a warning from beside him.

'My job is to think and decide how we act. Your job is to wait for orders and to obey those orders. ARE. WE. CLEAR?'

'Yes, sir,' Lee said.

'One more stupid act like that and I will shoot you myself. You could have put us all in jeopardy.' Having delivered her threat, Captain Kiandra appeared to have run out of steam. 'Come on. We've lost the militia, and the others are over this way.'

The scent is this way, Bruno said.

'Um ....' Lee's nerves seemed to have eaten his voice.

'What now, Private?'

'The scent leads that way.' Lee pointed in the opposite direction.

The Captain sighed. 'Wait here while I retrieve the others. And Private... try not to get yourself or anyone else killed while I'm away.'

Very funny! 'Yes, sir.'

As the sun sunk low in the sky, Captain Kiandra called a stop by yet another copse of trees. 'We need somewhere defensible to spend the night and I think this will do fine.'

Sergeant Rodgers pulled out the tent and arranged it in the middle of the small clearing with the opening facing the only track in. After making sure the bottom was secure, he pressed a button and it inflated. Sergeant Thea pulled an air filtration unit from her pack and set it into the vent.

Once inside, they removed their outer layer of clothing and laid their sleeping rolls across the tent. Finally, they placed their packs at the head of their beds away from the door, to provide additional protection.

It was all relatively comfortable. Lee had been on worse camping trips in his life, even if he had been forced to the outer edge of the group as a sign of the troop's displeasure. At least he'd get a good night's sleep with Bruno on one side and the tent wall on the other.

The dinner rations were cold and hardly filled the hole in Lee's stomach. He ate the tasteless food seated on his bedroll, took his radiation tablets, then lay down with his hands behind his head.

The others were in a group talking with their backs to him. Fine, if they didn't want to include him, he was good with that, really. He took his copy of *Lord of the Rings* from his pack and opened it to the first page. Reading and fantasy weren't his things, but if Alain said it was good, he was prepared to give it a go.

He had just started reading about the main character's elevenety-first birthday when Bruno stretched out beside him, his head resting on his paws.

Not eating? Lee asked, staring at the still full bowl of dog biscuits he had put out for the Guardian.

I am not eating that! Bruno said, disdain lacing his voice.

Lee chuckled. *You needn't think our rations were any better. In fact, I'd go as far as to say your food looks more appetising.*

The dog sighed a doggy sigh, humphed, then stood and chewed a couple of biscuits. Lee poured some water into another bowl so Bruno could have a drink as he ate the dried offering. The bedroll moved as Izzy joined them.

'What was that all about today, Lee?' she asked, making herself comfortable. 'You know, with the militia.'

'It wasn't them. It was the kids,' he said. 'They called them zombies. I knew something horrible was going to happen to them, and it wasn't their fault they have radiation sickness.'

'Surely you could've come up with something better than "run".' Izzy smiled to soften her words.

'It was a sort of spur of the moment thing.' Lee grinned.

Izzy smiled back. 'Well… I sort of get it, but next time maybe just give a heads-up first.'

Glancing at the others, Lee asked, 'Are they very upset with me?'

'They'll get over it,' Izzy said before reaching over and ruffling the dog's fur. *Bruno, do you actually have any idea where we're going?*

I smelt the boy exactly where Captain Kiandra said I would. Other scents around him indicate someone picked him up, and they were heading in this direction, towards Southampton.

Are you sure he's still with them? Lee asked.

When they rest they put him down, and his scent is mingled with theirs, Bruno confirmed.

Well, at least we're going in the right direction, Izzy said. *Have you or Thea heard from the Time Guardians?*

No, nothing, Bruno said as he wormed his way in between the two of them.

Izzy moved a little to make room for him. *Everything's silent from our lot too. Have you tried contacting them?*

No. Theta is in charge of this mission, so I'm leaving that up to her. I'm concentrating on what needs to be done by Bruno the dog, and of course making sure Lee is safe.

Izzy returned to the others and Lee slipped into his bedroll. Knowing Izzy was on his side gave him a warm glow inside—which disappeared soon after Jason took the spot beside him and hissed, 'You're a liability. You shouldn't be on this mission. You're gonna get us all

killed.'

Izzy turned and said, 'Shut up, Jason. If anybody is going to put our lives in danger, it will be you and that big mouth of yours.'

Stunned into silence, Jason made as if to say something meaningful, then sniggered. 'Well, Izzy, if you want to blame everything on me— go right ahead, it's par for the course for you.'

What's going on with them? Lee wondered. He got the impression the two knew each other well, and not in a good way. Bruno sat up and, when Jason tried to move him away, a low, rumbling growl came from deep in his belly, and he bared his teeth. Unsure of what to make of the dog, Jason shuffled away and started getting ready for bed

The tent was soon quietened down. Corporal Rodgers turned out the lamp, plunging them into darkness, before taking a seat by the clear doorway.

Lee barely slept that night. His mind was working overtime—mostly questioning why he hadn't stayed in England for the Christmas holidays before returning to Australia to start officer's training in February. Why had he chosen now to do something on the spur of the moment?

It was almost a relief when he felt a cold nose on his face sometime in the early hours of the morning.

Pleased you could join us. Thea's voice invaded his thoughts as her body moved in the bedroll beside him. She must be returning from guard duty, Lee thought.

Lay off him, Bruno said. *He's had enough of a whipping for one day.*

Sorry, we haven't much time before the others wake,

and I want to make sure we're all up to speed before I update Jason and Isolde, Thea said

You've spoke to the Guardians? Bruno asked.

Yes. Alpha contacted me while I was on watch. They have nothing new to report. She chuckled, which sounded odd in Lee's head. *I don't think he's enjoying working with the World Fixers. He seems to have taken a particular dislike to one of them, some chap called Gerald.*

Bruno laughed along with her. *He was never one of the most flexible members of the Guardian Council.*

Anyway, all he said was that they're still working on some guidelines for us. The time blip hasn't altered, so, at best, we're not making things worse.

The lack of control over what we are doing must grate on him, Bruno said, and the two laughed again.

Hold on. They said we're not making things worse, but that means we're not making them better either, Lee interrupted.

The current line of thought is that we won't see any change until we catch up with the boy who escaped, Thea said.

They didn't report on anything from the World Fixers? Lee asked.

I suspect their update will come via Jason or Isolde. It appears working together still means having information silos, Thea answered, then added, *I'm not sure that Jason is up to much. He's a little bit...*

... flaky? Lee offered.

Yes. I don't believe he takes any of this seriously, and he spends his time winding up Isolde.

The others are stirring, Bruno warned as he rose to

his feet and stretched, ready to start the day.

Captain Kiandra ordered them to eat a quick breakfast. She wanted to be on the road early. While they packed up camp, Jason and Izzy argued in hushed voices, Izzy's face growing more flushed as the conversation dragged on.

Lee was strapping on Bruno's pack when Izzy sidled over. Glancing around to make sure Jason was distracted, she whispered, 'We have nothing new to report. Jason wanted to make out we had something concrete we were keeping from you. The prat!'

Lee said, 'We don't have anything either.'

'I know Thea told us. Her being so open is why I shared our update with you.'

Thank you, Bruno said.

As he continued rolling up his bedroll, Lee mused out loud, 'Can't you guys just get along?'

Izzy paused, and asked in a low voice, 'Do you mean me and Jason? Or the World Fixers and the Guardians?'

'Yes,' responded Lee.

CHAPTER THREE
A SOLDIER'S LIFE FOR ME

They finished dismantling the camp and packed up before Captain Kiandra led them out of the copse. Dew still clung to the grass and the early morning sun, causing a mist to rise across the field.

'Righto, Private. You and the dog pick up the trail while I see if I can contact base,' the Captain said the minute they left the shelter of the trees. As she spoke she pulled some sort of communication device from her jacket and typed in a message.

'Are you waiting for something, Private?' she barked, finding Lee still standing in front of her.

'No, sir,' Lee responded, turning on his heel. 'Come on, Bruno. Let's find that scent again.'

I'll be lucky to catch the scent with all this moisture on the ground, Bruno grumbled, but he obediently stuck his nose into the grass and rooted around where he had last smelt their quarry. He shuffled forward a bit and swivelled his head this way and that before turning to Lee. *I can't smell much at the moment, but I am pretty sure they're still heading towards Southampton. If we take it slow, I am sure I will pick the trail up again soon.*

Lee was about to inform the others when Captain Kiandra joined the group.

'Good news. They sent through background on the boy we're tracking and, even better, a recent image,' she said.

'That's a bit of luck,' said Rodgers and he took the device. 'We're almost out of comms range.'

The Captain frowned. 'Luck had nothing to do with it. Patrols always check in before losing contact, and command tracks our progress, so they would have been aware this was the last chance for an update.'

Lee was beginning to get the impression from the way Captain Kiandra spoke to her corporal that, although she respected Rodgers as a soldier, she didn't much like him as a person.

Rodgers handed the device to Thea and Jason, who passed it on to Izzy. As she looked at the screen, Izzy's face froze, and her gazed flicked across to Lee. Taking this as an invitation, he glanced over her shoulder at the screen and the reason for her reaction hit him like a slap. The screen displayed an image of Alain, only it wasn't quite Alain. Izzy scrolled upwards to the description of the subject.

What's happening? Bruno asked.

Alain's on the screen. Well, not exactly Alain, but a boy called Allan who's an apprentice gardener from Portsdown.

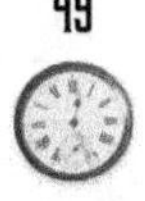

Only, it might as well be Alain from the looks of him.

Lee read the physical details of their quarry with his fists clenched and his stomach knotted. They could be describing Alain. Suddenly his concerns about being in a post-apocalyptic wasteland seemed unimportant—they were hunting his friend as if he were some sort of criminal.

Now I understand why your presence on this mission was so critical, Bruno said.

What? Lee shook his head, trying to clear it. *What do you mean?*

You and Alain are friends in many lifetimes. Perhaps you're destined to always find each other and renew that connection.

Lee was stunned. *You mean you're more likely to find this Allan because I am with you?*

Bruno sat up and stared at Lee, who could see his helmeted reflection in the dog's liquid brown eyes. *Yes, probably.*

Lee did not respond. He wasn't sure how he felt about being used as bait. He hadn't even met this boy but, if he was a reincarnation of Alain, he wasn't sure either person was capable of doing anything to warrant a group of soldiers tracking him down.

'Private. PRIVATE! Are we ready to go?' Captain Kiandra jolted Lee from his thoughts as she took the communicator from him.

'Sorry?' He shook his head. 'What? Oh, yes, Bruno has the scent. This way.'

'Right, you heard him. Let's go.' The Captain's voice rang clear in the morning air.

Izzy joined Lee and Bruno as the rest of the troop fell

in behind. 'Are you okay?' she asked.

Lee wasn't sure how to answer. On the one hand, he'd never met Allan, but his stomach and head were certainly reacting as if he was a friend.

'He isn't Alain,' he said, his voice low so only Izzy could hear.

'From experience I can tell you that is both true, and it isn't. Reincarnations often hold the essence of previous lives.'

'Thanks, that helped a lot,' Lee groaned.

Izzy laughed. 'It helps if you remember we're soldiers and we're here to do a job. All we need to do is follow orders.'

'If I do that, what do I do with all these conflicting emotions I'm feeling?'

Ask Sergeant Thea. She'll tell you to push the emotions down as far as you can and forget about them—all that matters is the job, Bruno said.

'What about you, Izzy? What do you say?' Lee asked.

'Is there a problem, Private?' Captain Kiandra called from behind.

'No, sir,' Izzy answered.

'It's a little difficult to track in the wet,' Lee said.

'Make sure you don't lose the trail,' the Captain commanded.

'I won't, sir,' Lee said, but his heart wasn't in it.

Following orders was easy when you had no stake in the outcome. Lee had never been in a situation where he had to put his personal convictions aside and do as he was told. How had his father managed it in his military career? It wasn't something he talked about, but Lee knew his dad lived by a strong moral code. Had he ever been ordered to do something contrary to that?

Lee wished he could ask his father's advice. With that thought a wave of homesickness washed over him. He wanted to see his sister, Bee, and his mother. To walk along a Sydney beach with them, the wind in his hair and salt water running over his feet—to behave like nothing had changed.

He gave himself a mental shake. 'Get a grip,' he said under his breath.

'What?' Izzy asked.

'Nothing. Just talking to myself.'

She shrugged.

His family wouldn't always be with him. Whether he was in an apocalyptic world sometime in the future, or in the middle of a war zone in his time, this was his problem to solve. He would gather more information, but in the meantime he would follow Izzy's advice and concentrate on the task at hand.

The trail Bruno followed led them away from roads and across overgrown fields full of rocks and potholes. Lee concentrated on doing his job and not twisting his ankle, pushing thoughts of their end goal from his mind every time they threatened to surface.

Around midday they stopped briefly for a mouthful of water and to chew on a bar of dried fruit and nuts. Picking up his pack to head back out, Lee turned to Bruno.

Are you sure we're still heading the right way? he asked. *If Alain, sorry Allan, is being carried, we should be moving faster than the people who found him. Surely we should've caught them up by now?*

You will remember I said "they" picked him up. Bruno stood before continuing. *Those carrying him are fit and healthy, and probably used to carrying extra weights. Also, they're likely local so aren't stopping to check the way every few minutes. At best we're keeping pace with them. At worst they might actually be pulling ahead.*

Before Lee could respond, Izzy joined them, saying, 'The tracks aren't getting any fresher.'

Lee's eyes widened. 'You can actually track? I thought that was a ruse to give you a place in the troop,' he said quietly.

Izzy glared at him.

'Oh, right, I need to be able to tell the Captain how I know why we haven't caught the boy up.' Lee sighed. 'I guess I should go and let everyone in on the bad news.'

Ever since the incident the day before, Lee had been keeping his distance from the Captain. Putting his fears aside, he wandered over to where she was talking with Sergeant Thea.

'Yes?' Captain Kiandra paused as Lee approached.

'I wanted to report, Captain. We're still going the right way. Izzy—Private Isolde—says whatever tracks she finds are not getting any fresher.'

'Can you tell me how many we are tracking?'

'We think perhaps two, and of course the escapee,' Lee answered.

'So, we're about keeping pace with Allan and whoever

he's with?'

'That is what we believe,' Lee confirmed.

The Captain stood and said, 'Right, gather round, everyone.'

Relieved to have the Captain's focus off him, Lee shuffled to the back of the group behind Rodgers and Jason, who had become quite pally.

'We're not gaining on our prey, so we need to up our pace to double time,' Captain Kiandra informed them.

Jason groaned, earning a glare from the Captain. Rodgers chuckled beside him and said quietly, 'Careful, boy, she's the type that'll make us go even quicker if she thinks we're bucking her command.'

I can't track as well if we go too fast, Bruno said.

Lee stared down at the dog. *Is that for real, or are you merely trying to make things easier on us?*

I'm new to this tracking thing. I can't guarantee I can keep us heading in the right direction if we speed up too much.

Lee sighed. 'Excuse me, Captain. We might lose the scent if we go too fast. Bruno and I are still only in training.'

Captain Kiandra humphed and drummed her fingers on her thigh. Everyone watched, waiting for her decision. 'Right, we move at a slow jog. Tell me immediately if we lose the scent, Private. I don't want to backtrack too often, or we'll lose even more time. I want this guy back in our custody before he wakes up or ends up somewhere we can't access him. Move out.'

The last comment caused Lee to frown. Where on earth would this boy go that they couldn't get to him? Lee started walking, Bruno and Izzy at his side, and the others falling into formation behind. An hour or so later, when they were approaching the outskirts of Southampton, the group stopped for a rest break.

'If he's in there, he'll be lost to us,' Corporal Rodgers said. 'I can't see those militia types letting us anywhere near him.' Rodger's lips curled back in a sneer. 'Not that we'd want to get too close to any of those radiation-drenched ba—'

'CORPORAL!' Captain Kiandra interrupted.

Although his glare was mutinous, Corporal Rodgers closed his mouth. The fingers began drumming against Captain Kiandra's leg again, then stopped abruptly. She turned to her team. 'He may well be in there, but we can cross that bridge if we come to it. We keep going until we lose the scent or reach their borders.'

'But—'

'Corporal Rodgers, I don't believe the Southampton Militia would pick someone up so close to Portsmouth. Firstly, because their relations with Portsmouth are volatile at best. Secondly, why would they drag one of ours so far? I cannot think of a single reason.'

'With all due respect, sir, I believe those militia mongrels would do just about anything to find out more about our city.'

Captain Kiandra started to speak, then shook her head. 'We can't say for certain he's with the militia—Portsmouth or Southampton.'

'Well, if the militia don't have him, then likely the zombies do. If that is the case, he's dead meat and we are wasting our time,' Corporal Rodgers grumbled.

Captain Kiandra adjusted her pack as she glared at

Rodgers. 'We in the Portsdown Regiment act on facts. While there is evidence that the fallout impaired will eat raw animals, there is absolutely no indication they eat human flesh. We also have no reason to believe they picked up the escapee. So, I'd appreciate it if you kept your opinions to yourself.'

Not hearing the message to leave well enough alone, Corporal Rodgers spoke again. 'I'm just preparing us for the worst.'

Captain Kiandra's chin rose as she ignored this last remark and ordered them to move on.

The sun had started its descent when the company caught their first glimpse of Southampton. Many buildings still stood, but they were more overgrown than derelict.

'How come Southampton did better in the war than Portsmouth?' Lee asked Izzy.

'Because the naval base at Portsmouth was bombed early on to prevent the navy from entering the conflict. Being a commercial port, Southampton was mostly left alone.'

About a kilometre out from the city limits, Bruno paused and sniffed the air before dropping his muzzle to the ground and snuffling around.

Please don't tell me they went into the city, Lee said. On the one hand, he didn't want to confront another militia group. On the other, Allan being out of reach would solve his ethical dilemma. On yet another, he was interested to meet this version of Alain.

Bruno walked around in circles, trying to find the scent. Fortunately, instead of wandering closer to the city, he was walking away from it. He finally stopped and stared up at Lee.

Whoever's got the boy went this way, around the outskirts. I think we can speed up for a while if we follow those perimeter markers, the dog said.

Izzy and Lee crouched and found the old roadside markers Bruno was referring to. Most were overgrown, but there were enough of them to show a route around the city.

'I don't think these guys wanted to encounter the Southampton Militia any more than we do,' Izzy observed.

Lee made a great show of searching for and finding markers while Izzy went back to report to the Captain. The group caught Lee up, and he pointed out the way around Southampton.

'Righto, it looks like we have a solid trail to follow that doesn't rely on scenting. Jason, I want you and Rodgers to take point—double time. Sergeant Thea and I will take the rear. I want you trackers safe in the middle,' the Captain ordered.

They formed up, and before anyone moved, the Captain leaned forward and added, 'We will stop and check our course every fifteen minutes. I don't want to lose that scent.'

Lee would have loved to have taken a look at the city as they ran. Unfortunately, although close to Southampton, the area was clear enough for anyone approaching to stand out like a sore thumb. Their side of the markers was completely overgrown.

We haven't seen any locals, Lee said as they ran. *Don't you find that strange?*

There's a group following us to make sure we don't stray too close to perimeter, Bruno informed him.

Lee dropped back a little to tell Captain Kiandra the news.

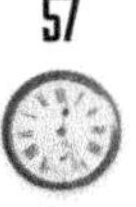

'Already on it, Private,' the Captain said. 'But good to know you're keeping your eyes open.'

Lee blushed at the praise as he returned to his position.

Soon they veered away from the city, and Lee tensed again. How easy it would have been if Allan was with the militia and out of their reach. Now he faced a restless night wrestling with his conscience.

By the time they started raising the tent that night, they were well on the other side of Southampton and heading into the New Forest. Once again the Captain directed them to a copse of trees with a place to raise the tent in an easily defensible position.

'We're out of militia-controlled territory, so we need to set an armed two-person watch tonight. We're on a four-hour rotation. Private Jason, Corporal Rodgers, take first watch—'

'But sir—' Jason started.

'Sergeant Thea and I will relieve you.' Captain Kiandra glared at Jason, daring him to say another word.

'We did it last night. How come the other two get to sleep in?' Rodgers argued, backing his new mate.

'Because we need them fresh and on their game in the morning.' Captain Kiandra's tone was firm but impatient.

'I don't know why we're doing this anyway,' Rodgers grumbled as they made camp. 'He's most likely with the zombies, and if he's not dead yet he soon will be. If they don't eat him, they're bound to pass on some filthy disease. We should just head home now.'

'Rodgers, for the last time!'

'I'm only saying, Captain, it's been years since anyone patrolled out this far. Even the militias don't come here. Everyone who was living in this area before the war is probably one of the zombie crew now.'

Captain Kiandra stood, hands on hips. 'The next person to use the z-word will be on latrine duty.'

'But we've been digging our own,' Rodgers complained, not knowing when to give up.

'For now....' The Captain turned away.

Thea moved closer to Bruno and Lee, pretending to ensure they were correctly setting up the tent for inflation.

'Captain Kiandra's older sister was on a patrol in the early days after the war. The wind changed direction and a radiation storm caught her troop. She's been ill ever since,' she told them.

'Well, that explains her dislike of the word zombie,' Lee said.

'In Portsdown there is a lot of mistrust and disinformation about what has gone on above ground,' Thea continued. 'Many people think like the Corporal because they know no better. Others think that way because it helps them deal with the guilt of leaving people outside to die.'

Captain Kiandra interrupted their conversation. 'Right, it's late and I don't like us being out here in the dark. Let's inflate and get inside.' Something moved in the undergrowth as if to emphasise her point.

Tonight the group included Lee in their conversations. Although he sat with them, he didn't say much. Too many

thoughts raced each other through his head for him to take part in the banter.

After they had eaten, Rodgers and Jason had suited up and were sitting just outside the door when Lee plucked up the courage to ask the question nagging at him all day.

'Captain?'

'Yes, Private.'

'What will happen to Allan—I mean, what happens to returned escapees in Portsdown? We lock them up in London... but what happens to them here?'

'That depends.'

'On what?' Lee pressed.

'On how long they've been away. On their reasons for leaving. And....'

There was a long silence.

'And?' Lee prompted.

'Well, I guess on how much their parents are able to influence the Representative Council.'

Lee considered this information for a moment. 'Will Allan's parents be able to influence the council?'

'I think it unlikely,' Captain Kiandra admitted. 'His father is a high school teacher and his mother is a microbiologist. While their skills are useful, they're not influential enough to change the outcome for their son.'

'And that would be?' Lee asked.

'Once we have found out all we need from him, I'm afraid... we only bring them in, Private. What happens after that is someone else's responsibility.'

'Just following orders,' Lee said, his tone a little sharp.

'Go to sleep, Private. Tomorrow will be another long day.'

Lee shuffled over to his bedroll and slipped inside, snuggling around the warmth of the dog beside him.

Bruno, we're not really taking him back, are we? We're not going to give Allan to them to be interrogated, and goodness knows what else?

We don't know what we're meant to do yet, Bruno responded.

But if those are our orders, will you do it?

There was silence in his head, and the dog shifted his weight beside him.

I hope not to be put in that position but, yes, if that is what the Guardians decide is for the best, then I will do it. I believe the Guardians only ask us to do what is best for the future of the world.

What about Allan's best interests? Lee asked.

We don't know enough about what is going on to go against orders, so we need to trust the Time Guardians. Now, I need to get some sleep.

It was like Bruno had erected a wall between their minds, signalling an end to the conversation.

'You might have to do what they say, but I'm not a Guardian,' Lee muttered under his breath. 'I can do what I like.'

'Go to sleep, Private! And that's an order.' Captain Kiandra's voice cut through the darkness.

Lee rolled away from Bruno, as if to make a point, although he wasn't quite sure what that point was. Would he actually disobey an order? It went against everything he believed in. Then again, so did betraying a friend.

He might never have met Allan, but his gut told him Allan and Alain were one and the same person. He had

never let a friend down in his life. Could he start now? Still, what if supporting his friend brought about the end of time?

Was Allan's escaping from Portsdown really that bad? It was not like he had killed anyone. However, a single person could spread sedition and bring down a whole regime, and that would be wrong. Then again, if the government was corrupt....

Now he had arrived at the heart of the matter. He was joining the Australian Army because it protected his home and answered to a democratically elected government. He might not have agreed with everything they asked the military to do, but he knew the majority of Australians voted for them to protect their interests.

The Time Guardians were selected, not elected. He hadn't chosen to join their cause. He knew nothing about how the Portsdown representatives got to sit on their council, or anything about how the local militias governed themselves. So, where did that leave him?

He chewed the inside of his cheek. Normally, if he did not have enough information to make a decision, he would do some research on the internet. He needed to find out more and there was no internet here, so he would watch and learn.

Just like that his stomach stopped churning, his eyelids dropped, and his mind stopped whirring. Until he had more information, he couldn't do anything. So he would gather intel, especially about the people who lived outside Portsdown, then he would be in a better position to choose a side.

He stretched, rolled back into Bruno's warmth, and was asleep moments later.

CHAPTER FOUR
AN UNEXPECTED GUEST

Basia laid down the ax before dropping the split wood into the wicker basket. Wiping the sweat from her brow with a sleeve, she then hefted the basket onto her hip and headed inside.

The logs made a satisfying clunk as she dropped them into the wood chest sitting by the old Aga that served as oven, heater, and water heater for the whole house. Popping the basket back in the pantry, she took the opportunity to pour herself a large glass of water from the pottery purifier. Refreshed, she returned to the kitchen.

'What now, Mum?'

'Our meat supplies are dwindling, so we'll have to use some of the root vegetables from the cellar to make dinner go a little further. If you could bring me some, then collect the eggs, I'll go milk the cows.'

Basia bit back a protest. Life was busy enough, but when her brother and father went on hunting trips, it was busier still because she and her mother covered the work of four people. Even so, her mother knew she hated going into the cellar and usually took on those tasks herself. She must be tired to have forgotten.

A lantern hung on a hook beside the stairs. Basia lit it and let the flame settle before opening the door. Waiting for the stale smell of animals and dirt to hit her, she took a deep breath and descended into the darkness.

The cellar was spacious. Its three rooms spanned two-thirds of the house above and half the barn. The door on the far wall led to the bedroom her family had slept in during the years after the war. Now it was a dumping ground for everything broken or useless—things that might one day be stripped down for parts, or might work if they fixed the old generator.

In the corner opposite sat an ancient air filtration system—a useless piece of junk now that the generator was broken. Beside it was the door leading to the underground barn. Although this section was closed off now, the stalls where the ancestors of their animals had weathered the aftermath of the war still stunk out the lower level.

Tucked underneath the steps were the wooden storage bins containing root vegetables, and beside them were the shelves holding muslin-covered blocks of cheese and pats of butter. Then, next door, jars of pickles and preserves stood in a row—although at the moment it would be more correct to describe them as jars waiting for pickles and preserves. Soon they would begin the process of stripping down the garden and preserving produce for the winter.

Ensuring they had enough to eat was a continuous grind. How she longed for the times she read about in books when you took money to a shop and simply bought what you needed.

She held out her apron before grabbing some carrots and potatoes, then almost lost the lot when she was distracted by the sound of scrabbling in the corner. It won't come near the light, she told herself, but still, she rushed back up the stairs.

Even though she spent the first four years of her life living in these rooms, she always heaved a sigh of relief when she returned to the warmth of the kitchen. Perhaps it was because she was leaving the ever-present rat population behind.

After returning the lamp to its hook, she dropped the vegetables on the table. Picking up a bowl, she used the hand pump over the sink to half fill it. As she grabbed the handle, her mother said, 'Don't use too much. It takes time to collect the water and then filter it, and with the others away....'

Every moment in her life contained a constant reminder of the war. Water had to be filtrated and tested for general use, then filtrated a second time for human consumption. The soil had to be turned over every year and tested before planting. Animals and humans were tested regularly for radiation exposure. Every night she took a cocktail of pills to combat radiation particles that might have entered her system in spite of all the other measures taken.

While she peeled and chopped the vegetables, she imagined herself living in an easier time: a time when

everything didn't have to be done by hand, and people did things other than work all day. So caught up was she in her daydream, she didn't even realise her mother had left until she come back into the room carrying two pails of milk.

'Basia. *Basia.*'

'What? Sorry.'

'Can you get the cellar door for me?'

'Sure.' She opened the door for her mother and kept it open to provide a little light as she navigated the stairs. When her mother returned, Basia went back to her work as her mother checked the bread cooking in the Aga. Deciding they were done, she removed the two loaves, releasing the aroma of fresh baked bread.

'Mum, did you know Johan said the boys from over at the Simpson farm went into Southampton to see if they could find some solar panels? They think they may be able to generate enough electricity to at least light the farm, and maybe run a few small appliances.'

'Mm, what...? Yes, your father told me.'

'Do you think we could do something like that?' Basia asked.

Her mother paused, glancing up from checking the bread. From the look on her face, Basia prepared for yet another lecture on the evils of everything that made life easier in the past. Instead, her mother sighed, and her face softened.

'Basia, I know this isn't much of a life for you. You're young, and you want more than working on the farm to look forward to. I wish I could offer more, but this is all we have. Perhaps once you complete your training, we might be able to find a place for you in a settlement. That will be a little more exciting than this.'

Basia wanted to say, 'But that is years away, I want something to happen now.' She didn't, though, because without medical training, life off the farm would be no easier. Her mother had begun training her to do more than just assist with the trickle of patients who made their way to the farm for help. She had dusted off her old nursing books and began teaching Basia medicine.

In the end she said, 'I guess they still need to figure out how to get the panels working, and also fix the appliances. Dad said he might look out some of his old technical manuals for them.'

'Yes, we could do with someone who knows how to fix these things in our little community. But I guess people like that prefer larger settlements where there is a small supply of electricity and a heap of salvaged appliances and parts.' Pushing a stray strand of hair from her eyes, her mother turned back to the bread.

'I thought this house to be so grand when your father first brought me here,' her mother sighed. 'The local stone pillars out front made it appear so imposing. Such a shame they didn't survive the war. Still, enough was left to make a lower level for the house and a sturdy barn. We should not complain.'

Basia smiled. She liked it when her mother talked of the nice bits of the past—of times before the war, or when she was little. She had been told that when the family emerged from the basement after five years of living underground, the top story was gone—destroyed in the aftermath of the fighting. Her father repaired the bottom level, making it secure enough for them to live in before tackling the barn. He and her brother Johan finished adding a wooden second story the year before last, giving them all their own rooms for sleeping.

'It was a real English manor. Many generations of your family lived here,' her mother continued, reminiscing. 'When your father brought me from Southampton for the first time, I could not believe a man from such a background, an architect in a fancy firm, had fallen in love with me, a Polish immigrant training to be a nurse.'

Basia paused to listen. This was special, the story of how her parents had overcome his parent's objections to their marriage.

'Your father was an architect for such a short time. First his parents died, then war threatened. We moved back here, and I worked for the local doctor. Johan was a baby when your father began building the shelter downstairs, a small underground life for us. We stocked it with everything we needed, and when it was time to go below, I took Johan downstairs while your father brought down the sheep, chickens, and cows. Now that was fun to behold.'

Her mother chuckled at the memory of her husband coaxing the reluctant animals below ground.

Basia added the familiar next line. 'And he wouldn't have been able to do it without the dogs.'

'Yes, Whip and Sheba were most helpful. They left their puppy with Johan and went to herd the sheep.'

Basia took the vegetables over to her mother, who stirred them through the thick stew.

'Did you collect the eggs?' she asked, as if just remembering.

'Not yet. I'll go now.' Basia was reluctant to break the storytelling spell, but the chickens needed to be locked up tight before darkness fell.

As she rounded the side of the house, two great lolloping dogs bowled into her, almost causing her to lose her footing.

'Jasmine and Baby, you're back.'

Baby rolled over for a tummy rub, while his mother stood quietly by. Looking into the dog's intelligent brown eyes, Basia paused. Something was wrong.

She lifted her head and raised a hand to shade her eyes. In the distance two figures appeared, silhouetted against the grey-blue sky, one tall and one slightly stooped under an indiscriminate load. Her mouth watered—there would be venison for the winter. Deer were elusive, but they occasionally appeared in the deepest reaches of the forest where fallout had not penetrated.

No, Juniper would not act like this over a deer. As they drew closer, she realised it was not an animal they carried, but a human.

Forgetting all about the chickens, Basia sped back to the house. As she left the garden, her father called, 'Basia, tell your mother we have a badly injured boy, so she'll need to set up a bed.'

Flinging open the door, she gulped in some air before stuttering, 'Dad and Johan have a boy. He's injured...

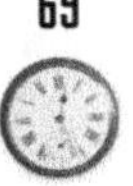

quite bad.... We need—'

'I've got this. Catch your breath, then go fetch what we need for a bed,' her mother said as Basia dropped into a chair.

Things moved quickly after that. Johan and her father took the boy into the front room and laid him out on the divan her mother used for patients. Basia put some water on the stove and went to fetch blankets while Johan left to lock up the rest of the animals.

'Thank you. Just put the bedding on the chair,' her mother said when Basia entered the living room. 'Then go and finish getting dinner ready. Your father and brother haven't eaten a proper meal in days.'

Hovering in the doorway, Basia attempted to catch a glimpse of their guest, but her mother and father presented a rather solid wall.

'Basia, dinner,' her father said without looking behind in a tone she knew not to disobey.

Johan was placing a basket of eggs on the bench and she crossed the kitchen to shut the door behind him. A flurry of dog fur flashed past her, almost knocking her over for the second time that day. Once the animals were safely inside, she closed up, turned the key, and dropped the stout wooden bar. Moving the rifle from where her father left it leaning against a chair to its position beside the door, she turned back into the room.

'Can you do the shutters in here while I close the others?' Johan asked, and she nodded.

This dusk ritual happened every evening: securing the property and animals from marauders and goodness knows what else roamed in the dark. No one stayed out in the open once the sun went down unless they carried weapons and were able to defend themselves.

Basia hustled the dogs to their beds in the washroom and gave them each some dried meat before filling their drinking bowl. Having seen to the animals, she closed the shutters and lit the lamps.

With everything secure, she checked on the stew. It simmered nicely, its rich aroma filling the room and causing her stomach to rumble. Cutting thick slices of bread, she piled them on a plate before fetching a round of cheese and some butter from the pantry. As she worked, the murmur of her parents' voices drifted through from the other room, but they were speaking too low for her to make out actual words.

'If they want you to know, they will tell you,' Johan said from behind, making her jump.

'Not everyone is prepared to wait until information is handed to them on a—'

She stopped suddenly, realising her brother was so calm because he knew something. If she antagonised him, he would not be interested in sharing it with her.

'Clean up, Johan. Dinner is almost ready.'

Frowning at her, Johan paused, then shook his head as if the reason for her abrupt change of heart was beyond him. Good. If he was off balance, he might let something slip.

He took his and his father's travel packs into the washroom, returning in a fresh set of clothes, his hair wet and sticking to his head. Basia ran the radiation detector over him, looked at the reading, and smiled. 'You're all good.'

Ladling out two bowls of stew, Basia placed them on the table, and waited for Johan to sit before beginning to eat herself.

'I hope you brought home more than that boy from your hunting trip,' she started. 'We're running short on meat.'

'I can tell,' Johan smiled, raising his fork to display the carrot on the end.

'So?'

'So what?' Johan smirked, enjoying needling her.

Basia bit back her frustration. 'Did you bring back any meat?'

Johan laughed. 'A couple of rabbits—they've been gutted and cleaned. We saw some wild beef, but their radiation levels were too high for us to be interested.'

'Well, it will be dried pulses and root veggies all winter then.'

Johan did not take the bait. 'We're planning to go out for a couple of days again tomorrow and return via the fishing hole.'

'And what about the stranger? Would you leave us alone with him?'

Johan shrugged. 'He was barely breathing when I put him on the bed. He'll be lucky to survive the night. I don't know why father insisted we bring him home.'

Basia punched her brother on the arm. 'He couldn't just leave him out there. That's not who we are.'

'You're right. We are people who look out for others.' Johan and Basia turned to find their father standing in the doorway. 'Is there any of that for me?'

'Yes, I'll dish you some. Should I get some for Mum too?' Basia asked.

Her father shook his head. 'No, your mother will be a little while longer yet. Can you make some tea if that water is boiled?'

Basia moved to serve her father's meal while he went to clean and change. By the time she placed his bowl and a steaming cup of tea on the table, Johan had checked him for radiation and he was ready to tuck into dinner.

'So, who is he?' Basia asked, unable to contain her excitement. Nothing this interesting ever happened in their quiet, boring life.

'An injured boy we found on the old motorway. He's been unconscious the entire time, so all we know is that he is badly hurt.'

'Isn't it dangerous bringing him here?' Basia said. 'I mean, the community doesn't like strangers.'

'If we're lucky we won't need to tell them anything. If he comes to, we can find out where he is from and send word to his family, and if he doesn't, well....'

As her father finished talking, his wife entered the room, poured some water from the kettle into a bowl, then left. They finished their meal in silence, then Basia and Johan cleaned up while their father went into the pantry to joint the rabbits.

'No use putting them up for winter, Basia,' he said when he returned. 'They can go into the stewpot tomorrow.'

Basia nodded, not looking forward to a winter with little or no meat. Sometimes when a cow was no longer good for milk they would butcher it for food and to provide something to barter with. Unfortunately, all their cows were currently strong and healthy.

Johan reboiled the kettle, and Basia pulled down the

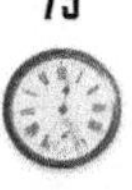

jar of dried chamomile, ready to make more tea. Her father joined them at the table just as her mother came through the door from the living room.

'How is he?' her father asked.

'The wound in his side is nasty, Simon, but it seems to have missed everything vital. I've given him antibiotics for his infection. He is young, well fed, and strong, so there's a good chance he will recover,' her mother informed them as she dished some stew into a bowl.

'So, no radiation disease?' Basia asked, and her mother shook her head.

'Unusual for a person living away from a community.' Basia fished for information.

'He has a community...,' her father said.

Basia caught the look between her mother and father—it was her mother's "not in front of the children" look.

'And ...,' Basia encouraged, hoping for once her father would ignore her mother.

'Where he's from isn't something we need to worry about at the moment. What is important is that I need someone to watch him tonight. Someone to give him a second lot of antibiotics, and to keep his temperature down.'

'I guess that will be me,' Basia said with little enthusiasm. The part of being a trainee medic she hated the most was sitting with patients through the night. She was a person who really needed her sleep to be able to function the next day.

'Are you sure that's a good idea, Tanya?' her father asked.

'Given the sedative he took, he's unlikely to wake,' her mother said.

Basia's eyes widened. 'Is there a chance he might be

dangerous? Why ever did you bring him home, Dad?'

'He's unconscious. And if he wasn't, even you could best him in his current condition.' Johan laughed.

'He doesn't pose a physical threat,' Tanya said as she stood to rinse her plate in the sink. 'Simon, could you please help me with some bedding for Basia?'

As their parents left the room, Basia leaned towards Johan and whispered, 'He's from the underground city, isn't he?'

Johan froze, his cup halfway to the table.

'Basia, what do you know about the city?' His tone was wary.

'I know there is one.'

'Basia, please keep this to yourself.' Johan's eyes pleaded. 'If anyone finds out who he is, we will be in a lot of trouble.'

'Then why did Father bring him here?'

'You said it yourself: Dad couldn't leave a wounded human to die, no matter where he comes from.'

Any further conversation was cut short by their parents' return. The family began to ready themselves for bed, and Basia did not get another chance to talk alone with Johan. In fact, it was almost as though he was avoiding her.

While she was in the pantry, she heard his footsteps on the stairs and then his bedroom door close. 'You don't get away that easily,' she said under her breath as she wrapped the cheese. 'Tomorrow is another day.'

By the time she returned to the kitchen her parents had cleared everything else away and moved the dogs' beds in front of the Aga.

'The painkillers and antibiotics should last him through the night. Call me if you need anything else,' her mother said before disappearing up the stairs.

Basia wandered into the living room and went around the furniture to get her first look at her patient.

The pale face framed by a blanket and a shock of wavy black hair was handsome enough to have come from one of the books she read. He appeared well fed and relatively healthy, as her mother had said. This meant the chances of him living as an outcast were slim, making it more likely he came from the underground city near Portsmouth—the one she heard so much about but must never speak of.

Reaching out her hand, she felt he was a little warm. She turned and removed the thermometer from the table and placed it on his forehead. His temperature was up a little, but nothing to be alarmed about yet.

Placing the thermometer back within easy reach, she picked up her comforter and a book from the coffee table. Taking them to the chair on the other side of the fire from the boy, she curled up under the blanket and opened her book. *North and South* by Elizabeth Gaskell had always been one of her favourites. In fact, she enjoyed most of the books her parents called the classics. The England they told of was very different to the one she lived in, but she felt an affinity with the female heroines.

Although they wore beautiful gowns and attended parties and balls, like her their options for the future were narrow. If they were strong enough willed to want to be independent, they must choose a husband who would allow them to do what they wanted.

Sighing, she looked over at the patient—he was the most exciting thing to happen in her entire life, and she would probably still be saying that ten years from now.

She smiled, imagining herself as Margaret Hale to his Mr Thornton. He could whisk her off her feet and take her home to be waited on hand and foot for the rest of her life. Well, at least she might have a stab at a life somewhere where women were not held back because of their ability to breed.

This was just as big a fantasy as *North and South*, and never likely to happen. Her eyelids began to droop closed. Sleepily, she rolled over to check the alarm clock would wake her in time for her next check. Snuggling under the covers, she dozed to visions of balls and of dashing young men who wanted nothing more than to take her away from her life of drudgery.

Simon flopped back on the bed and sighed. No words could describe the pleasure of sleeping in his own bed again after four nights alternating between keeping watch and sleeping on the ground.

'I'm getting too old for these long hunting trips,' he said.

'You're fitter than most men your age—even half your age.'

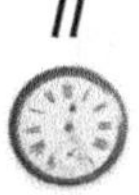

He smiled at his wife as she hung her shirt in the wardrobe. 'Although I appreciate the sentiment, you are more than little biased.'

Tanya paused halfway through hanging her trousers, as if waiting for him to continue.

'The reality is I'm not as young as I once was, and this life is hard on us all. I don't know how much longer we can go on without extra help on the farm,' he said.

His wife looked over her shoulder with the piercing gaze she used when trying to search for the meaning beyond his words. He often felt like she was attempting to pluck the very thoughts from his mind.

'Ah, so your intention was to supplement our labour force when you picked up the stray downstairs.'

Simon chuckled. 'Perhaps not consciously,' he said. 'But it certainly wouldn't hurt to have another pair of young hands around and put into practice that idea of adopting a couple of children without parents from the settlement. We could even go as far as Southampton if needs be.'

'You think they will want to live on a farm?' Tanya's eyebrows rose skeptically.

'I'm sure we could find one or two, and we have the spare room for them. Perhaps even a few older children ready to leave home might be interested in fixing up the old house on the other side of the pond.'

'And in the meantime, it might bring potential partners for our children right to our doorstep?' Tanya chuckled as she closed the wardrobe.

Simon sat back up. 'You make it sound like I brought back a husband for Basia.'

Tanya raised an eyebrow.

'It's still not safe out there, is it so wrong of me to prefer opening our doors and offering them an alternative to leaving home?'

Tanya sighed. 'You can't protect them from the big bad world forever.'

'I know, and I also know there is a chance they may leave anyway, in which case we would still need new people to help work the farm.'

Again that eyebrow rose. 'And you had to start with that particular boy?'

'He was injured,' Simon said, defending his actions.

His wife's hands moved to her hips and his stomach sank. The look on her face was another familiar one. It said, 'What were you thinking?', and he braced himself.

'Simon, that boy's from Portsdown. You took a huge risk bringing him here.'

'Perhaps not so big. No one's patrolled this far out for at least ten years,' he said.

'Even so, the town elders won't let him stay—not when they find out where he's from.'

Simon shrugged. 'Perhaps they never need to know.'

'Huh. You really think they will just let a stranger slip into our midst without questioning his origins?'

His wife was right, but he did not want to admit it. 'No, I'm saying he might move on before anyone finds out he is here.'

Tanya's stance relaxed, but Simon didn't let his guard down quite yet. 'Putting aside how I feel about people from Portsdown, you have no idea if this boy will want to stay with us or go on his way. Basia already hankers for an easier way of life. What if he offers to take her back with him?'

'I don't think—'

'And Johan is also restless, he may consider leaving with them.'

When he had decided to bring the boy back with them, Simon's one thought had been not leaving him there to die. Everything else he rationalised away on the trek home.

'I'm sorry, Tanya. I didn't think beyond saving him. I have been trying to focus on the positives to justify my actions.'

Her face giving nothing away as she walked around the bed and slipped between the covers. 'Well, I guess we can cross those bridges as we come to them. Now, this weary old lady needs her sleep… and so do you.'

Simon grinned at her. 'Maybe I'm not so tired after all….'

The hairs on the back of Allan's neck stood on end. Someone was watching him. His fight or flight instinct suggested he open his eyes and at least find the cause, but in truth he didn't have the strength. He was so tired even his earlobes ached. Far away voices murmured. He moved a little, thinking he should sit up. Pain wracked his body and he started to drift back into oblivion.

No! He fought the exhaustion threatening to overwhelm

him, pushing the pain to the recesses of his mind. If he couldn't open his eyes, he could listen and try to figure out where he was—in Portsmouth, or back in Portsdown, or somewhere else entirely?

At least back in the underground city he would get decent medical treatment for his wounds before they interrogated him. If the Portsmouth militia had him, then who knew what his fate would be. They'd probably torture him for information about Portsdown.

Perhaps the radiation affected had found him? He had been so sure the rumours of their turning to cannibalism were fantasy, but he could be mistaken.

Was it wrong to hope he might have been found by the people he was looking to find? The people who had found a way to live a new life after the holocaust? Documents in the secret archives indicated radiation should have dispersed to livable levels years ago. Then again, when they had been written, no one had lived through a nuclear war of the scale the world had experienced. Perhaps the existence of people living above ground was nothing more than a pipe dream.

Pain threatened to overwhelm him again. He rolled to get more comfortable and the covers slipped. When the wave had passed, he snuggled back into the warmth, his mind drifting back to the events that led him here.

For a moment he wondered if he had done the right thing leaving Portsdown. Food was plentiful, education was free to all, and he and his parents had lived in a comfortable apartment.

No, that was his fear talking. He needed to remember his reasons for wanting to leave—to choose the life he

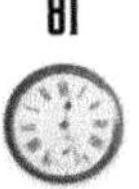

wanted to live.

All his life he dreamed of being a teacher like his father. When he turned eighteen, he found the Representative Council had other ideas. They informed him Portsdown needed soldiers more than they needed teachers. They needed farmers more than teachers. They needed carpenters more than they needed teachers. They invited him to choose from a range of jobs they said the community required to survive, and not one of those had anything to do with teaching. In fact, not one of those jobs required him to undertake any further study.

Swallowing his disappointment, he took the list home to discuss his options with his parents, certain he could find a way to work for the good of the community in a fulfilling job. On the way he bumped into a school friend Daniel, whose father was head of the hospital laboratory where Allan's mother worked. They had gone through school together, and Allan had spent many a lunch break helping Daniel keep up in class.

Preparing to commiserate with the shortlist of options they had to choose their future careers from, Allan drew back in surprise when he found Daniel's list looked very different to his. His list contained vacancies in university courses leading to professional careers.

Allan had been aware his whole life that there were those in charge and those who weren't, but until that moment, he had not fully understood how determined those in charge were about keeping power for themselves. Daniel's acceptance of the different futures available to them made this all the harder to take. He remembered the rest of the conversation well.

'We can still be friends,' Daniel had said. 'I mean, I might need some help with my courses and you can learn as I do.'

'And would I eventually be able to be accepted into university?' Allan asked.

'Well, of course not. If you're not admitted directly from school, you can't ever attend.' Daniel's brow furrowed, as if Allan's anger confused him.

'And would you have me as best man at your wedding?'

'But Carmel and I are not engaged,' Daniel said, bemused. 'Besides, when we do tie the knot, it will be a stuffy society affair. You would hate it.'

There was so much Allan wanted to say, but in the end he brushed past Daniel and muttered, 'See you round.'

That night he complained to his parents, hoping for some sympathy, but instead he got a lecture about how many babies had not survived the war, and he should be thankful for whatever life offered him. Allan's frustration grew. It wasn't that he believed any job to be more or less important than another, it was the way people's choices were limited by who they were, not by what they could do.

As his distrust of the ruling elite grew, he pulled further and further away from his parents. They would be forever grateful to Daniel's father for wangling a precious place in the city for his favourite assistant. They would never question the gift they had been given, or the treatment of their offspring.

In the end he chose a career in horticulture. Not because he had any affinity for growing things, but more because it came with a small room of his own close to the underground farms.

While Allan learnt about hydroponics and growing food under artificial light, he also learned more about why the people in charge of the underground community kept such tight control of their citizens. It was a question of balance, they explained to him. The city needed a certain number of labourers to run the basic services and provide amenities for the ruling elite.

His new friends thought moving above ground was the answer to their problems, except the people leaving threatened the balance, so it was prohibited. Besides, no one could say what it was like above ground, not really. Others escaped trying to find out, but no one ever returned. When one of their number found a back door to the city, Allan volunteered to go above ground and report back on the state of the world.

Getting to the entrance had been easy, as had opening the secret door. As he slipped into the cave on the other side, he sensed someone watching him. He turned to check if he was being followed, but there was no one there. He should have listened to his gut. Making his way down the incline towards and old motorway, he paused, and someone yelled, 'Halt.'

He responded by breaking into a run and was almost at the road when a cry rang out, 'Halt, go no further. In the name of the Portsdown Regiment, you are under arrest for unauthorised activity.'

At those words he ran faster, weaving through vehicles abandoned before he was born. Unauthorised activity was a euphemism for sedition and mutiny, and it was likely his life was already forfeit. He decided being killed outright while running for freedom was better than being made an example of in front of the entire community.

Pain shot through his side and he slipped, losing his footing. Using an abandoned vehicle to pull himself to his feet, he carried on moving, looking for somewhere to hide. He slipped under a nearby car and listened until the sun began to set and the soldiers finally gave up their search. As they departed, he overheard them calling for reinforcements.

Although the wound hurt like hell, he managed to struggle out from under the car. Leaning against it, he enjoyed the feeling of the setting sun on his face before he fell to the ground. As he fell in and out of consciousness, he was aware of someone picking him up and carrying him for what seemed like an age. Then all he knew was darkness and the warmth of a fire.

Icy drafts of air crept up his back. He pulled the blankets back over his shoulders and gasped at the pain in his side. That at least he hadn't imagined. He tried to will his eyes open so he could find out where he was, but they still wouldn't obey. He drifted again, back into dreams of sun on his face and the blue sky above.

CHAPTER FIVE
TIME FOR A PLAN

Basia was rudely awoken by the sound of footsteps thundering down the stairs. She was rubbing the sleep out of her eyes when Johan rushed into the room.

'Wake up, sleepyhead and let me out the door.'

'Mmm... why?' She tried to grasp what he was saying, but her brain still was not functioning.

'Just let me out and lock up after.'

'What's the rush?' Basia asked.

'Some men from the town are heading this way. You'd best go make sure Dad is coming down too.'

'What...?' A horrified thought struck her. 'They must have travelled in the dark.... I mean, the sun's not even up.'

Johan tugged at her blanket and it fell to the floor. 'Come on, get a move on or they'll be here already.'

Exposed to the cold morning air, Basia's skin goose

bumped as she swung her legs around, then slipped and almost fell as her feet found the comforter Johan had discarded. Reaching down, she plucked it up and tucked it securely round her shoulders as she walked to where her brother was waiting impatiently. She glanced over at the boy, pleased to see the noise had not woken him.

Johan grabbed the gun that stood beside the door and tapped his foot, waiting for her to pull herself together.

'Patience. You know I'm not a morning person like you,' she hissed.

'All right, I'll just tell the men outside to come back later when you are ready for them, shall I?'

She stuck her tongue out as he slipped past her through the opening. The key snicked in the lock and she turned to head upstairs. Knocking quietly on her parent's door, she said, 'Father. Father. Johan needs you. Men from the town are coming.'

Heavy footsteps sounded from the other side of the wood, and there was a creak before her mother's head appeared through the crack. 'I heard Johan go down. Your father's sound asleep. Can he not handle it?'

Basia shrugged. 'He sent me up to make sure Father was coming, so—.'

'It's all right. I'm awake,' came the sleepy voice from inside.

'We'll be down in a minute. Can you make sure the boy's okay for me... and start the breakfast.' Her mother closed the door before Basia's lips formed her assent.

She was stoking the fire into life when she heard her parents descend into the living room. She finished placing a couple of logs on the glowing embers in the Aga before rushing to meet her mother by the door.

'Make sure you lock it behind us,' her mother said. 'I don't want anybody slipping past and getting inside until we are sure of their intentions.'

Her father joined them, rifle cocked over his arm. As they left the warmth of the living room, her mother shivered and Basia glimpsed her brother leaning against the veranda post, his own weapon held casually across his body. He appeared relaxed, but the set of his jaw told Basia he was anything but.

She turned the key a second time, then quickly nipped in behind the sofa their guest slept on, opening the shutters a crack so she could watch the action. Her father had joined Johan, while her mother took up a position in front of the door. At the edge of her vision, Basia could just make out a group of men coming into view. It took an age before they were anywhere near close enough to speak.

'Good morning to you, Simon, Johan... and to you too, Tanya.'

Her mother frowned at the implied insult of being acknowledged after her son, but before she could respond with something cutting, Basia's father spoke.

'Councillor Johnson. What can I do for you this morning?'

'No need for all these weapons, Simon. This is just a neighbourly visit. We aren't armed.'

From her vantage point, Basia saw six of the men carried pistols in their holsters. And even if she could not see the others' guns, no one would be foolish enough to come this far from the settlement without some form of protection—especially not at this early hour.

'If this is a friendly visit, then why are there so many

of you?' her father countered.

'Simon, why not invite us inside out of the cold and we can talk over a nice cup of tea.' Councillor Johnson took a step forward, but something in her father's face must have caused him to pause.

'I'm fine where we are,' her father answered. 'At least until I know why so many of you have turned up on my property unannounced, uninvited, and just as dawn breaks.'

'I think you know why,' Councillor Johnson said, all pretense of friendliness gone. 'One of our patrols saw you and your son carrying a body, a human body, yesterday. A rather unusual thing to be doing, don't you think? We have come to investigate.'

'Johan and I found an injured boy while on our way back from patrol. I assume you mean him? We brought him back for Tanya to tend to. I see nothing in our actions that would warrant you and your mob turning up on my doorstep like this.' Her father's voice was calm, but Basia could hear the underlying anger.

'Come now, we were the ones who asked you to patrol near Portsmouth. We know you were close to the underground city. You can't blame us for wanting to check the origins of your guest,' the councillor pressed.

Tanya took a step towards her husband, although she didn't take her eyes off the men for one moment. 'What do you mean you were patrolling near Portsdown, Simon? You told me you were on a hunting trip.'

'It *was* a hunting trip, but the council asked us to have a look at what was going on around Portsdown while we were out,' her father said without taking his eyes off the men in front of him.

'I'll get right to the point,' Councillor Johnson interrupted. 'Is that boy a runaway from the underground city?'

'I knew it,' Basia muttered. 'I knew there was an underground city close by, and that he was from there'

It seemed her mother was not interested in answering the councillor's question. 'What were you thinking, Simon? Our family relies on you and Johan, and you risked yourselves by—.'

'To be fair, Mrs Pettigrew...'

Her mother swung around and glared at the man who had dared speak while she was. 'My name is Tanya!'

'All right, Tanya, your husband has allowed your son to patrol and scout for us for the last year, so you can hardly call foul now.'

The fury on her mother's face caused Councillor Johnson to take a step back. Even Basia could feel the waves of anger rolling off her, and she tensed, waiting for the explosion.

To her surprise, her mother pursed her lips and gave her husband a look that said, 'You and I will talk about this later.'

Oblivious to the tension, Councillor Johnson continued. 'There is a high likelihood this boy originates from the city. If by a slim chance he doesn't, you still haven't declared the presence of a new person in the settlement as our rules of association decree.'

Her father ran a hand through his hair, a sure sign he was stressed. 'Goodness, Charlie, give a man a chance to breathe. The boy is not from the city and I am not hiding anything.'

Councillor Johnson moved as if to interrupt, but her

father held up his hand. 'I brought the boy straight here because he was barely alive and he needed immediate medical care. We only got home at dusk, I planned to come into Lyndhurst to declare.'

The Councillor frowned and took a step back. After a quizzical glance at her family, he turned to talk to the others. The conversation went on for quite some time, and Basia crossed her fingers, hoping her father had convinced the men to leave them be.

Councillor Johnson finally emerged from the group and said, 'We were perhaps a little premature in our actions, but given what happened last time an escapee found their way here, can you blame us?'

'We all know of the farmstead that was burned to the ground as a rebuke for harbouring the escapee—but that was over ten years ago. We haven't seen one of their patrols around here since,' her father pointed out.

The Councillor smiled a smile that did not reach his eyes. 'Listen, why don't you invite us in for that cup of tea and we can sort all this out like civilised men.'

Basia gasped and cast a worried glance around the room. She should have trusted her father though; he was a wily campaigner.

'I see no reason why all seven of you should traipse around my home first thing in the morning when my daughter's not even up,' he said.

Councillor Johnson laughed. 'I can see her peeking through the shutters.'

Basia ducked back behind the curtain.

Her father didn't falter. 'Give me fifteen minutes to ensure she is suitably attired to receive males into the

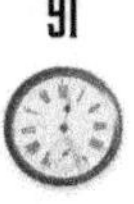

house, and then one or two of you can come in, meet the boy, and put all your fears to rest.'

Councillor Johnson checked with the others, then nodded. 'That's a reasonable request. I will check out your guest, but don't keep me waiting too long, or we will think you are still hiding something.'

Basia closed the shutter and went to open the door to admit her family. This time when she locked it, she dropped the bar back down. She did not trust any of the men outside, especially Councillor Johnson, who was known for saying one thing and doing the opposite.

'Into the kitchen. We haven't much time to save ourselves from the wrath of the Council.' Her mother's tone was brisk as she bustled them though the living room.

Johan frowned. 'Don't you want to talk about—'

'Time enough later for that, after we have dealt with the men outside,' her mother said.

Basia's father and brother exchanged a look, worried the longer Tanya had to stew over things, the worse the eventual outcome would be for them. When they were all in the other room, her mother began barking orders.

'Johan, go get a pair of your shorts and a T-shirt.' A relieved Johan immediately departed. 'Basia, stoke up the fire until it is raging. Simon, come and help me get that boy out of the rest of his clothes—one look at them and they'll know exactly where he came from. We'll burn them before we let anyone in.'

'Won't they be suspicious about that?' her dad asked.

'Of course, but we can tell them they were so covered in blood and crawling with lice we had no option but to burn them. Charlie Johnson is so fastidious he won't even blink an eye.' Her mother's lips curled disdainfully when she spoke about the Councillor.

Her father chuckled as he moved to help his wife.

When her mother returned moments later with a bundle of clothing, Basia shoved it into the fire. It started to burn... slowly.

'Pass me a log,' her mother said. 'I'll put it in front to hide the evidence.'

Basia complied, and then said, 'I'll put on the porridge for breakfast, and the kettle for tea. That can be our excuse for the fire being so hot.'

'Okay.' Her mother rubbed her forehead. 'Actually, I'll get things started. You go on up and get dressed.'

Basia moved swiftly to do as her mother asked, not wanting to test her mother's temper under the current circumstances. By the time Basia returned, the boy was dressed in a pair of Johan's cotton shorts and a T-shirt and her mother was pulling the blanket up to cover his chest. He appeared more pale and grey than he had been, and the sheen of sweat on his brow highlighted the cost of moving him.

Seeing she wasn't needed in the lounge, Basia went through to the kitchen to finish preparing breakfast while her father went to let the Councillor in. Basia kept herself quiet so she could hear what was going on in the other room.

'Well, Simon, you're right, it looks like this boy could be from anywhere. Perhaps his clothes might be of some help?'

'If only I'd realised you would want to see them—I burned them last night,' her mother's voice answered. 'His top was so caked in blood it was unwearable, and his trousers were so riddled with lice I got rid of them too.'

Oh no, his boots, Basia thought. *Where did Mother put them? There, by the pantry.* She tiptoed over and grabbed the tell-tale items along with another log of wood. Opening the door to the range, she pushed them in, placing the log in front so they couldn't be seen. She hoped it was enough, although a strange odour began to fill the room. Leaning over the sink, she opened the shutters. before pushing up the sash window to let in some air.

No, she could still smell it. Frantically glancing around the room, she remembered the rabbits in the pantry. She rushed over, opened the door, and retrieved the skins. Laying them out on the bench furthest from the food, she just had time to get back to stirring the porridge as her parents came through with the Councillor.

'Basia, what's that smell?' Her mother's nose wrinkled. Spying the rabbits, she raised an eyebrow as she said, 'Take those back into the pantry. We can cure them later. We can't have out guest putting up with that horrid smell.'

Basia moved quickly to do as she was bid, bringing back a citrus pomander they used to scent rooms after any particularly smelly work.

Her mother leaned over to check the porridge, and when Basia returned to take over from her, she whispered, 'What was that about?'

'Boots,' Basia replied, her lips brushing her mother's

hair as she answered.

'That wound. I haven't seen anything like it before. Could it have been made by a laser blaster?' Councillor Johnson's voice boomed.

Her mother turned and walked to the cupboards and began gathering mugs for tea as she answered. 'To be honest, I'm not sure what made it. I have to say I was thinking it was more like someone had tried to cauterise an injury.' She placed the mugs on the table and said, 'I didn't find a bullet, so I thought maybe a stab wound. I hadn't considered a blaster.'

'Mmm, he might have come across one of the city militia. They have some blasters... or if he travelled with someone, they may have tried to help him then given him up for dead.' the Councillor mused.

Basia smiled. The pompous prat was taking the bait.

Her father now spoke. 'Perhaps we can sit down. We don't want to wake the boy.'

'Hasn't he said a word the whole time?' The Councillor's voice was moving closer, so Basia stared intently at the porridge, covering the stove door with her body.

'Not a single thing,' her father confirmed.

'Good morning, Basia.'

Basia had hoped he would ignore her, but no such luck. His over familiar attention always set her teeth on edge. Still, she could not afford to be rude, given the current circumstances.

She half turned to find the ruddy-faced man standing a little too close to be polite. His smile was almost a leer, and she forced herself not to shudder in response. She could not believe some women in their small community thought this tall, fair-haired widower was a catch. All she saw was a man of around her father's age, running to fat and full of his own importance.

'Morning,' Basia mumbled, turning her eyes forward and watching the spoon as she stirred the porridge, hoping she had satisfied the requirements of politeness.

'My, young lady, you've grown since I saw you last.' Basia's stomach heaved. 'Simon, perhaps the time has come for us to find somebody who will take on your daughter.'

Basia froze, unsure how to respond, but her father came to her rescue. 'She is still young. There's plenty of time. Besides, she's studying with Tanya. Our community needs more than one person with medical knowledge if we are to thrive.'

'I'm sure we can find a boy to take her place when the time comes for her to marry. I mean, the females of the species hold a special place. Our future survival relies on them.' The Councillor had not moved, and Basia was holding herself very still so she did not brush against him.

'Come, take a seat, Charlie,' her father said as the sound of wood scraping across the flagstone floor filled the room.

Councillor Johnson paused, and it seemed as if he wanted to say something else. Slowly, perhaps reluctantly, he pulled away from Basia and sat down in the chair her father offered.

'Don't leave it too long to match your girl or all the strong men will be gone,' the councillor insisted. 'You want to find her someone who can look after her, don't you?'

'I can look after myself,' Basia whispered furiously.

'And we don't want the Council to have to make that

decision for you,' Councillor Johnson continued, his voice hiding Basia's comment.

Her mother's laugh was brittle. 'Come, we are not barbarians. We don't arrange our children's mates.'

'Perhaps it is—'

'Anyway, Charlie, we're here to discuss the boy, not Basia. If you are happy, he can stay here until he is ready to travel. We will bring him into town in a couple of days to answer all your questions.'

'I am not sure.... There is still a risk, you know... um.... and what if a patrol comes searching for him?'

'A small risk, Charlie. It's been an age since soldiers came out here. Besides, do you think I would place my family in that sort of danger?' her father asked.

'If it would make you feel better, we have a spare room. One of your men could stay here until he is well,' her mother added.

'Umm, it could be days. We have businesses and family to consider....'

'So, it's decided. He'll stay here until he's well enough to be moved.' Her father's tone was decisive.

Smiling to herself, Basia had to admire the way her parents had handled the Councillor.

Not to be outdone, the Councillor said, 'And perhaps you can bring your lovely daughter into town when you bring him in—give her a chance to look over our fine male population.'

Basia shuddered and whispered, 'Over my dead body.'

'We shall see.' Fortunately, her mother was noncommittal. 'Now, if you're happy, perhaps I can escort you out. I am sure we all have much to do and we can't stand around here gossiping all day.'

'Well, yes.' The Councillor sounded like he would like nothing more than to while away his day in the kitchen.

Her parents bustled their guest out before he could find an excuse to stay. As the kitchen emptied, Johan appeared as if from nowhere. 'That old creep. He was leering at you the whole time.'

'Eww, I don't want to know,' Basia said, placing her brother's breakfast on the table and wishing they could forget the whole terrifying morning.

Grabbing a bowl, she sat down beside Johan, trying to ignore the voices in the other room.

'What are you doing today?' she asked conversationally after they had eaten in silence for some moments.

'Father asked me to hunt close to home. I think he wants me to keep an eye out for any unusual activity. What about you?'

'Mother is going to the Watson place. Ma Watson hasn't been well. So, I guess I will be on patient watch here,' Basia said, picking at the food in her bowl.

'I think Dad is staying close to home too, so at least you won't have to lock up and stay inside.'

You mean at least I won't be treated like a child, Basia thought, but said, 'I'm perfectly capable of looking after myself. I'm a better shot than you, and almost as good a fighter as Mum.'

Johan snorted as Basia "accidentally" kicked him on the shin as she placed a fresh pot of tea on the table. The relaxed air was sucked from the room as her parents returned, and she and Johan stared into their tea as they waited for their mother's explosion.

SOLDIER

Their parents ate in silence and Basia could feel Johan's tension as he sipped his tea. Their mother still said nothing. Johan left the table to get his hunting gear, and Basia took the leftovers into the pantry. Taking her time putting things away, she eavesdropped on the conversation in the room next door.

'I want an explanation before I leave, Simon. I want you to tell me why you risked our family's wellbeing for ... for ...'

'... for our neighbours,' her father finished. 'For the people we trade with, who provided the horse you ride to visit patients, and who provide many of the things we need to survive.'

'I appreciate you and Johan have a valuable skill they don't, and that it makes more sense for the farmers to range around keeping our protectorate clear. We've discussed that, and we agreed it was right for us to contribute in that way. What we didn't talk about was going up to Portsmouth, and we didn't talk about Johan going out on patrol by himself.'

'Hardly by himself. The scouts go out in groups of four, and he was put with experienced men,' her father said, defending himself.

There was a long silence. Basia took the opportunity to nip through the kitchen to the lounge to tidy up from the night before. As the silence in the room next door drew out, she cuddled the comforter to her chest and slumped in an armchair. She hated it when her parents fought.

Finally, her father broke the silence. 'Portsmouth was spur of the moment. We ranged close to Lyndhurst on our outward leg, and the guards at the gate were talking of trouble between the city militias. Charlie joined us and asked if we would investigate while we were out. We agreed to go as far as the boundaries of Portsmouth Town.'

Silence again.

'There was no time to tell you, Tanya. I thought we were doing the right thing.'

Still nothing from her mother. Mum must be really angry. Basia wondered why her father hadn't sent someone back to tell them where they were going. Apparently, her mother was thinking exactly the same thing, as she asked her father the very question on Basia's mind.

'I asked Charlie to, and he said he would. But you know Charlie Johnson. He says one thing to your face while knowing he'll do no such thing.'

'What would I have done if you had got caught up in some inter-town war and not come home?' Basia's heart almost broke at the sound of fear and hurt in her mother's voice.

'I'm sorry, Tanya, I truly am. I thought you knew where we were.'

There was another long pause.

'And Johan—why on earth would you let him join the scouts?'

The words her mother uttered were so quiet Basia was not sure she heard them correctly.

'He's getting restless, Tanya, and wanting to break

away on his own. He's all but a man now, and he needs to set his own path,' her father said.

'He didn't say anything to me.' Her mother's voice was weary.

'Of course not. You're his mother and he didn't want to hurt you. But there comes a time when all young men, even those with a gentle nature, need to prove themselves. He wanted to move to the township, and I struck an agreement with him. I would allow him to go out on patrol with one of the groups once a month. They teamed him up with Paul and a couple of the older men.'

'Paul? The son of the woman who runs the cooperative store?'

Basia thought her mother's voice sounded lighter and she relaxed a little.

Her father sounded a little less defensive when he answered. 'Yes, him. He was in the same boat, except he was looking to move to Southampton if they'd have him. This way they both got a touch of independence, and a chance to stretch their wings before flying the coop.'

'Okay, but I still don't understand why you didn't tell me. I would never have told Johan I knew.'

How can this be all right? Basia thought, feeling betrayed by her mother's acceptance. *I'm not allowed to go anywhere without an escort, so how come Johan gets to do what he wants?*

'I ... I don't know what to say, Tanya. It seemed like the right thing to do at the time. I thought after a while he would tell you himself.... On reflection I can see how we have hurt you.'

The conversation was now too personal. Basia bundled

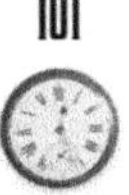

her bedding together and headed upstairs. By the time she returned to finish her chores, her father was sitting at the table having another cup of tea. In the distance she could hear the hooves of her mother's horse as she departed.

She grabbed a clean cup and sat down just as the legs to her father's chair scraped across the floor, and he said, 'Well, I guess the jobs your mother left for me to do won't get done while I sit here drinking tea.'

'Dad?'

'Yes?'

'That boy. He's from the underground city, isn't he?' Basia blurted out before she lost her nerve.

Her father sighed and ran his fingers through his hair. 'Yes, Basia, I believe he is.'

'The one near Portsmouth?'

Her father raised his eyebrows and Basia added, 'I've known about it for a while. We all do, us younger ones, even though you older people don't want to talk about it.'

Her father's response to that revelation was not at all what Basia expected.

'We're not keeping secrets from you,' he said. 'We all have our own reasons for not wanting to talk about the city or the people who live in it.'

'Why don't you talk about it?' Basia pressed her father, unable to let this rare openness pass.

Her father sighed and leaned forward, arms resting on the back of the chair. 'For me it is because of your mother.... It was a death sentence, not to be let into the city. Our government abandoned us to the ravages of war, while choosing to save others. It was not an easy time.'

Basia tried to imagine what it would be like to be locked out of your one chance of survival in a nuclear war. 'Why? Why would they keep some people out and take others? Wouldn't you want to try and save everyone?' she eventually asked.

'In the time they had, it wasn't possible to create sustainable communities for the entire population of England, so the government made choices. And they chose the people they wanted to populate their new world with and some of us weren't considered to have the right... um... skills,' he told her.

His answer confused Basia. 'But you were an architect and a farmer. Wouldn't they need you to build a new world?'

'Yes.'

'And Mother's a nurse—'

'And a Polish immigrant,' her father interrupted. 'When the whole world is in crisis, no one trusts people born elsewhere. They wonder where their loyalties truly lie.'

'So, you could've gone, but Mum couldn't.'

Her father nodded. 'Your mother... and Johan. I couldn't leave them behind, so I decided that instead I would make our home our sanctuary, and I would ensure our family survived.'

Basia was quiet for a moment, chewing over this new information. She finished the last of her tea before saying, 'I always think of the underground city as being just like life in the books that I read. Holidays and parties, going to school with other people my age—'

'We have no way of knowing how people live in the city, Basia.'

'Still, I like to dream of a place where things are easier than they are here. Where I don't have to wait until I am older to be valued as more than just as a potential incubator for babies.'

'We all like to dream, Basia, but as I said, there is one thing I am certain of—each community and country throughout time has good points and bad points. I'm sure some things in Portsdown aren't as agreeable as they are out here, and vice-versa.'

Basia was not yet ready to give up her escape from her daily drudgery. 'But I can still dream, can't I?'

Her father smiled as he straightened up. 'I wouldn't take that away from you, not for anything. Come on now, we've got jobs to do and we may as well get them done while the sedative your mother gave the boy is still working.'

Basia spent the rest of the morning doing the things she normally did: cleaning the house, preparing dinner, then checking the garden and pulling a few weeds. After lunch she sat down in the kitchen to study her medical books and complete the worksheets her mother had set. As she was about to break for afternoon tea, a groan from the lounge interrupted her thoughts. Walking in, she found herself confronted with a pair of intense green eyes.

'You're awake,' Basia said, stating the obvious.

'You're real,' the boy shot back.

Basia laughed and was rewarded with a smile that

crinkled his eyes. 'Would you like some water? Or maybe some soup? I have some on the stove.'

'Water would be wonderful, thank you.'

Basia propped the boy into a sitting position, leaning him back against the pillows to catch his breath while she went next door for water. Supporting his head, she allowed him to take a few small sips, and stopping when he winched in pain.

'Just go slowly,' she said. 'Too much water and you might throw it right back up.'

'I'm all right now,' he said.

She placed the glass on the table within easy reach, then settled him back into a more restful position. Pushing all the questions she had for him down, she put on her best nurse face and said, 'I'll come back soon and give you some broth.'

'Wait,' he said. 'Please, I need to know where I am. Your mother.... She is your mother, isn't she? She wouldn't tell me much. She said I should concentrate on getting well and worry about everything else later.'

Basia frowned and drew her bottom lip between her teeth and considered what her mother would expect her to do. She would say not to agitate the patient, but would he be more agitated by her answering his questions, or by her staying silent?

'I'm not sure. Perhaps you should rest and wait till Father comes in for a break, or Mum returns,' Basia finally said.

'Please.' His eyes and his voice both pleaded with her to make her own decisions.

She closed her eyes and took a deep breath. Why

shouldn't she answer his questions? If it was good enough for Johan to have some independence, it was good enough for her to make decisions too.

'All right.' Taking a seat, she smoothed her cotton print skirt over her knees and placed her hands in her lap. 'All right, ask away.'

'Firstly, where am I?'

Laughing out loud, she relaxed a little. 'That's an easy one—you're on my family's farm, about five miles outside of Lyndhurst, in the New Forest.'

The boy frowned, almost as if he was trying to comprehend what she was saying.

'You do know where the New Forest is, don't you?' she asked. 'Lyndhurst is not far from the old city of Southampton, now called The Southampton Protectorate.' The boy's expression didn't alter. 'You've seen a map of Southern England, haven't you?'

The boy shook his head. 'The only maps we had at school were maps of the old world, pre-war, and of all the underground towns.'

It was Basia's turn to draw her brows together, wondering what they taught in underground. How could she explain where they were in a way he would understand? She had an idea. 'So, you can visualise where your community is and where the Portsmouth Protectorate is?'

He nodded. She rose walked to the bookcase built into the wall between the kitchen door and the staircase. Pulling down the atlas, she flicked to the pages showing Hampshire. She pointed. 'This is Portsmouth, this is Southampton, and here is Lyndhurst, which is near where we are now.'

The boy's eyes widened in surprise. 'How did I get this far from where I was shot? I had only made it to the outskirts of Portsmouth.'

Returning the atlas to its home, Basia sat down again before answering. 'My father and brother found you and brought you home for Mother to tend to your wounds. She's a nurse.'

The boy smiled tentatively. 'She's done a great job. I was sure I would die. I managed to crawl away from the soldiers and hide. When they gave up and left, I tried to crawl away, but I fainted, and that is the last thing I remember.'

'Why were you running away?' Basia asked, then clasped her hand over her mouth. Her mother wouldn't like her tiring the boy with questions.

'It's okay. I wanted to find out if people were living out here, or if they had all died from radiation poisoning.'

Basia leaned forward, her elbows on her knees, and peered suspiciously at their guest. 'Of course there are people living out here. We do have to take some precautions, though. Some people still become sick from radiation when a nasty pocket of air comes through, or they eat food from contaminated sources. But we're not barbarians. We have medicines and very few die from the sickness anymore; well, at least in our community, they don't.'

The boy half rolled so he could see her better, his eyes bright with interest. 'What do you live on? I mean, do you grow your own food. Is the soil okay? What about meat sources? Do you have your own currency, or do you barter?'

'Whoa, slow down. Our protectorate has a number of

farms, and yes, we grow our own food and keep animals. When we have surplus, we barter for other things we need with Lyndhurst, and sometimes with Southampton. When you're more mobile we can show you around and you can find out more for yourself. That reminds me—are you hungry? Would you like some broth now?'

As if on cue, the sound of a stomach rumbling filled the room. The boy looked down at the sound, and they both laughed. 'I'll take that as a yes,' she said.

Nipping to the kitchen, she half filled a bowl with broth from the pot of soup on the stove and returned to the lounge. She helped the boy to sit up.

'Would you like me to feed you, or are you able to do it yourself.'

'I should be fine.' He took the bowl she offered, but his hand shook so much he almost spilled the lot.

Deftly, she took the plate, perched on the edge of the bed, and fed him small sips from a spoon. He managed to get halfway through before he said, 'Thank you, that's enough.'

Leaving him propped up a little, she said, 'You should get some rest now. I'll come back and check on you later.'

The boy's eyes were already drooping closed, but at the sound of her voice he forced them open. 'I'm Allan, by the way.'

'And I am Basia,' she said, but Allan was already snoring gently.

SOLDIER

Johan surveyed the clearing in front of him, thanking his lucky stars he had heard the group before he stumbled into their midst. It was only due to his and Baby's hunting skills that they hadn't heard him approach.

From his vantage point, he observed the group. They were covered from head to toe in black. The material of their suits appeared similar to clothing on the boy Johan and his father had rescued. The way they interacted told him they were trained soldiers, and well-armed ones at that. His father had been wrong; a patrol had come searching for the Portsdown escapee.

Crouching in the cover of the bush, he calmed his heart and signalled for Baby to wait before he tried to hear what they were saying.

'What do you mean the dog lost the scent?' the one farthest away asked, a woman from the pitch of the voice.

'He can't find it. It is as if someone has broken the trail and we can't find the next bit,' the lanky soldier standing beside the largest dog he had ever seen explained.

Without moving, Johan tried to pinpoint where they were, and he smiled. Yesterday, about half an hour from home, his father had suddenly worried what might happen if someone decided to track them.

They had stopped in a clearing, then carefully back-tracked out about a hundred metres. His father gutted a couple of rabbits, fed the innards to the dogs, then he and Johan smeared some gore on their boots and the dog's paws. Father then sent the dogs home one way, and they left in the opposite direction, avoiding the clearing all together.

'Go back and check if the dog can pick anything else

up,' the first voice commanded.

Two soldiers and the dog peeled off and retraced their steps, returning a few minutes later.

The smaller of the two soldiers reported, her clear voice carrying all the way to Johan. 'Still nothing. There are other tracks, but they are all intermingled. Some are from hunters, we think, and others from animals. Everything is mixed up, but we identified at least two distinct trails—we're not sure if either of them are the one we want though.'

The soldier giving orders cursed, then said, 'So, we have nothing?'

'Not quite,' the lanky soldier said. 'I asked Bruno to see if he can scent humans. He indicated there are traces that way.' The soldier pointed in Johan's general direction. 'But the scent is strongest there.'

Johan's stomach clenched because the soldier indicated the way he and his father had gone. It also happened to be the direction of the Watson farm where his mother was today. Neither option boded well for their family.

The best thing would be if they went the other way. If they didn't though, maybe if he timed it right, he could run into them and send them off in the wrong direction. Luck was not with him today. The woman in charge chose to head directly towards the Wilson's place.

The soldiers moved out in formation, with the trackers in front, two soldiers in the middle, and two dropping behind to make sure they weren't ambushed.

'Damn,' Johan muttered. The path that was too narrow and overgrown for him to get ahead and force a chance meeting. And he would not be able to follow them without being seen.

Waiting until they were out of sight, he told Baby, 'Home.' The dog obediently trotted off. Johan skirted the clearing and sped to a jog, taking the long way to the Wilson farm, hoping to reach it before the soldiers did.

CHAPTER SIX
MEETING THE LOCALS

Bruno and Izzy took the lead. Lee wandered after them, marvelling at how different this place was to the New Forest in his own time. The area appeared greener, more wild somehow, in spite of the war it had lived through.

Do you feel that? Izzy asked.

What? Lee looked around to see what she was talking about.

Izzy nudged him with her elbow. *Not you, Lee. I was talking to Bruno.*

You mean that tingling? Bruno asked. *I think magic is starting to regenerate here. Perhaps enough for us to be able to speak with our handlers tonight.*

As he half listened to the others, Lee allowed his senses to expand as much as they were able within the constraints of his suit. The dappled sun warmed his skin even through the protective layers, but he longed to take off the mask, if only to feel the sun and the breeze on his face.

What was that? His skin tingled with tiny electrical pinpricks.

I felt you reaching, Lee. You almost had it. The joy in Izzy's voice was infectious.

Is this what Alain felt when he did magic? he asked the girl.

Yes. If we find more pockets of magic, I might be able to teach you a few simple spells, Bruno said.

'Izzy, we have work to do tonight. I trust you can pull yourself away from your new friends for long enough to see to your duties.'

At the unwelcome intrusion of Jason's whiney voice, Lee's hackles rose and Bruno bared his teeth. Izzy placed her hand on the dog's shoulder to calm him. No matter how irritating Jason was, she clearly did not want any trouble.

'Oh, look, you have protectors.' Jason's supercilious smile grated.

For a moment Lee pondered how liberating it would be to tell Bruno to attack. He bit back the urge, and merely moved closer to Izzy in support, his clenched fist the only indication of his anger.

'I always do my duty, Jason.' Izzy's tone was icy. 'Now, go away.'

Jason's smile froze in place, and he glared at them. 'How dare you give *me* orders.'

'Private Jason, the Captain would like a word—something about not distracting our tracking team.' Thea's timely interruption prevented Izzy from cutting Jason

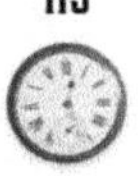

down to size.

Jason didn't move. In fact, he looked about to object to being ordered about by anyone. Izzy tensed beside Lee.

'Now, Private,' Sergeant Thea commanded.

Jason actually huffed as he turned on his heel and headed back towards the Captain. Izzy relaxed, and Lee released his fingers from their fist.

'Must you aggravate him?' Sergeant Thea asked the trio.

'Must he continuously annoy us?' Izzy responded.

'He is like a child who must always be appeased. On the other hand, you are all adults and should be able to take the high ground,' Thea told them.

'You sound like my mother,' Lee said.

'Only because you are behaving like children,' the Sergeant fired back.

Lee had another retort lined up but laughed, suddenly seeing the absurdity of the situation. 'Fair point. We'll try to behave better.'

Sergeant Thea didn't smile often, but when she did it lit up her whole face and her blue eyes twinkled. 'Thank you, Lee. I am sure it will make life easier for all of us.'

Lee thought he would take advantage of her goodwill. 'Sergeant, may I ask a question?'

'Go ahead, Private.'

'Has anyone said why Allan ran away from Portsdown?' he asked.

Thea didn't answer immediately. She stared at Bruno for a long while before pulling her attention back to Lee.

'Our briefing was a little sketchy. We believe Allan ran away to find out if people were doing more than surviving above ground, and report what he found upon his return.'

'And is that really possible? Thriving above ground? I mean, our radiation tags indicate very little exposure these last two days. And the Portsmouth Militia looked quite healthy,' Lee pointed out.

Thea checked behind to ensure Captain Kiandra could not overhear their conversation before saying, 'The truth is, we don't know. I can feel a little magic now, so the earth is healing. Two city-based communities are active in the area, but the Captain tells me the actual townships and farms are comparatively small in number.'

'Perhaps they would welcome some new blood,' Lee suggested.

'They spend a lot of resources protecting themselves from marauders. Life is very hand-to-mouth, and most people no longer live to a ripe old age. Who would choose that life?' Thea responded.

'Doesn't sound like much of an existence,' Izzy commented.

'Compared to what I saw underground, it probably isn't,' Thea agreed.

But should they be given the choice to try living out here if they wish? I guess that that is the question, Bruno added.

Thea considered Bruno's answer for a moment, then shook her head. 'In this instance that point is moot. Our role is not to interfere, but to work with the local people—'

'You say that, Thea, but in this instance both our roles are the same: to find out why time ends and prevent it. Can you honestly say that taking this boy back to the city will achieve that?' Izzy asked.

'Can you be certain it won't?' Thea countered.

No one can be certain. All we can do is wait, watch,

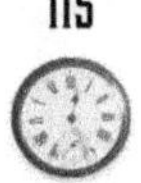

report back to our handlers, and hope they will provide us with useful guidance, Bruno said, playing the peacemaker.

'What does Captain Kiandra say?' Lee asked Thea. 'You and she are quite chummy I imagine she's said something.'

Thea's eyes widened in surprise. 'An interesting question, Lee.'

Don't look so surprised. He was sent along for a reason. Was Bruno smirking? He certainly looked like he was to Lee.

Ignoring Bruno, Thea continued. 'Kiandra believes the balance of life in the city must be maintained at all costs. When the needs of the few were put before the needs of the many, the world went to war. That has scared her, and many others.'

As I am sure it has done to many survivors, Bruno said.

'She is a strong believer in sticking together and following their leaders. She joined the guard to help maintain law and order, and to help prevent another war, so I guess she supports bringing Allan back to face the music, although she hasn't specifically said that,' Thea concluded.

'Would another war be on such a grand scale?' Lee asked. 'Surely all the weapons of mass destruction are gone?'

Theta laughed out loud. 'What makes you say that?'

'Well, I just assumed....'

From what we understand, the world was decimated by only a small proportion of the weapons that had been stockpiled over the years, Bruno said.

'History shows the underground cities in the old United

Kingdom were built around or close to stockpiles of weapons.' Izzy said.

'So... they didn't use them all, but they didn't think to dispose of them either when they witnessed the devastation they caused?' Lee was incredulous. Was humanity destined to repeat its mistakes?

'We do not believe so,' Thea said. 'Part of my mission was to find out what weapons were in and around Portsdown. Unfortunately, a number of the more heavily guarded areas were off limits to me. Given more time I might have found a way in....'

The group fell silent, and Lee was left to his own thoughts. He didn't like where his head was going. Not only was he in a post-apocalyptic future, but the locals still had enough firepower to annihilate what was left of the world.

Moments later the trees began to thin, and Izzy halted them until the others caught them up. As Captain Kiandra led them out behind the back of a house, they were greeted by a horse's knicker. It eyeballed them, then calmly went back to munching grass.

'We'll go round the front,' the Captain said.

'Perhaps we should take off our masks before we do. I mean, we look a bit intimidating like this,' Lee suggested.

'Are you mad?' Rodgers spluttered. 'You want to expose us to radiation just so we don't scare the locals? No way am I doing that—you're on your own, boy.'

Unfortunately, the others agreed, and they emerged into the clearing in front of the house as an imposing group of soldiers armed and with their faces covered. Lee hung back a little, thinking there was no way this encounter was going to go well.

The two tall, well-muscled young men on the veranda froze mid conversation when they spotted the intruders. They spoke quietly before walking down the stairs towards the group, their weapons casually hung across their bodies. The glint in their eyes told Lee it wouldn't take much for them to use those guns.

The men stopped about ten paces away and glared at them, waiting for someone to speak. Captain Kiandra moved forward. 'Good day, we are from Portsdown and we—'

The door to the house creaked open, causing Captain Kiandra to pause. An elderly woman walked out, leaning heavily on a stick. Behind her followed a tall blonde woman carrying a rifle, looking as though she knew how to use it.

The younger woman remained on the veranda while the older one made her way forward until she stood by the men. Out of the corner of his eye, Lee saw two other men emerge from nowhere. They stood by the house with guns cocked and ready to fire.

As the woman stepped forward to speak to them, Captain Kiandra took a step back, raising a cackle from the other woman, who said, 'I'm suffering from old-age, not the plague—and not radiation sickness.'

Captain Kiandra straightened her back. 'Old people live underground too.'

'Well, we have nothing like you guys out here.' Pleasantries over, the woman's voice turned cold. 'Why are you wandering across my property as if you own it?'

'We mean no offence. We were not aware anyone owned this land—' Captain Kiandra started.

'You know now, so you can be on your way.' As the woman spoke, the boys beside her moved their guns, ready to fire at her command.

Captain Kiandra tried again. 'I apologise. It has been a long time since someone from Portsdown has been out here—'

'I'm old enough to remember the last time your lot came around this way hunting down strays. You are not welcome here. I want you gone from my property.' The woman held a hand out, inviting them to leave.

'We are not here to harm you. We simply want some information, then we'll be gone.' The Captain's tone was neutral, but it did not soften the look on the older woman's face.

'About one of your own?'

Captain Kiandra nodded.

'A runaway?'

Captain Kiandra nodded again. 'He didn't request permission to leave they city.'

The old woman's face hardened almost imperceptibly as she asked, 'Is he over eighteen?'

'He is.'

Shrugging, the woman smiled, and Lee could see gaps where her teeth had once been. 'Seems to me since he's over eighteen, he should be allowed to come and go as he pleases. Makes no difference to me though. I have no

information for you.'

Lee made ready as if to leave, but Captain Kiandra had other ideas. 'He broke the laws of our community. Would you harbour a law breaker?'

Again the woman laughed. 'Not all laws are equal. Did he harm anyone, or steal from your people?'

'No, but—'

The woman folded her arms across her chest. 'Then as far as I can see, his actions won't impact anyone else.'

Captain Kiandra started to speak, but the woman held up a hand. 'We can debate the morality of his crimes all you like, but it will make no difference. As I said, I haven't heard anything, and I can't tell you what I don't know. Now be gone.'

Thea moved alongside the Captain, and Lee heard her say, 'Do you know the saying "there's more than one way to skin a cat"? Perhaps if we camped close by tonight, we might be able to root around and find out if there's anything they're not telling us.'

The Captain nodded slowly, then said, 'It's getting late. Would you mind if we slept in your barn tonight?'

'I would,' the woman answered almost before Captain Kiandra had finished speaking.

Lee smiled at the abrupt answer, finding himself warming to the elderly head of the family. Captain Kiandra obviously did not feel the same as she attempted to negotiate for them to at least make camp at the edge of the woods.

As the conversation drew out, Lee caught sight of a skinny boy clambering over a tractor in the barn to the right of the house. The boy jumped down, picked up a wrench, then clambered back up, making eye contact with Lee as he did. It gave Lee an idea.

He stepped forward and said, 'What if I work on your tractor? I used to tinker with engines, so I might be able to get it going. Would you let us stay then?'

The woman's grey eyes swivelled towards him, assessing him and his offer. At the same time, Captain Kiandra hissed, 'Private, what do you think you're doing?'

'I thought you wanted to stay the night,' Lee whispered he as rolled up his mask to reveal his face, then took it off all together.

The woman smiled, and this time it even reached her eyes. 'The tractor is dead. I doubt anything but a miracle can save it.'

Lee grinned at her. 'I love a challenge.'

She chuckled. 'All right, young man. It's a deal. And if you actually manage to get it running, I'll throw in a homemade meal.'

'Done,' Lee said, then realised his mistake and glanced sheepishly at his Captain.

'We accept,' Captain Kiandra confirmed. Turning on her heel, she glared at Lee before saying to the others, 'Right, let's set up camp.'

They started moving as one towards the barn.

'Wait, nobody enters my buildings without being checked first. I don't want any of you getting sick and dying on me. Someone might assume it was something we did.'

Lee waited by with the others while one of the boys pulled something from his pocket and ran it over Captain Kiandra. Lee realised the device checked radiation levels.

Once they were all deemed safe, the old woman said,

'Make yourself at home, but stay in the barn. The privy is round the back, but tell one of the boys if you need to use it—we don't want one of them shooting you for an intruder.' She turned to Lee. 'Knock yourself out with the tractor.'

Having dismissed them, she made her way slowly back to the blonde woman on the deck. As Lee headed to the barn, he watched as the two women talked for a moment before the younger one handed over a bottle, hugged their host, and departed round the side of the house. He turned to enter the barn only to find Captain Kiandra had also watched the exchange.

'I wonder what that was about?' Lee said.

'I would be wondering more about what your punishment might be for acting without orders.' The Captain's voice was cold.

'But I was only trying to help,' Lee said, defending himself.

'You are a soldier. You take orders. When you act on your own initiative, you put us all at risk. One of these days you might get us all killed. I will be taking a note of this, and you will face disciplinary action when we return.' The Captain stalked away, leaving a speechless Lee staring after her.

Shrugging, Lee muttered, 'If I return,' before following her into the barn.

'Lee, what on earth possessed you to take your mask off?' Izzy asked as he entered the barn, and he imagined her face screwed up with worry. 'Put it back on,' she ordered. 'The air purifier will soon be running, then you can remove it safely and play hero with the locals.'

'Come on, Izzy. Didn't you take notice of the radiation levels on their monitors? They hardly registered anything, not even in the air when they moved it away from us.'

Lee stepped to move past her, but she blocked his way.

'Why did they want to check us if the levels are as low as you say?' she said, challenging him.

Lee thought for a moment before answering. 'It could be habit, but I think that although these people do all right for themselves, they don't have enough resources to take care of the long-term sick.'

Izzy's head dropped to the side. 'Mm.... That's definitely possible. These people seem remarkably healthy, as did the Portsmouth Militia, for people living in radiation saturated air.'

Smiling triumphantly, Lee said, 'I don't think we need to cover up so much. With care, people are actually living a normal life out here.'

Izzy rubbed her chin with her forefinger, and Lee could almost hear the cogs whirring inside her head. 'Mm, you may be right,' she said. 'Perhaps it's time people from the underground city took a closer look at how people are living outside of its walls.'

A movement behind Izzy caught Lee's eye. Glancing over the girl's shoulder, he saw that the boy who had previously been crawling over the tractor had stopped his tinkering and was staring intently at them.

'Good afternoon,' Lee said, and the boy's eyes rounded with curiosity—but he said nothing.

Lee shrugged off his pack and handed it to Izzy, who left to go help set up with the others. Lee wandered over to the tractor with Bruno padding alongside.

'Nice John Deere you've got,' he said conversationally.

The boy's mouth dropped open before he managed to stammer out, 'You... you know about tractors?'

Lee laughed and pointed to something on the side of the vehicle. 'I can read,' he said. 'What's wrong with her?'

The boy shrugged. 'I'm not quite sure. I turn her on and nothing happens.'

'Did you check the spark plugs?' Lee asked.

The boy snorted. 'First thing I tried,' he said. 'We had a man with the sickness stay a while a few months back. He used to be a mechanic and he showed me a thing or two before he passed.' The boy stopped talking, and looked a little lost.

'And?' Lee asked.

The boy's face was blank.

'How were the spark plugs?' Lee prompted.

'Oh.... They're shot, but we ain't got no more here. When one of the bigger boys goes scavenging on the motorway... well.... Gram won't let any of them leave while you're here, so it's no use wondering about that.' The boy's brows drew into a frown as he spoke.

'Still—'

'But you'll be gone tomorrow, so we might be able to get her running then if Gram will let one of the boys go.' He turned a gap-toothed smile towards Lee.

'How long since the old girl started?' Lee said.

'A month or more. She's a good runner, just needs a few parts.'

'Well, if we can't get any new spark plugs, perhaps we can take the plugs out and give them a good clean,' Lee offered. 'My grandad taught me there is always something to do to make a machine run a little more smoothly.'

The boy grinned and deftly removed the spark plugs, handing them to Lee so he could climb down.

'We can clean them in the workroom.' He pointed to a door behind the tractor.

For the next hour the two worked in silence doing what they could to revive the clearly very old spark plugs. As they worked, Lee's mind drifted back to the days he spent with his grandfather in his garage at home, helping him restore classic cars.

With the army regularly sending his father away, the older man had taken Lee under his wing, rescuing him from a house dominated by women. Those times they spent pottering with engines were some of the happiest Lee could remember, and his heart had nearly broke in two when his grandfather died earlier that year.

Shaking his head, Lee dispelled any lingering sadness and decided to befriend the boy. 'I'm Lee,' he said.

'I heard the girl say your name already.'

'And you are?' Lee prompted.

'Colin,' he said.

Lee hid a grimace. This was going to be hard work.

'Where do you find fuel for the tractor?' Lee asked, spying a number of gerry cans around the room.

'Same place we hunt for parts—abandoned cars on the motorway.'

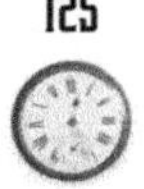

Lee was surprised. 'Not from pumps in Southampton?'

Colin shrugged. 'Sometimes, when we have things to trade with them. Siphoning diesel from car tanks is cheaper.'

'What do you do when the tractor is broken?'

'Some neighbours have horses. They loan them to us, just like they use our tractor when it goes.'

Interesting, Lee thought. *This area has a good support network.*

'Are there many other farms around?' he asked, wondering just how big their local community was.

Colin frowned. 'Gram wouldn't like it if I told strangers too much about the people round here.'

It was a statement of fact, and Colin would not budge from his position, no matter what questions Lee asked. The sun was setting when Lee and Colin had the spark plugs back in their original positions.

'Give her a go,' Lee said.

Colin turned the key and the tractor spluttered.

Lee jiggled the plugs and tightened some connections. 'Try it again.' He held his breath and crossed his fingers. The tractor finally chugged into life.

The grin on Colin's face was enough reward for Lee, but the pot of stew he bought out to them later was most welcome. Sitting down beside Lee, the young boy joined in their conversation, though the rest of the family continued to keep their distance. And Colin didn't appear to mind that Lee, Izzy, and Bruno were the only ones eating Gram's thank you meal.

'What's wrong with the food?' Lee had asked the others.

'It will be radiation riddled—the ingredients were

grown out here.' Rodgers grimaced as he spoke.

Asking Colin for a radiation detector, Lee swept it over their plates and the pot, and the dial didn't move. Still, they carried on eating their own dried rations, although Thea was looking longingly at their hot meal.

It's delicious. Why don't you try some? Bruno asked her.

I want to, but I also don't want to break my cover. A Sergeant with my supposed experience wouldn't make that leap. Thea's voice in Lee's head sounded disappointed.

Suit yourself. Bruno licked his bowl clean, then ran his tongue around his muzzle to mop up every last bit.

That night Lee had a full belly and the best sleep he'd had since arriving in this weird and warped version of the world.

CHAPTER SEVEN
A DECISION IS MADE

Basia was so engrossed in her studies, chin leaning on her hands while she read the text in front of her, she jumped when the door hit the kitchen wall with a loud bang. Her mother entered, followed moments later by her father, who let Jasmine and Baby in by the stove and shut the door.

'Where's the fire?' she asked as she closed her books. Frowning at Baby, she thought, *Hadn't he been out with Johan?*

'Fire would be preferable to the situation we find ourselves in,' her mother said as her father went into the washroom to clean the mud from his hands.

'What's going on? Did something happen at the Wilson's place?' Basia stood to move the kettle over onto the hob to boil. Unused to seeing her mother so flustered, she felt the need to do something.

'Wait until your father is finished, and I'll explain everything to you both. How's the boy?'

Shaking her head at the swift change in direction, Basia focused and reported, 'He woke for a little while. He was coherent and it looks like his temperature has dropped almost to normal. I gave him some broth and he's been sleeping for the last hour. He was restless a few moments ago, so he'll probably wake up again soon.'

'Excellent. I'll just go and—'

The door was flung open again, and Johan rushed in. 'I found soldiers from the underground city in the forest,' he blurted out, then he spotted his mother. 'But you already know that, don't you, because you met them at the Wilson's place?'

'What's that you're saying?' Her father emerged from the washroom, drying his hands on a towel. He closed the door for a second time as he said, 'There are soldiers from the underground city? Here?'

'Stop panicking. We are okay for the moment. Ma Wilson's let them stay in her barn overnight.' Tanya turned to Basia. 'Do you think the boy would be ready to travel into town tomorrow? I am thinking we might all be a little safer if he moves to Lyndhurst.'

'Hold on a minute,' Simon said. 'Let's not panic. Firstly, the Council won't want to come under fire for harbouring a citizen of the underground city. And we've no chance of convincing them now that he's from somewhere else.'

Her mother's hands planted themselves firmly on her hips, which was never a good sign. 'You want him to stay here and put us all at risk, Simon?'

'Both of you, please calm down,' Johan said. 'This arguing isn't helping anyone. Mum, after you left the Wilson's and the soldiers were setting up in the barn, Ma Wilson sent one of her boys into town to inform the Council. It won't be long until they put two and two together.'

'Then we need to get the boy to Lyndhurst quickly,' her mother said. 'We need to tell them that as soon as we realised who the boy was, we brought him straight in. If we don't, we risk being kicked out of the protectorate. Lord knows we won't survive for long without being part of their community.'

'But they'll decide to send him back with the soldiers to save their own necks,' Basia said. 'I can't imagine his treatment will be fair when he gets there.'

Her mother placed a hand on her shoulder. 'We don't know what will happen to him when he returns home. On the other hand, your father and I experienced firsthand what happens to people who harbour escapees from the underground city.'

'Are they killed?' Basia asked, not actually believing they would be.

'No, worse than that,' her father said. 'Their homes are burned, their livestock butchered, and their crops spoiled. They're forced to rely on others to survive—if anybody will agree to care for them after the pillaging soldiers depart.'

Basia's mouth formed an "o" as she realised the full extent of the risk her father had taken by bringing the young boy back here in the first place. 'So, it's Allan or us,' she said.

'I'm afraid so,' her mother answered.

'You must give me to them. You can't put your own lives at risk,' a voice said from the other room. It still sounded thin and frail, but full of determination.

Her mother left Basia's side and moved to the doorway, where she could still see her family, but could also talk with the boy.

'Tell me the truth, young man. What did you do in the city that they sent out soldiers to hunt you down?'

Her mother was using her "don't mess with me voice", and Allan acknowledged that by giving her a direct answer. 'I swear, all I did was leave. Even so, you must hand me over to them.'

'That is not our way. If the Council agrees, we may be able to offer you sanctuary. Young, strong people are needed if our community is to survive, and they may take that into account.'

'But the soldiers will simply return to Portsdown and bring back a larger force to take me home. The backlash would devastate your whole community,' Allan said.

'That is if the soldiers ever get back.' A fierce look of determination set itself on her mother's face as she crossed her arms over her chest.

Her father tensed. 'What exactly do you mean by that, Tanya?'

Shrugging, her mother said, 'If the soldiers never return to Portsdown, what are the chances the city will send anyone else out this far to search for them? They'll likely assume it's wild and dangerous out here and let it go.'

If Basia had been surprised by her father putting them at risk in the first place, she was shocked by what her

mother was suggesting. 'You mean the Council might—'

'I'm not saying anything… yet,' her mother said. 'Although many of us would not bat an eye at doing harm to soldiers from the city.'

'We can't do anything more tonight, so let's take a step back and sleep on this,' her father said. 'Perhaps we can approach it with clearer heads in the morning. Kids, go lock up.'

Basia held her breath until her mother nodded her agreement. 'Yes, it would be too dangerous to leave tonight. Come on, you two.' She gestured to Basia and Johan. 'Evening chore time.'

Heaving a sigh of relief, Basia left the room before her mother changed her mind.

The others had gone to bed. Allan was dozing. Basia curled up in a chair by the fire, the book in her lap sitting unopened. Now that she was alone, she had time to consider the events of the afternoon and their dinnertime conversation—or the lack of it.

With four people living in the house together with few visitors, you would think a meal eaten in silence would be a common occurrence, but it wasn't.

The lack of banter unnerved Basia, perhaps more than anything else that had occurred in the past couple of days. In fact, she was still unsettled, even though her father had decided they wouldn't make a decision about what to do until the morning.

'You must convince them to let me go my own way tomorrow,' the boy's voice said, interrupting her thoughts.

Basia looked up and found Allan regarding her with those cool green eyes. He wriggled a bit and used his elbows to prop himself up a little. The pain on his face as he moved himself into a more comfortable position told her he was still not ready to do things by himself. Still, she liked that he had tried.

'Basia? Did you hear what I said?'

'What? Yes. Sorry.' Basia took a breath to centre herself. 'They'll do what they will do, and I'm afraid nothing I say will change their minds. In fact, I'm the last person they're likely to listen to.'

Allan's jaw tensed, giving a stubborn set to his face. 'The soldiers from my home are worried about what I will do. They won't just let me go my own way, and they won't show mercy to anyone who has helped me.'

'Surely they would let you stay here.... Hold on. Are you sure you didn't do something awful?'

'You mean, like kill someone?' he asked, a smile playing around the edges of his mouth.

Basia felt a blush rising. 'No, well, yes.... Something they could not let you get away with.'

He drew a cross over his heart with his index finger. 'I promise you, I didn't hurt anyone, or steal anything. I merely left the city boundaries.'

'Phew.' Basia was strangely relieved. 'In that case, the soldiers might let you stay here with us.'

He gave her words serious consideration before answering. 'You're right, they might be convinced to leave me if

I swore never to return—if that was my intention.'

Basia's hopes of a peaceful resolution were not looking good, and she wanted to know why. 'What do you mean?'

Allan closed his eyes. 'I came out here to find out what it was like outside so I could return home and tell everyone whether or not it was safe to live above ground.'

Frowning, Basia asked, 'Why would you want to do that? Surely your people can come and go as they please?'

The boy's laugh was hollow. 'Where I come from, we can choose very little for ourselves. Unless of course your parents have money or power.'

'So you can't leave Portsdown? Ever?'

Again that hollow laugh, and it chilled Basia to the core. She leaned in closer to the fire, stirring the embers with the poker while she waited for Allan to answer.

'That's the funny thing about the underground community: it needs a certain number of people to maintain itself. Too many and resources are stretched. Too few people, and there aren't enough hands to produce everything the community needs.'

Basia drew her bottom lip between her teeth, then asked, 'How do they maintain the balance? You must practice some form of population control... am I right?'

'Yes, you are. When someone dies, a token is created, and people who want children participate in a draw to win it.'

Basia shrugged. 'Sounds fair. A life for a life.'

'It would be if it were as simple as putting your name in the draw, but there are rules.'

'Of course. All societies agree on rules to ensure fairness.'

'Oh, nothing is fair about these rules, I assure you.' Allan rolled over and reached for the cup of water on the table. Basia forced herself to watch him strain, not wanting to help unless he asked for it. He took a sip from the cup, placed it back on the table, then relaxed before he continued.

'Only married women can apply for the lottery, and they must be able to pay the application fee—which is about six month's wages for the average worker.'

'That's a little discriminatory, but not drastic,' Basia said when she had worked through the implications. Men could not apply, nor could same sex couples, and some people would have to save for years to get the application money.

'The worst part is, you can apply more than once.'

It took a moment, but then the penny dropped. 'So people with money apply more than once and stack the odds in their favour?' she asked.

'Exactly.'

They were silent for a while as Basia considered everything he had said about the city she had always believed to offer a perfect alternative to their way of life. Finally she asked, 'If you return and tell people they can come up here and live, wouldn't you be helping out the city by reducing mouths to feed, and increasing the number of people allowed to become pregnant?'

Allan smiled a sad smile that told Basia she had not fully understood the problem.

'Unfortunately, I believe the number of people who would want to take their chances above ground is high, and they're mostly from lower orders—the people who work at keeping those with money comfortable.'

Basia mulled over his words, comparing his reality to her fantasy of what life in the underground world was like. Between them, Allan and her father had dispelled any idea of a better, easier world she could escape to. That ease of living came at a price, and she for one would not be able to live with it—not that she would ever really get the chance.

'Okay, the soldiers want to make sure you don't tell people they can leave Portsdown. That, in turn, will maintain the status quo for an elite group of people?'

'Exactly, although the soldiers might not be aware of the true reason for their mission. I hope if they did, they might be inclined to support me—but I doubt I'm best placed to convince them of the error of their ways.'

It was Basia's turn to chuckle. She held up the book in her lap, *Middlemarch*, so he could see the cover. 'Have you read any of the old classics?' she asked.

He half shrugged. 'A bit of *David Copperfield*, and some of *Great Expectations* when I was at school—English wasn't my favourite subject. I was more a maths and science kind of guy. I don't see the relevance of an old book though.'

Basia smiled. 'In nineteenth-century England, the upper-class elite made the rules and the bulk of the people, the workers, kept society going, maintaining the status and power of those in charge. What you are describing to me is exactly what used to happen then.'

'Is it any different out here?' Allan asked.

'We are much more like the American frontier. Our community, and I believe many others, are run by white men who believe their superiority gives them the right to be in charge, which derives from their certainty that they are best placed to physically defend us.'

'White men?' Allan raised an eyebrow.

'Yes. We're in the English countryside. The few people who had enough resources to survive out here during and after the war were farmers and landowners who were predominantly white middle-class males. The mix in the protectorates is a little different— though men are still in charge. Only the skin colour changes.'

'What about women?' Allan asked.

'Older woman born pre-war are an independent lot. Most of the businesses in Lyndhurst are owned and run by them. A couple even sit on the Council,' she told him.

'I sense you're holding something back.'

This was a sore point for Basia, and she tried not to let her voice sound too bitter when she replied. 'Younger women are a rarity, and because mankind relies on us to reproduce, everyone else thinks they should be able to decide what is best for us.'

'That sounds bleak.'

'Fortunately, my father is different. He trained me to fight and defend myself, and I'm studying to be a healer. The rest of our community may value me as a brood mare, but I am lucky my family values me for being me.' Basia gnawed her lip. 'Even so, I probably have less control over my life than you.' As she finished speaking, Basia relaxed back in her chair, feeling a little less satisfied with her lot in life now her fantasy of escaping to the underground city was gone.

'I am sure your parents will do their best to ensure

you choose your own future,' Allan said.

'They will try to give me a say, but in the end, it may come down to politics.'

'Doesn't it always,' Allan said.

They fell into silence.

'Did yours not stick up for you?' Basia asked a little later.

'I don't think they would have, but to be honest, I never gave them the chance,' Allan admitted. 'We were never close.'

The room fell silent again. The only sound was the crackling of the fire. Allan took another sip of water before asking, 'What about the militia-controlled territories?'

'How do you mean?'

'I came across the Portsmouth Militia on the way here, although they didn't see me as they chased my pursuers from their territory. Perhaps your future lies in one of the old cities.'

'Life in the towns is pretty hand-to-mouth,' Basia said. 'They farm what they can, but most of the people spend their time defending themselves against marauders.'

'I see. Perhaps not the best option for you.'

'There are so many small groups in England now. Maybe what we need is someone to inspire us to join up and do something better,' Basia sighed. 'I don't know where that came from.'

Allan chuckled, and this time the laugh was genuine. 'Perhaps from your books.... Still, you're right. There are so many little groups dotted around spending all their resources on surviving, when what they actually need is someone to show them a better way forward together.'

Each sunk back into their own thoughts until Allan tried to sit up and winched in pain. 'Nice though this dreaming of a great future is, if your parents won't listen to reason, I'm just going to make the decision for them.'

He tried to swing his legs around to stand, but his brow knitted in pain and drops of sweat stood out on his forehead. Basia shook her head as he struggled.

Finally he stopped and stared at her. 'I could do with a little help.'

'You're kidding me, right? If you can't get out of bed without my help, how do you think you would survive out there? Let alone get back home.'

'But—'

'Not to mention it's nighttime,' she added. 'There are all sorts out there: bandits, fallout victims, people ejected from other communities for their crimes. The night belongs to the desperate. You won't last five minutes before you're stripped bare and left to fend for yourself without food or weapons, and probably clothing as well.'

'Wow, sugarcoat it, why don't you?' he said, flopping back on the bed. 'I guess we're back to trying to convince your parents of the right thing to do.'

Basia moved to help make the boy more comfortable again. 'Good luck with that. I've been trying my whole life and never changed their minds a single time.'

Once Allan was settled, she curled back up in the chair and opened her book as he dozed off. This time she concentrated on the words, trying to block out the bleak images of her world their conversation had raised to the surface. It didn't work. Her mind was too active to lose itself in fantasy. Something had shifted inside of her, jerking her out of her complacency.

She knew now there was no ideal world to escape to, no magic wand to give her a better life. If she didn't like the life she had, it was up to her to do something to change it. And she decided she would start with ensuring the soldiers didn't take Allan back to Portsdown. She would help him return on his own terms.

CHAPTER EIGHT
A CHANGE IN TIME

Beta took a deep breath and willed himself into physical form. Clasping his hands behind his back, he made to enter the conference room, then paused. This was his third meeting with Alpha and the two representatives from the Time Fixers. Rather than bringing their actions more in line, each meeting escalated tensions between the two groups.

Actually, that wasn't quite true. He and Cynthia had been working together to find a way to use both parties' unique set of skills to help their teams on the ground save humanity.

In stark contrast, Alpha seemed intent on aggravating Gerald, and the other Time Fixer acted like he just didn't care. They squabbled incessantly, which often resulted

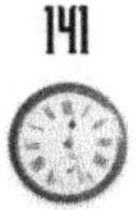

in Alpha storming off and Gerald retreating into himself.

Earlier today he suggested he meet alone with Cynthia. Of course, Alpha overheard and said, 'I think not, Beta. We will make more progress if we work together.'

Beta responded, 'Maybe that would be true if you did something other than stir up Gerald.'

'I wouldn't need to prod and poke at him if he actually contributed something,' Alpha said and nodded towards Gerald.

Gerald leaned laconically back in his chair. 'I would make an effort if I thought we could do something, anything, to change the course of time.'

Alpha had picked up his tablet and winked out of the room.

Oh well, best he get on with it. He pushed the door open and, plastering a grin on his face, he entered the room.

'Good afternoon, everyone,' he said. 'Are we all ready to see how we can help our friends on the ground?'

Cynthia smiled and he momentarily allowed himself a small sliver of hope that things would be different this session. It lasted until he turned to Alpha and Gerald. They sat on opposite sides of the conference table, locked in a staring contest.

Stifling a sigh, Beta took the seat beside Alpha and placed on the table the papers that a monitor handed him on the way in. They contained detailed reports from the monitoring stations both here and at the Time Fixer's headquarters—carefully approved reports.

A furrow formed between his brows as he scanned the summary sheet. They were no further forward than they had been this time yesterday. He raised his eyes and caught Cynthia watching him.

'This isn't good,' he said to her.

'No, it isn't. I am uncomfortable having a team on the ground when I can't provide them with directions,' Cynthia said.

His brow furrowed. 'We only sent them because we had expected to see changes in the timeline which would have helped us direct them.'

'It is disheartening. Our people are having no impact at all,' Cynthia said.

Beta's fingers drummed on the table as he considered his next words. *I had forgotten some of the satisfying things about having an actual body,* he thought. 'At best, this tells us we haven't made anything worse....'

'Which is saying very little at all,' Alpha said, not taking his eyes off Gerald for even a second.

'It shows you're not mucking anything up.' Gerald smiled at Alpha.

'Should we be doing something different? Change it up a little...,' Beta trailed off as Alpha directed his scowl at him.

'It would be a stretch to say we are winning this battle at the moment, but we are making progress, even if the teams monitoring cannot see it,' Cynthia said.

'How so?' Beta asked.

Cynthia leaned forward, resting her arms on the table. 'People from our organisations are on the ground for the first time ever. We are getting occasional reports, which add to our pool of information on the period. In time, we will be able to stitch these pieces together to give us a more complete picture if we get another chance at fixing things.'

The Time Fixer paused. When no one else said anything, she spoke again. 'Plus, our team at Time Fixer headquarters have been relaying to us occasional thoughts from our operatives registered on our recording equipment over the past couple of hours.'

Alpha frowned. 'I don't remember reading anything about a change in the documents.'

'No,' Cynthia confirmed. 'Our information is reviewed before being included in the reports we share. I was just told the good news now, and it will no doubt be in the next release. I simply wanted to give us a little hope in advance.'

'Interesting,' Beta mused. For a moment he considered not saying anything else, but he felt Cynthia's leap of faith deserved an equal move from him. 'Just before I came in, our monitors told me they can now track our people on the ground—they are in the New Forest area of Hampshire. The monitors suggest this shows a regeneration of magic in parts of Southern England.'

Alpha swivelled in his chair, again turning his glare on Beta. 'Should we be sharing that if it hasn't been approved?'

'In the light of Cynthia's revelation, I thought it only fair.'

Alpha continued to glare at him. Beta decided to ignore his colleague. 'All indications are that we should be able to contact our operatives and provide more direct support from here on in.'

Cynthia smiled. 'Perhaps we should each try to contact our teams tonight and regroup tomorrow to share what we find.'

'I think that's a brilliant idea. What do you say, Alpha?' His colleague mumbled something Beta took to

be agreement.

'I feel we've turned a corner. Now more than ever I believe our people will change the future for the good of all humanity,' Cynthia said.

Alpha humphed, turning in his seat with his back towards her. Gerald's eyes followed him as the Time Fixer leaned back in his chair, folded his arms, and chewed his lip as if he was thinking.

Beta smiled at Cynthia, hoping to transmit his support, but she was too busy trying to attract Gerald's attention to take notice.

Clearly there was nothing more to be done here. He stood, gathered his papers, and said, 'See you tomorrow,' as he left the room.

He decided to return to his quarters via the flow of history, which ran through the centre of the city and appeared as an infinite number of strands of light energy. Like so many others, when he first joined the Guardians, he had been awed by history, and honoured to be chosen to protect it. Back then he had not realised how restrictive the Time Guardian's approach to protecting the timeline was. Nor had he understood how dogmatic they would be.

Then he began mentoring Sigma. The issues he raised started Beta thinking, and he began questioning the Guardians and what they were doing. Since then, he found the eternity he had chosen increasingly frustrating.

Recently he had wondered if Alpha was losing touch with his humanity and should perhaps stand down from the Council. Over the last few days, Beta's thoughts ran more along the lines that perhaps it was he who should be reconsidering his own future.

Once Alpha blinked out of existence without even a goodbye, Cynthia finally managed to attract Gerald's attention. It infuriated her that he only responded because he could no longer play his mind games with Alpha.

'Really, Gerald, we are not in the war with these people. If we don't work with them, we risk all humanity ending here.' She could not keep her exasperation in check.

'Come on, Cynthia, there's nothing to say we can't have a little fun while trying to save the world.'

'You're such a child. We're the first ones to get a chance to fix this mess, and I won't let you screw it up.'

Gerald laughed. 'Whatever we do, history will continue to run up until the point that it doesn't, and time will carry on whether or not humans populate the earth. Whatever happens on the ground, Time Fixers still be able to move backwards and forwards through the time periods populated by humans, trying to save people from themselves, and trying to prevent this event from continuing. So chill out. Take a moment to enjoy this experience.'

Cynthia's jaw dropped. She couldn't believe what she was hearing. Gerald stood and picked up the reports and flicked through them. 'Have you ever considered that nothing we changed over the years, or the Time Guardians changed, for that matter, has altered the end of humanity?'

'If you believe our work is futile, what are you even

doing here?' Cynthia's tone was icy as she posed the question.

'I made a commitment and I am in this till the end. Besides, what else can we do? I'm going to live forever, and that is a lot of time to fill.' Gerald smirked.

Disgusted, Cynthia said, 'If you are weary of all this, then why don't you will yourself out of existence—you don't need to put yourself out trying to save the human race.'

'But this game we are playing with the Time Guardians has given me a whole new purpose, and hours of amusement.'

Cynthia glared at Gerald, not sure whether he was having her on, or whether he was truly this self-centered. She half stood, then sat again, not quite sure what to do next. Her shoulders slumped with defeat.

'Are you ready to go?' Gerald asked, unaware of her internal conflict.

Shrugging, she decided he was not her problem to deal with. She had a job to do, and she would do it regardless of whether or not Gerald was engaged and effective. She owed it to Izzy.

'Jason is your man. Do you want to contact him this evening, or shall I?'

'Knock yourself out,' Gerald said. 'He's all yours. You might find him a little tedious, though. Perhaps you will have better luck getting him to listen to your directions than I've had.'

Again Cynthia didn't know whether Gerald was serious, but she took him at face value, if only to end this conversation as quickly as possible. Closing her eyes, she reached out and felt for the magic. It was easy to link with Gerald, but it took some time to find a sense of Jason. Eventually she found his personal signature.

Jason?

No response.

Jason? Isolde? Are either of you in a position to report?

A slight tingling tickled at the edge of her senses. She drew a bit more power to herself and concentrated.

Cynthia, is that you?

The voice was weak, but she could hear it.

Isolde—can you report? Or can you ask Jason to?

Jason has just arrived to relieve me from guard duty. We can't gather enough magic for both of us to speak. I will talk and relay messages, Isolde sent.

Cynthia looked up and Gerald nodded. 'We're likely to get more from her than we ever would from him.'

The two of them listened while Isolde went through the events of the last few days up to their arrival in the New Forest. *We think we're close to finding the boy who escaped, but....* Isolde stopped.

What? Cynthia asked.

Can you provide clearer instructions on how we should proceed once we catch up to him?

Cynthia shook her head, then remembered Isolde could not see her response. *With no significant changes showing up on our equipment, your only option is to continue to work with the guard troop.*

There was silence. It lasted so long, Cynthia was beginning to wonder if the link had disappeared. *Isolde?* she asked.

Sorry, I was thinking. There was another short silence before Isolde spoke again. *Some of us are worried that if*

we take the boy back as we are expected to do, they will end his life. I am not comfortable with that. How can sending a person to their death be the best way forward for humanity?

Cynthia considered this for a moment, then said, *Isolde, we all understand that sometimes the sacrifice of one is needed for the many to survive.*

Isolde was silent again. *Isolde? Izzy?*

Wait a moment. Jason is saying something. He says to tell you he is good whatever you decide.

Gerald smirked. 'What a surprise. That guy has never had a unique thought in his head—ever.'

So, you have nothing more for us? Nothing at all?

I don't know what you want me to say, Cynthia said.

All right.

Wanting to give her something, Cynthia said, *The only consolation I can give you is that the blip alerting us to the possibility of change is still showing. We know you're in the right place and in the right time, and that's all we know.*

Okay, Isolde said. *We will try and contact you this time tomorrow.*

The girl's presence blinked away, but Cynthia kept her eyes closed for a moment, not wanting to open them and face the inadequacy of their support of the team on the ground.

'And you still see value in doing this?' Her eyes flew opened to find Gerald leaning on the table, a smirk on his face.

Cynthia fought the urge to slap him. Rising in a single movement, she gathered her papers and left the room before she said something they would both regret.

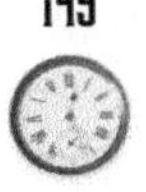

'Really, Alpha, must you bait him so?' Beta asked as his colleague joined him by the flow of history.

Then he mentally kicked himself. Why did he bother? Alpha simply didn't care whether or not they got on with the Time Fixers. He thought trying to work with them was beneath his dignity.

'You must agree he is incredibly irritating,' Alpha said. 'I am sure that was why they chose him.'

Beta sighed, unable to deny Gerald rubbed him up the wrong way too. He was also aware of how annoying Alpha was being, which prevented him revealing this fact—so he said nothing and changed the subject. 'Have you tried reaching out to Theta?'

'Not yet. I assume you talked with Sigma already?'

'No, although there is something pulling at the edge of my consciousness. It could be him trying to activate our link, or it could be the boy he took with him. Lee is quite strong, and he hasn't learnt to dampen his psychic thoughts yet.'

'It might be one of our other prospective Guardians too. That boy Alain—Allan—was close to becoming a Guardian before the war erupted. It was a shame he died so suddenly. In this incarnation he might actually be ready to make the move. Perhaps we should talk to the Council about recruiting him before time ends. What do you think?'

SOLDIER

Bringing a new person into the ranks of the Guardians was the last thing on Beta's mind. He really just wanted to go home, power down, and be by himself. The frustrations of working with Alpha and Gerald these last three days had worn him out.

Ever the diplomat, though, he said, 'I think that is a discussion for another time. Do you want to try and contact Theta, or shall I try for Sigma?'

Alpha closed his eyes, and the air around Beta began to tingle.

Alpha, is that you? a female voice said in his head.

It is. Beta is with me. Is Sigma around?

Yes, we're both here, she said before launching into her update.

We are currently staying on a farm, she informed them as she finished up.

So, you are finally in contact with the locals? Beta asked.

I wouldn't quite put it that way. They allowed us to camp the night in a barn in exchange for Lee fixing their tractor.

And how is Lee doing? Beta had been concerned about the Council's decision to send an untrained boy on this mission. Especially as their ability to maintain contact was severely limited, not to mention the worry that they might not be able to portal him to safety should anything happen.

Funny you should ask that, Theta said. *He has raised some interesting issues these last couple of days. He is concerned about taking Allan back to the underground city. He believes they will terminate his life.*

Your orders are to support the soldiers on the ground, Alpha said.

I understand that, sir, but things are very different here than we imagined. The world has started to regenerate, and there appear to be communities living quite happily above ground. From what I can make out, the stringent rules required to maintain life in Portsdown are no longer essential for the survival of the human race. It all leads me to wonder if we are doing the right thing.

Alpha's energy became more red tinged as Theta continued speaking. *It is not your job to wonder. You have your orders and you will continue to follow them.*

The silence after Alpha's remark was heavy, and Beta felt compelled to add, *I think what Alpha is trying to say is, nothing in the timeline or in history has changed–*

No change at all? Theta's voice sounded dismayed.

I am sorry, Theta, but your presence so far has not done anything to change the future, Beta said.

There was a longer silence this time, long enough for Beta to wonder if they had ended the conversation.

Theta? Alpha asked.

I'm still here. Please wait a moment. Sigma asked me to tell you that a couple of our team are unwilling to return the runaway to Portsdown. They won't hinder the mission, but nor will they actively assist either, Thea said.

Alpha sighed, then sent, *The Council says–*

Which leads us to the end of humanity, which is what I thought we were all sent here to prevent, Sigma interrupted.

The appearance of Beta's protege had an immediate effect on Alpha. His energy changed from red tinged to bright red.

You must not interfere, Alpha barked.

They know they cannot take direct action and are not

asking for you to agree to that. I guess in the light of no new direction from you, we would all like some leeway to react to what we find, and be allowed to follow our instincts.

Sigma's proposal sounded reasonable, but the tension in the air around him signalled Alpha's disagreement.

How would you behave differently if I were to say go ahead, follow your instincts? Beta asked, hoping to diffuse the situation before Alpha exploded.

We have not discussed this, Theta said, sounding a little flustered. *An example might be for Sigma as Bruno to run off, meaning we can no longer track scents. The team would then need to return to Portsdown to arrange a new tracking team.*

Beta had hoped that by Theta showing some support for Sigma's suggestion, Alpha might be more amenable to the change. However, he had severely underestimated the Guardian's dislike of Beta's protege.

I find no reason to change what you are doing, Alpha said. *Proceed as is, and report back tomorrow night.*

Alpha cut the conversation short before Beta could say anything. 'That was a bit abrupt, don't you think?' he said. 'They raised a fair point. If they don't change anything, then their mission might be a failure.'

'It's the Council's agreed course of action. We can't change that without going back to them. And I, for one, am not prepared to take such a step at the moment. Are you?'

Not when you obviously won't support me, Beta thought. He tried a different approach. 'Sigma and Theta have more current information, and Theta is a seasoned operative, so perhaps we should take their concerns to the Council.'

Alpha said nothing, and the crimson hue of his energy told Beta any further discussion would be futile.

'Just think about it,' he said before turning and heading towards his quarters.

'See you tomorrow,' Alpha said as he departed.

As he moved through the other light beings, Beta pondered the events of the day. More and more he was becoming convinced the Time Guardians must change the way they approached history. They could not change things directly or history itself would redress the balance, but perhaps they could review how they chose who to support in any given situation. Or at the very least, give more control to operatives on the ground to adjust their approach as events unfolded.

Perhaps this minor tweak to procedure might help deal with the problem they always had with preventing the end of human history. This was their first opportunity–perhaps their only opportunity–to save humanity at the point of extinction, and they were not rising to the challenge.

He sighed as he reached his dwelling. He was only one voice on the ten-person Council. What could he do? Still, there was another day tomorrow.

CHAPTER NINE
THE LOCAL PROBLEM

Lee opened the barn door, blinked, and squeezed his eyes shut in the glare of the morning sun. Without his protective helmet, it was almost blinding. He stretched long and loud before opening his eyes and freezing, arms still above his head.

'Um, Captain Kiandra, you might want to come here,' he said, slowly lowering his arms by his sides. 'We have a bit of a situation.'

'A bit of an understatement, Private,' the Captain said under her breath as she joined him in the doorway.

Lee smiled warily as he surveyed the thirty or so men surrounding the barn, weapons raised and pointed directly at them.

'I don't think they're friendly,' Lee observed dryly.

'You don't say?' she responded. Turning to him, she

added, 'Private, I'm giving you fair warning. This is not the time for one of your inspired off-reservation ideas.'

'As if,' Lee said under his breath, then added, 'Understood, Captain,' for his boss' benefit.

The group had joined them in the doorway and Thea asked, 'What do you want us to do, sir?'

'I'm not sure yet, Sergeant. Where was our warning? Who was on guard duty?'

Lee looked around and spotted Jason standing at the back of the group surrounding them with his hands behind his back.

Captain Kiandra's gaze found him around the same time. 'I might have known,' she said. 'How that boy ever made it through basic training, I will never understand.'

'Indeed,' Corporal Rodgers said. 'He must be supported by some powerful sponsors.'

'I don't see much point in fighting,' the Captain said. 'By the time we draw our weapons, we would most likely be dead. Let's see what negotiating will do.'

As the Captain stepped forward, Lee felt movement beside him and he glanced down to find a worried face staring back.

'It wasn't me,' Colin whispered. 'Gram said we needed to tell the town Council you were here, otherwise we'd be in trouble. We didn't know they'd do this.'

Lee ruffled the boy's hair. 'Don't worry, Colin, it'll all sort itself out. Just in case, you'd best hurry back inside. I don't want you caught in any crossfire.'

He turned his attention back to the Captain as she slowly walked forward, hands in front and palms facing outwards to show she would not do anything stupid—like make a move for her blaster. The rest of them remained where they were, hands visible so the townsmen could see they were no threat either.

Lee noted that, unlike his troop with it its mix of gender and race, the group in front of him was all white and all men. He briefly wondered where the women were.

Bruno shuffled forward to sit in front of Lee before laying down to make himself less conspicuous. *I guess we should have seen this coming,* he said.

If Jason had only warned us, we would not be in this position, Thea commented. *Why would the Time Fixers send someone so clearly incompetent on this mission?*

Rodgers couldn't have been more right if he tried, Izzy said. *Jason's family have been supporters of the World Fixers since time began. Most of them are pretty decent operatives, but I guess every family has one exception.*

'Good morning,' Captain Kiandra was saying, and they turned their attention to her. 'There's no need for guns. We are not here to harm any of you.'

One of the men stepped forward. He was perhaps in his thirties, lean and weather-beaten. His face was all hard lines, displaying no obvious signs of welcome.

'Places around here are still suffering from your kind's last visit. We're not taking any chances with you. One of my men will remove your weapons. Then we'll be taking you to town with us to talk with the Protectorate's representatives.'

Captain Kiandra paused for a moment as if she was considering this as a request rather than an order. 'I can agree to that,' she said. Turning back towards the barn, she spoke to her team. 'Come forward, slowly.'

Two men broke away from the main group and entered the building, probably to collect their gear, while a third removed blasters from those who had thought to grab them. Lee was pleased they didn't search for any handheld weapons—they all had at least one knife about their person. At least he could still defend himself should it come to a fight.

When the man in charge was certain all their gear was rounded up, he said, 'Right, let's head into town.'

'Can we at least put on our anti-radiation gear?' the Captain asked.

Everyone except for the soldiers laughed. 'This is one of the most radiation free areas in the Southern Zones. You'll be fine for the little walk we'll be taking.'

The Captain didn't look convinced, but with the number of guns pointed at her and her troops, she didn't have much choice. 'Fall in,' she commanded.

Thea joined the Captain, and Lee and Izzy dropped in behind them, with Rodgers bringing up the rear. As they walked forward, Jason was pushed into line beside the Corporal, still bound. Bruno padded up beside Lee, but the leader of the local guard halted the group.

'The dog can stay here. Ma Wilson and her boys will look after him.'

'He comes with me,' Lee insisted, not willing to leave his friend behind.

Izzy placed a hand on his arm and sent, *He'll be fine here, and it won't hurt to have someone on the outside.*

Lee was about to object when Bruno said, *Don't worry. I'll slip away and follow behind.*

The walk into town was taken at double time. Lee

was pleased he had spent the last three days walking so he didn't embarrass himself by dropping back too far. Throughout the journey Captain Kiandra attempted to engage the guard captain in conversation. He either ignored her or told her to shut up.

She's trying to force him to identify with us as guards like him, as people following orders, Izzy said.

It isn't working. In fact, Lee would say she was actually annoying the guard leader, causing him to push on faster, almost as if he wanted to be rid of his troublesome charges.

The sun had barely warmed the earth when he spotted a series of dilapidated buildings on the edge of the settlement. The group joined a road crisscrossed with a barrier at the entrance of Lyndhurst proper.

Two guards appeared as they drew closer. One raised the barrier to allow the group through while the other had a brief word with the man who had led them.

Lyndhurst, Izzy said. as they walked along the road. *This was the old High Street.* The bottom level of the buildings had obviously once been shops. Wooden barricades covered the windows on the left-hand side. On the right, everything had been collapsed so the area beyond could be seen from the top floors on the left. The debris also made it difficult for anyone to rush in and attack. Lee admired the ingenuity.

In behind there is roughly a triangle of suburbia, Izzy continued, pointing towards the boarded-up shops. *It looks like they are set up to defend that area as the centre of their community.*

Even though it was still early, he expected to see more

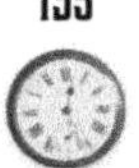

people. It was surreal walking through what had once been a thriving town and not seeing a sole person.

As they reached a lane on left, the guard leader caught them up. 'Down here,' he said, then proceeded to lead them through an old carpark, past a building with a dilapidated sign proclaiming it as "The New Forrest Heritage Centre", to a small building on the right.

'You lot you can wait inside.' The leader gestured towards the open door.

'No way! That's an old public toilet,' Izzy said, taking a step back.

Lee wasn't particularly keen either, but the guards did not give them a choice. The old building had been repurposed as cells. It was relatively clean, even though it still retained the distinct whiff of public toilets the world over. They had left a stall intact at the back, which meant they could at least use the bathroom in private. The rest of the room contained bunk beds behind some pretty hefty iron bars.

'I thought you said we were going to meet with your Council,' Captain Kiandra said as the metal door was closed behind them.

'You will,' the guard leader said. 'When they're ready to see you.'

Left alone in the rather bleak building, Captain Kiandra told them, 'You might as well make yourselves comfortable. No telling how long we might be here before we get a chance to speak to the people in charge about being released.'

'You seem certain they will let us go,' Izzy said, skepticism lacing her words.

'Of course I am. With their limited manpower, small communities like this would struggle to stand up to Portsdown,' the Captain said as she lay down on a bunk.

'They looked well armed to me, and they had enough men to come get us and leave the town well defended,' Izzy insisted.

'You are obviously new to interactions with the locals,' Corporal Rodgers said. 'They like to show their power, but our forces are superior, and they always roll over in the end.'

Izzy shook her head. 'I am not getting the feeling these are people prepared to give way to anyone. They are a disciplined unit who are annoyed at our wandering over their lands.'

Lee had to say he agreed with Izzy, but Corporal Rodgers had other ideas. 'They're the dregs, the leftovers. They can never defeat us.' He took the lower bunk beside the Captain, ready to make the most of the downtime provided.

'I think you're wrong,' Izzy mumbled, moving to the bars and peering out.

Lee also moved to the bars and peeked through the door. A couple of guards stood about outside, but the street was clear.

Bruno? he sent.

No reply. Sighing, he took a bunk opposite the Captain and Rodgers. Theta joined him, easily swinging herself up top and rolling over to look out the slit window across the way. Izzy kept her vigil by the door.

Bruno? Lee tried again, his stomach sinking as he was met with silence.

Bruno padded through the undergrowth, staying a little way behind the last of the Lyndhurst guardsmen. It was difficult to remain close enough so their scent was still fresh, but far enough away that they would find it difficult to pick him out of the surrounding greenery.

He had gone some way when he began to suspect he himself was being followed. Slowing down a little, he cocked an ear, but couldn't quite make out where the footsteps were coming from. Sniffing, he recognised the smell and he waited until its owner drew a little closer before revealing he knew of their existence.

Timing it just right so he barred the pathway as a figure emerged around the bend, Bruno bared his teeth and growled menacingly at Colin. The boy stepped around him and carried on towards Lyndhurst. Frustrated he couldn't make the boy understand the danger he was in if he continued, Bruno trotted after him, wondering what else he might do to send the boy home.

He caught Colin up and tried leaning into the boy's legs in an attempt to use his weight to turn him around. When that didn't work, he gripped at the boy's clothes, only to find himself swatted on the nose. It seemed Colin was determined to follow the others to their final destination.

In light of such stubbornness, Bruno wondered if Colin was actually meant to be going to Lyndhurst. If that were the case, stopping him would be interfering directly with history. Dropping behind, he allowed the boy to take the lead as he clearly knew where he was going.

When they reach the edge of the forest, Bruno's skin stopped tingling and he realised the magic around him was thinning out; it appeared regeneration had not yet reached the Lyndhurst settlement.

Plonking himself down, he surveyed the open road. The rear guard were still filing through the barricade, but he couldn't find Lee and the others. Not wanting to be seen, he slunk behind a bush. Colin joined him.

'Ah, smart dog,' the boy said. 'Best to wait until they're inside the settlement before we approach.' He dropped to the ground and sat cross-legged beside the dog.

Their spot under the shady tree was pleasant and Bruno relaxed a little, leaning into his companion. Comfortable for the moment, Bruno decided to make the most of his enforced break.

Beta, he sent. *Where are you?*

Nothing came back.

Beta. Beta, I need to talk with you.

Still nothing. No, there was a faint buzzing. Bruno expanded his senses and drew a little more magic to himself.

Sigma, is that you?

Beta? Yes, thank goodness, Bruno sent, then tuned his thoughts until the voice of his mentor came in loud and clear.

I'm here, Sigma. What is it? You're not due to report again until this evening. Has something happened? The urgency in his mentor's voice highlighted his concern

Calm down, Beta. I'm not sure it is anything to worry

about—yet. Some local guards escorted the others from the New Forest a little while ago. I will be joining them soon. Magic is weaker around here, so I'll keep you posted when I can.

This is not good, Beta said. *No, not good at all. We were waiting for something different to happen, but not something like this.*

Bruno resisted the urge to say, 'I'm still here.' One of the downsides of taking animal form was that others often disregarded him. *I wouldn't be too worried. The original team on this mission may have been taken into Lyndhurst—*

Sigma, I thought about things after we spoke last night. It is possible Lee offering to fix the tractor, which in turn allowed your troop to stay at the farm, may have already altered the timeline. Beta could barely keep the excitement from his voice.

Bruno didn't answer immediately. Had Lee actually changed history? Could this be the real reason he was with them? He shook his head, and Colin rubbed the fur round the ruff of his neck as if he needed calming. The action helped him focus his thoughts.

It is possible, Beta, and we should definitely discuss the potential ramifications... some other time. For now, I must focus on going after the others.

Oh, right... of course. Perhaps I will head to the monitoring station and keep an eye on what's happening, Beta said.

Of course, you must go help them. Just call me tonight as agreed, no matter what! Updates are critical at this point.

Understood, Bruno said and opened his eyes to find Colin staring down at him, his mouth hanging open.

'Was that you talking? Who's Beta?'

Bruno shook himself and stood. Had he been speaking out loud? No, he was a dog, and dogs can't speak. He had been worried about the magic, so he hadn't shielded his thoughts. *Can you understand me?* he asked.

Colin shook his head as if trying to clear his ears.

Bruno drew and a bit more magic and tried again. *Can you hear me, Colin?*

The boy's eyes widened in surprise and he stuttered, 'Y... you can talk. But you're a dog.'

I'm a special sort of dog, and I can only speak to special people.

Colin giggled. 'It's like you're whispering in my ear, but you're really talking to me. This is so cool. Wait until I tell my brothers I met a talking dog.'

No, stop, you can't tell anyone I talk to you, Bruno said.

Colin considered the dog for a moment. 'Okay. But only if you tell me what you're doing.'

If Bruno had been anything but a dog, he probably would have sighed, but instead he flopped to the ground and rested his head on his paws. *Well, obviously I'm following my friends to make sure they're going to be okay.*

Colin laughed. 'I'm going to help Lee and his friend escape.'

You can't. I mean, you're just a boy. What are you going to be able to do against a group of armed men? Bruno laughed

'More than a dog can do,' Colin said disdainfully.

Bruno thought about this for a moment before letting out a sharp bark. *I think you may be right. So, do you have a plan?*

'Sort of. I'm good at distracting people. I thought if I

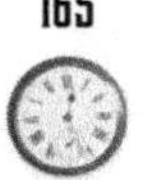

annoyed the guards, Lee and Izzy might be able to escape.'

Only Lee and Izzy?

'The others weren't too nice to me, but I guess if they got away too, that'd be okay.'

Bruno bared his teeth in a grin and rose to his feet. *Come on. Let's go see what havoc a boy and a dog can cause.*

Standing in the stuffy room at the back of his troop, Lee shuffled uneasily from one foot to another. The Council had summoned them over an hour ago, then made them wait until they had attended to everything else on their agenda. Now it was their turn to stand in front of the sixteen men and four women who represented the Lyndhurst Protectorate.

A rather pompous looking middle-aged man, whose stomach almost popped out of his clothing, called them forward. Although he was nominally in charge, Lee noticed that the woman sitting on his right actually ran things. Dressed in brown, with an angular face and piercing eyes, she appeared more predator than person. Her sharp eyes narrowed as they focussed on the confident figure of their Captain as she introduced them.

'I am Captain Kiandra from the Underground City of Portsdown. The motley crew behind me are my troop. Our current assignment is to return a runaway boy to our city elders for judgement. We respectfully request your help to apprehend him.'

The pompous man continued to smile inanely while the hawk-like woman sat forward in her seat and pinned the captain with her gaze.

Lee's stomach did a flip. *This isn't going to go well,* he sent to Izzy.

Shush, she said. *I want to listen.*

'You ask for our help, yet you sneak into our community bearing arms, and only come before us once you have been found out,' the woman said.

Although it was difficult to see from behind, Lee thought Captain Kiandra's cheeks reddened under the scrutiny. He couldn't tell whether it was from embarrassment, or anger at being challenged.

'We had no way of knowing the region had formally organised itself, otherwise we would have come here first. But, as I told your men, we are not here to hurt anyone. When we find the boy we are looking for, we will leave you in peace.'

The bird-like women scowled at the Captain. 'You want us to help you return one of your own because he has broken your laws, yet you walk around our protectorate without paying any heed to ours.'

The pompous man shifted in his seat as if he wanted to say something, but the bird-like woman held up her hand, cutting him off before he could get a word out, saying, 'No, Charlie, this is important. If we are to exist this close to the underground city and stay independent, we need to set some ground rules. We can't just roll over and die every time they send a few soldiers our way.'

'I apologise if we offended you,' Captain Kiandra said,

but the hesitation in her voice was obvious even to Lee. 'We will, of course, update our command upon our return and ensure any future soldiers who come into your area contact you first.'

'That's a start,' the woman conceded. 'If we were to help you, what would this look like?'

'We would want access to any new people who entered your community in the last week. If we don't find the boy amongst them, then we would want to question anyone who has been out and about during the last few days.' The Captain was back in command, her voice more certain.

'And were you told to bring him back even if he doesn't want to go with you?' the woman asked.

'Yes.' The Captain's answer was crisp and direct. Lee thought she should have been a bit more wary. He sensed a trap.

'Were you told to bring him back at any cost?' the bird woman pressed.

Captain Kiandra chewed on her lip, suddenly seeing where this was going. Standing a little more erect, as if she intended to confront this assault head on, she said, 'Yes, that is exactly what I was told.'

'And would that mean forcing us to bend to your will if we did not agree with you?' The woman leaned forward so she could better peer at the Captain.

Captain Kiandra didn't flinch this time. 'That would only ever be as a last resort—for instance, if some of your people attacked us in an effort to prevent us from carrying out our orders.'

'Well, I guess that says it all,' the pompous man said

as he leaned back in his chair, indicating the discussion was over.

'No! No, it doesn't,' Captain Kiandra insisted. 'I cannot imagine a situation where your people would attack us—can you?'

'Yes,' one of the other men said. Lee turned to meet the gaze of an elderly man on the far left. 'By our laws, anyone eighteen or over has the right to decide to leave the community and make their own life elsewhere. Many of us would see handing this boy over to be breaking one of our own laws to meet one of yours. Not many here would be prepared to do that—well, for you and your kind anyway.'

Sergeant Kiandra assessed the man before allowing her gaze to wander over the faces of the rest of the Council. From his own position, Lee saw the same thing she did: a group of people hostile to their mission. No, not to their mission. They were hostile towards *them*.

The Councillor's demeanour threw the Captain and she was momentarily speechless. On the way here, she had given the impression that soldiers from Portsdown were treated with deference, or at least kept at a wary distance by above ground dwellers. First they had been challenged by the Portsmouth Militia, and now it appeared the Lyndhurst Protectorate would not help them.

Much had clearly changed since soldiers from Portsdown had last been here. For all their sakes, Lee hoped Captain Kiandra would take this into account when she answered.

'Well... it wouldn't be optimal to attack your people for sticking to their beliefs... but we were given a mission... and... we can't return home until that mission is completed.

So all I can do is hope that your people do not force us into that position.'

Lee's stomach sank. This was not going to go down well.

The bird-like lady leaned forward again, clasping her hands on the table in front of her. 'Last time your people came out here with a troop the size of yours, we were a people beaten. We were barely surviving in the harsh post-war environment, and you were all well armed and well trained. In the last ten years, we have grown. As you can see, we are no longer at your mercy. We have much to protect, and much to defend, with the people and resources to do it.'

'Does that mean you will not help us?' Captain Kiandra asked, clearly a little bemused by how these people were reacting.

The pompous man answered, almost as though making a proclamation. 'We are not so inclined to be of assistance at this time. Our guards will escort you to our boundaries and you may leave.'

Captain Kiandra took a deep breath. 'I am sorry, but we cannot do that because it would be going against orders. We tracked the boy to your lands, and we need to check whether or not he is here.'

The woman turned in her seat and considered the Chairman. 'To avoid a confrontation, I believe we should let these people go back to the cell and give them time to consider whether or not they might want to proceed a little differently with their mission. Perhaps find a compromise solution to how the boy is dealt with if he is found on our lands.'

'Whoa, hold on a moment,' Rodgers said, stepping

forward. 'We are soldiers of the Portsdown Army, who are part of the largest fighting force in the country. We will not be locked up again like common criminals. You will let us go so we can complete our mission.'

Whirling round, Captain Kiandra glared at her Corporal, but before she had a chance to speak, the chairman of the Council rose to his feet. 'We don't take kindly to threats—'

'I'm sure Corporal Rodgers didn't mean to threaten you—'

'Yes, I did. You can't let these... these above grounders treat us like this. We represent the ruling authority in England. They have no—'

'Shut up, Corporal. That is an order.' The commanding tone of Captain Kiandra's voice silenced everyone in the room.

Sergeant Thea shuffled closer to Corporal Rodgers and gripped his arm tightly in warning. Once she was sure Rodgers wasn't going to say anything else, Captain Kiandra turned back towards the Council.

'In light of recent events, I think we will take up your kind offer to return to our quarters and discuss the situation amongst ourselves.' She turned on her heel and led her troop out of the chambers, gripping Sergeant Rodgers firmly by the other arm as she did.

'Well, I thought that went well,' Jason said once they were alone in the cell, a bright smile plastered across his face.

'Went well! Are you serious?' Sergeant Thea asked incredulously. 'Corporal Rodgers all but invited them to take us out back and shoot us.'

Jason looked at the Sergeant, a picture of puzzlement.

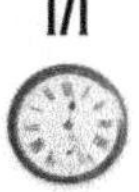

'What do you mean?'

'He basically told them if they don't do what we want, we'll return to Portsdown bringing the might of all the underground cities down on their heads,' Thea said patiently, using the tone people use when explaining complex issues to children.

'Yes, I know. I was there. And I say good on him too. They can't go around treating us like common criminals.' Jason clapped Rodgers on the back.

'You idiot,' Izzy said. 'He gave them incentive to see we never return home.'

They all waited a moment for Jason to figure it out. His mouth formed an "o" and he backed away from Rodgers as if he had a contagious disease.

'And for that, Corporal, you are not only on report, but I am demoting you back to the rank of Private for the rest of this mission,' Captain Kiandra growled.

'But—'

The Captain crossed the room and towered over the Corporal. 'And if you carry on speaking out of turn, I may decide to turn you over to these people as a sacrificial lamb.'

'Go ahead, do your worst. When we are back home, I will denounce you as a traitor for negotiating with these barbarians,' Rodgers said with a sneer, turning his back on the Captain.

'If we make it back, do what you will,' Captain Kiandra said, her eyes as black and hard as obsidian.

Izzy, would you be able to portal us out of here if we needed to leave in a hurry? Lee asked.

Not from here, perhaps if we could make it to the New

Forest....

Lee's stomach plummeted and he felt sick. Walking over to his bunk, he sat down and rested his arms on his knees.

Bruno, are you there?

Nothing. He tried again.

Bruno, we need you!

CHAPTER TEN
HISTORY IN PERIL

After his conversation with Sigma, Beta felt strangely reluctant to move. He knew he should head to the monitoring room, but part of him did not want to go to all that effort only to find out nothing had altered.

He could advise Alpha of the change in the ground team's situation. Perhaps he should, given Theta was potentially in danger. Not that they could do anything to help. If the team on the ground could not gather enough magic to portal out, there was no use sending more operatives to rescue them. Besides, he couldn't face another moment with the other Guardian without recharging his energy.

Before he raised any alarms, he should find out whether the team was still in the same timeline, or whether there had indeed been a shift—it was really better if he spoke to the Monitors first.

As he finished the thought, the light around him brightened, indicating someone wished to join him.

'Come,' he said.

A moment later the Chief Monitor herself joined him, almost as if he had summoned her.

'Sorry to bother you, Beta. I thought you would want to know that about half an hour ago, we identified a change in the timeline.'

'I rather thought you might have,' Beta said wryly before asking, 'For better or worse?'

'Difficult to tell,' she said. 'The original blip is still orange, and it is still in exactly the same place on the timeline....'

'If it hasn't changed, what is different?' Too tired to deal with this, Beta's tone was terse.

'The timeline itself, it appears to be.... I can't describe it... but it looks like it's quivering.'

'Quivering?'

'Yes. It begins to move like it does before it changes, then it snaps back in place. Moments later it starts to move again. We watched it for some time, but it does not appear to be able to keep to the current timeline, or move to the altered one.'

'Have you informed the Council? Or Alpha?'

'Well... I rather thought you might like to do that,' she said. 'Or maybe we don't need to tell anyone. I mean, we can't really say what is happening, can we?'

Beta sighed. 'You tell me.'

The Monitor coloured. 'It's just.... Well, you know how Alpha likes to deal in absolutes, and I can't say definitively what is happening here.'

'Humph,' Beta said, secretly pleased others also found Alpha difficult to deal with, but not wanting to face the Council of Ten with such flimsy information. Sighing, he added, 'All right, I'll deal with it. What exactly should I say to them though?'

Frowning, the Monitor did not immediately answer.

'Hm.' Beta cleared his throat. 'Chief Monitor?'

'Sorry, but there is no simple answer. At best guess, I would say something going on in Hampshire has the potential to change history.'

Hope wormed its way into Beta's heart, although he resisted letting it all the way in. It was still too soon to believe they had changed the future of mankind. 'Thank you. That is exactly what I will tell them.'

The Monitor beat a hasty retreat before Beta could change his mind. No sooner had she left then there was a tingling indicating someone else was trying to contact him. He opened his awareness and barked, 'Yes.'

'Did someone get up on the wrong side of the bed? Do you even sleep in a bed? No, forget I asked—'

Beta felt even less able to deal with Time Fixer business than tacking Alpha. 'Cynthia, I am kind of busy. Did you need me for something in particular?'

'No need to be so touchy.' Her tone switched from friendly to tart.

This was the first time the Time Fixer had contacted him outside of their conferences, and certainly the first time she had spoken mind to mind. Perhaps she had news from their side.

'I'm sorry. I'm still half asleep. Please excuse my abruptness. I'm sure you wouldn't have bothered me unless it was important.'

'I wanted to inform you that we've had a change in the last half an hour—an interesting one.'

'Us too. I was just talking to our Chief Monitor and the timeline is a little off... unusually off....'

'Mm... that is interesting. Our Head Timeline Specialist has reported a change too.' Cynthia's voice was excited.

The significance of the changes happening began to dawn on Beta. 'What are you seeing?' he asked, unable to keep the hope out of his voice.

'The future has split into three paths.' Cynthia's excitement was slow to seep through his fug of lethargy.

Beta changed into solid form and began pacing. Sometimes a being simply needed a body to be able to deal with life. 'I... I don't know what to say to that. Is this a good thing?'

'Maybe, maybe not. Normally when history splits, one line is clearer than the others. This time all three lines are weak. The only positive thing is that one of them extends beyond the last known end of the world.'

'Am I sensing a "but"?' Beta's stomach began to churn.

'One of the lines stops where we expect it to and—'

'Don't tell me—the third stops earlier?' Beta knew it was too good to be true.

Cynthia's silence confirmed his worst fears.

'I guess we had better meet. I'll call Alpha and we'll join you soon.'

CHAPTER ELEVEN
ESCAPE

Bruno, Bruno, can you hear me? Lee's voice sounded panicked.

No need to shout. I'm close by. Bruno tried to calm him down.

I've been calling you for ages, Lee said, desperation tinging each of his words.

Sorry, but there is not much magic in Lyndhurst, Bruno said calmly.

You've got to get us out of here as soon as possible, please. Corporal Rodgers has stirred up the Council and they're probably deciding whether or not to kill us as we speak.

I can't just wander in and take you away, Bruno responded. *Firstly, Captain Kiandra would have to want to leave.*

What? Why?

It was unusual for Lee to be this flustered. Things must be worse than he thought.

That pesky little rule about not being able to act on our own. We can only support a person living in this time, Bruno said. *If we don't follow the rules, history or time will balance everything out and we might end up with worse problems.*

Oh. I forgot about that. Lee's voice sounded sheepish.

If we can get past that little glitch, have you any ideas how we might physically be able to break you out? Bruno asked.

Well, I thought you might magically open the lock or—

Magic isn't the answer to everything, you know, Bruno admonished. *Is it digital?*

Is what digital?

Bruno sighed and slumped, dropping his head on his paws. *The lock.*

Oh.... No, it's an old style mechanical one.

Bruno said, *Give me a minute. Don't go anywhere.*

He chuckled at his joke, but Lee did not join in. Crouching beside the small figure of Colin, Bruno surveyed the area. There was an office building to his left, and a smaller structure to the right of it.

'That's the Council Chambers,' Colin said. 'The smaller building beside it is the prison. Your friends are probably being held in there.'

It looks like a public toilet, Bruno said.

'You're funny. A toilet for everyone to use? Why wouldn't they just go in the bushes?' Colin laughed.

For privacy—oh, never mind. Bruno had more important

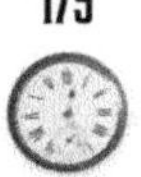

things to worry about than providing a potted history of toilets.

He surveyed the area, trying to think how he might get the others out of their cell. The street itself was deserted. It was the two men standing guard outside who were the problem. They seemed quite relaxed, but their guns were propped against the building within easy reach.

As he watched, the blonde-haired woman who had been at the farm yesterday walked down the road and entered the council building. She was the first person he had seen on the street since they had been here, so it was likely foot traffic would not be a problem.

So, your plan is to wait until the prisoners are being moved and cause a distraction? Bruno asked. And Colin nodded.

What if they don't move them today? he prompted the boy, needing Colin to come up with a plan.

Colin's brow puckered into a frown. 'I hadn't thought of that. Gram would be mighty angry if I didn't get home for dinner, so....'

Although he was aware this was on the edge of permissible interactions with locals, Bruno said, 'So, you might have to consider breaking them—'

'Breaking them out of jail is a good idea. You could help me do that.' Colin's face broke into a grin.

If that is what you want. Has anyone ever broken out?

Colin snorted. 'No. Most people aren't in there for long enough to try. Sometimes someone gets drunk, or some of the boys fight, so mostly people are only there for a few hours until they cool off. Except when it's something more. Then they are only held until....'

Bruno waited for Colin to finish, but when it became obvious he had said all he was going to, the Guardian asked, *Until what?*

'Punishment is administered,' Colin mumbled.

What sort of punishments are we talking about?

'For stealing you lose a hand, for anything worse banishment, or... you know....'

Bruno could well imagine. Justice in subsistence communities was often harsh. When people could barely look after themselves, they had little time and resources for rehabilitation and lengthy prison terms.

Interesting though this was, Bruno's brain needed to come up with a plan. Lyndhurst was pretty well set up to keep people out, but he hoped they didn't worry too much about keeping the locals in.

'Colin, are there any empty buildings down the end of the street? One close enough to the edge of town for someone to get to the forest without being seen by the guards at the gate?'

Smiling, Colin said, 'My friends and I play in an old shop down that way. It has a lane down the side where you can cut across the road and into the old town. From there you can slip into the forest without being seen—if you time it right, that is. Usually, the guards walk through town every hour to change posts.'

Excellent. And do you think you could distract those guards outside the jail long enough for me to get inside and talk to my friends?

'Of course I can. Gram says I'm good at being a nuisance.' The boy grinned from ear to ear.

A sudden twinge of guilt tugged at Bruno's conscience. He had led Colin into this plan, and he didn't like placing the boy in danger. Having second thoughts, he said, *This could be dangerous, Colin. You might get hurt. If you want to back out, it would be all right.*

'Pah, I'm not scared. Let's go.'

Shaking his head, Bruno stood to move, then paused as the sound of horse's hooves and the wheels of a cart filled the alley. Moments later a tall, lean man slowed his horse to a stop outside the Council building's door. He was joined moments later by a short titian-haired girl and a tall lanky boy, and a rather large shaggy dog.

The dog sniffed the air. Turning her head, she looked directly to their hiding spot while her owners conversed in muted tones. The door to the Council building opened, and the blonde-haired woman came out. She helped a young man out of the back of the cart while the man tied the horse's lead rein to a bollard. The group went inside.

Colin, do you know who those people are?

'Of course. Everyone round here does. The man is Simon Pettigrew. The woman is his wife, Tanya. The others are his children. The boy in the cart is not from the Protectorate. I have never seen him before.'

I think I know who he is, Bruno said.

'You don't mean....'

Yes, I think he's the one the soldiers are looking for.

With the arrival of Simon and his family, the guards outside the jail stood to attention, their guns back in their hands.

I think we might need to wait until the street is clear again before we move.

'I wonder why they're taking the boy in to see the Council?' Colin asked.

I don't know, but it won't be anything likely to assist us in getting our friends out.

Bruno slumped back to the ground, wondering if the arrival of the boy they were searching for was history's way of paying him back for overstretching his authority. Another thought occurred to him: perhaps this was a sign he should be thinking on a broader scale.

Hiding at the back of the room, Basia attempted to avoid the unwelcome attention of Councillor Johnson, who kept trying to catch her eye. When she had complained about coming into Lyndhurst today, it was this exact situation she had wished to avoid.

Her mother had overruled her, saying it was important the whole family come to present a united front to show they all supported a decision not to give Allan over to the soldiers.

When Basia went to raise further objections, her mother offered to take her to the recycle stores to look for some new books after this was over. The lure of something new to read was too much, and she backed down.

Feeling uncomfortable, she took the extra chair beside Allan under the guise of checking he was all right. Out of the Councillor's direct line of sight, she immediately relaxed.

Her charge's jaw was tense and he looked a little grey. Clearly the journey into town, even resting in the back of the cart, had taken a lot out of him. She hoped he would be well enough to speak in support of her father's plan when it was his turn to talk.

Their continued acceptance by the community relied on him confirming he had been injured during his escape from Portsdown. He also needed to confirm he had managed to steal some clothes, then when he tried to leave the area, he collapsed. Finally, he needed to testify that he had been unconscious until he woke up this early morning. Her father had tried to persuade him to request sanctuary in Lyndhurst.

Allan refused, saying, 'Please, just hand me over to the soldiers. It will be far better for everyone. Besides, I must return home and tell people what I found out here. Going back with the soldiers will achieve that.'

'You can't believe they will let you do that, can you?' Johan had asked.

'I am sure I will have to serve a sentence for escaping, but once I am out—'

'They shot you. You can't believe they will ever release you,' her father said.

'Even so, it would be safer for everyone if you handed me over to them.'

In a firm no-nonsense tone, her mother had explained in no uncertain terms why that was not going to happen. 'We are not handing you over to Portsdown.'

'I'm *from* there,' Allan countered.

'But you were trying to escape, so that makes you different. Anyway, we're not debating this. If you want

to return when you are well, that is your choice. Until then, while you're my patient, please let me negotiate some time for you to heal properly.'

It was her mother's way to end discussions, and Basia shook her head, warning Allan that saying anything now would not change her mother's mind.

A sharp laugh brought Basia from her reverie, and she leaned around to get a better look at what was going on.

'Any other day I would hand him over to the soldiers to keep the peace without batting an eyelid. But it seems like it's your lucky day,' Monica, the owner of the recycle shop, said.

'So what's different about today?' Basia's father asked.

'Less than an hour ago, a soldier from Portsdown threatened our very town with the might of all the underground cities if we did not allow them to do what they wanted on our lands,' Monica said.

Basia gasped at the implication, but the look on her face was nothing compared to the shock on her mother's.

'Monica, there are rumours that the cities still have missiles. We can't risk the whole community for the sake of one boy, much though I might want us to,' her mother said, turning and smiling regretfully at Allan.

'That is certainly something we must take into consideration,' Monica said. 'But we must also take into account that the numbers of people outside of the underground communities is growing. Perhaps it is about time we asserted our right to be here, and to be self-governing. If we don't take a stand now, they will forever be treating us like cast-offs and challenging our right to govern ourselves.'

'Hold on, Monica. Not all of us want to take on the underground armies. We should take a vote on this,' Councillor Johnston, the supposed head of the Council blustered, and a few of the other men nodded.

Monica turned in her seat. 'As Chairperson, of course it is your right to call for a vote. However, our constitution states we must invite all members of our community for a full vote when we are considering committing them to armed conflict.'

Bemused, Councillor Johnson said, 'We're only voting on whether to hand the boy over.'

'But are we? The soldiers told us if we decide not to help them, then they will bring down the full force of their military might on us,' Monica said. 'That means we are actually considering whether or not to enter an armed conflict with Portsdown.'

'Then let's call everyone in and take a vote,' Councillor Johnson said.

'All right. I think we should be able to get everyone here by tomorrow afternoon,' Monica calmly answered, which flustered the chairman even more.

'We would have to wait that long?' he asked.

'Perhaps longer if we don't get runners out now,' Monica said.

'And what do we do with the soldiers in the meantime?' Councillor Johnson sounded completely lost, and Basia had to smile.

'Totally up to you. We could let them go? Which means they could wander our lands doing what they will. Or leave them where they are, though they might not be too happy when we finally set them free, whether we give the boy to them or not.'

Basia bit back a smile, enjoying Councillor Johnson's discomfort. He had been outmaneuvered by Monica, and he didn't seem to realise it.

'Or you could decide we need a little more time to discuss the best way to handle this for the good of our community,' Monica suggested.

Councillor Johnson and the others nodded their agreement, and the deputy head turned back to her father.

'Simon, why don't you let the Council talk about this in private. Perhaps you and your family could go to the eating house and have some lunch while we do.'

'I'm afraid Allan is not well, and he wouldn't be up to that,' Basia's mother said.

'How about I have a guard take him over to the single men's quarters. They can find him a bed and he can rest while we sort matters out,' Monica allowed.

'I can decide for myself.' Allan's voice sounded thin and shaky in the cavernous hall. 'Rather than going through all this palaver, you should give me over to the soldiers.'

Monica glared at him. 'Your wishes are noted young man, but we must consider the bigger picture. If we hand you over, we are tacitly agreeing to remain subjugated to people who told us we were not good enough to be a part of their community. We will not hold you here against your will, but we ask that you work with us towards a solution that is in all our best interests.'

Allan's jaw set, and Basia placed a hand on his arm. 'You need to pick your battles. This one is lost. Don't waste your energy,' she whispered.

'But—'

'Shall we meet here at about two?' Monica suggested. 'That gives us ample time for a discussion, and you can still be back at your place before night fall.'

'Sounds fine,' said her father. 'Johan, go see to the horse and cart. Tanya and Basia, perhaps you could go and do your shopping and we will meet you at the eating house after we see Allan settled.'

As Basia helped Allan to his feet, she said, 'Trust me. I won't let them hold you here if you don't want to stay.'

'It's not that I don't want to stay.... I mean, I think I could quite enjoy sticking around.' His eyes crinkled with a smile and she felt a blush rising. 'It's just I made a commitment. I can't let all those people down. They deserve to know they might have a good life up here.'

'I understand, and we will find a way to get you home,' she promised as they followed her father.

Out of the corner of her eye, she caught Councillor Johnson watching her. She quickly turned away and shuddered.

'What's up?' her mother asked.

'Nothing,' Basia mumbled.

Turning to glance behind Basia, her mother found the cause of her unease. 'Oh, I see. We must do something to squash the Councillor's ambitions once this is over.'

SOLDIER

Crouching behind some bushes, Bruno was still waiting for an opportunity to break the others out of jail when Simon and his family emerged from the Council building. He was close enough to confirm the boy Simon helped into the cart was indeed Allan, the escapee they were looking for.

The group began walking and Bruno stood to follow. *Colin, wait here and keep an eye on the jail. I'll be back in a minute,* Bruno sent as he left.

Keeping the family in sight, he slunk behind bushes and fences until the group split. The two women went one way, and the two males led the cart along a residential street. Deciding to stick with Allan, Bruno found fewer places to hide as they meandered through the township.

He thought he was going to lose them when they turned a corner and the lack of cover meant he had to duck back. When the street was quiet, he peeked his head around to find the cart was stopped outside the two-story building taking up most of short road. Simon was helping Allan out of the cart. As they headed inside, the large golden retriever following behind turned and stared straight at Bruno and bared her teeth.

Bruno slunk behind a single rosebush in the garden opposite and peered through the branches. What seemed like an age later, but was probably only moments, Simon and his son reappeared. They spoke briefly before the son headed in one direction leading the horse and cart, and the father returned the way they had come.

The Guardian waited until they were both out of sight before crossing the road and nudging open the door they had come through. Laughter drifted from one of the rooms to the right. The noise made by the men sitting inside masked the sound of the door shutting behind him.

Down from the dining room the men occupied was a dark corridor. On his left was a closed door. In front of him was a set of stairs. The faint smell of dog drifting down told Bruno which way to go. Keeping to the shadows, he crept up the stairs and found himself in a large dormitory. At the far end of the room, a figure lay curled up on a bed, snoring gently.

Bruno approached, and a dog growled low and slow, rising to her feet from where she had taken a position under the bed. He stopped, wondering how to let the animal know he was a friend. For the first time in a long time, he wished he had taken human form; he didn't have time to establish a pecking order with this animal.

Keeping his head down, in what he hoped was a submissive stance, he moved forward again. This time the growl was louder and more menacing. The figure on the bed stirred and rolled. He saw Bruno, and leaned over to pat the dog. He said, 'It's okay, Jasmine. It's just another dog, and he seems friendly enough.'

Jasmine growled her disagreement.

It was now or never. Either history was with him and this would work, or it wasn't and he had lost nothing. Gathering what little magic he could find, he said, *I am a friend and I have come to help you.*

'Who's there? Is this your dog?' Allan asked, glancing around the room.

Jasmine took another step forward and growled again.

Must we go through this.... I'm no threat.

Allan's gaze returned to the dog. His eyes widened. 'Is

that you talking? No, you can't be. Must be the painkillers addling my head.'

The golden retriever whined and moved back towards Allan. Bruno couldn't tell whether it was because she heard the distress in the boy's voice, or because she sensed something odd was going on.

I am a dog, and yes, I am talking. I came to help you get out of here, if you want to leave, that is?

'That depends,' Allan answered. 'Where will we go after we leave here?'

Bruno could not believe he was having to talk this boy into accepting his help. *Wherever you want to,* Bruno said.

'If I say I want to go back to Portsdown, will you take me?'

Why would you want to go back after they shot you, then sent soldiers to hunt you down?

'Because I made a promise to return and tell people what it is truly like out here. I believe they deserve to know there is life again on the surface.'

Bruno frowned at the boy. *Very commendable. Still, it would not be my first choice of destinations. But if you want to return and you want my help to get there, then I guess we'll do just that.*

Allan stared at him, then shook his head. 'This is all very odd. How do I know this is for real? I mean, I could tell you to do something, but then you might just be a very well trained dog.'

We don't have time for this.... Look, why don't you think of something for me to do.

'Ah, like a telepathy sort of thing. Is that what we're doing?'

Yes, you could say that. It's actually more like magic, but who's to say what magic really is.

'Now I know I'm going crazy, talking philosophy with a dog.' Allan lay back down on the bed.

Look, there isn't much time, and I have quite a bit to organise if we are going to do this. Are you in or not?

'Roll on your back,' Allan said.

Are you kidding me? You want me to roll on my back with a killer dog in the room? Bruno looked at Allan's guard dog and she glared back as if she understood every word of the exchange.

'Jasmine, sit,' Allan said. The dog obeyed and relaxed a little.

'Okay, that was probably a bit much to ask. Jump up on the bed beside me and lie down,' Allan instructed Bruno.

Bruno did as he was asked. *Are you happy now?*

Allan's eyes widened in surprise. 'Who *are* you?'

I am a Guardian, a special being sent to help those in need, and I'm here to help you, if you want me to. Bruno jumped down from the bed. *But I need to know right now if you will work with me.*

'I guess. You're the only one who is listening to what *I* want. Worst case scenario, I have gone nuts and I'm agreeing to escape with a talking dog. Best case, this is for real and I actually get to go home,' Allan said wearily, lying back on the bed.

Can you walk?

Allan didn't move a muscle as he answered. 'What? Yes, but not very far.'

Okay, this might take a little longer than I expected. I

need you to wait here while I organise a couple of other things.

Without waiting for an answer, Bruno turned around and left the room, already moving on to the next part of his plan. Jasmine's low growl followed him out and he wondered what he was going to do about that dog when it came time to move Allan.

His tail held high, he trotted down the road. He had chosen his side and he somehow felt lighter and more purposeful. Now all he needed to do was to try and persuade the others to join him.

Righto, Colin. Do you have any objections to helping the boy the soldiers were hunting to escape? Bruno asked when he arrived back at the hiding spot.

'Boy? The one the soldiers are looking for? Won't Lee and Izzy hurt him? I am not sure I'm good with that,' Colin said.

Lee and Izzy want to get him away from the other soldiers, Bruno told him.

Colin looked doubtful, and Bruno wondered if he had overreached again.

He wants to come with us too, I promise, Bruno said.

Frowning, Colin pulled his bottom lip between his teeth. Bruno saw his escape plan slipping away.

How about we make a deal? If at any time you find he changes his mind, I will return him to Simon and his family, Bruno offered.

The boy shrugged. 'You absolutely promise?'

I do.

Bruno expected the boy to put up more of a fight, but he had forgotten how suggestible children were.

'Okay. There could be a bit of a problem though,' Colin said as he unwound himself from his hiding place. 'A little while ago, some guards arrived and took some of the soldiers back to the Council rooms—the dark-skinned lady, the tall lady with red hair, and the short grumpy man.'

Bruno took that to mean Captain Kiandra, Sergeant Thea, and Corporal Rodgers. He cocked his head to the side and considered his options. His plan still might work. Theta was a strong enough operative she would be able to ditch the others and catch them up if she chose, which he doubted she would. And now that he was supporting Colin and Allan, he no longer really needed Captain Kiandra.

I don't think the others would come with us if they were here. Let's go and rescue the ones we can for now, Bruno said.

The boy nodded before sauntering over to the guards with Bruno padding beside him.

'Good afternoon,' Colin said in an extremely polite voice. 'My tractor broke again and I wanted to please talk to the soldier who helped me fix it.'

'Sorry son, orders are not to let anyone in, no matter who they are,' the guard closest to them said before turning back to the conversation he'd been having.

'That can't mean me. I'm just a boy. I only want to...'

Bruno didn't hear the rest of the sentence because he

had slipped inside. Sitting down in front of the bars, he surveyed the room. Lee and Izzy were resting on the bottom bunks. Jason was lying on the one above the girl, one leg swinging over the side.

'How long do you think it's been?' Jason asked.

'About two minutes more than when you asked last time,' Izzy responded, not attempting to conceal the disdain in her voice. 'And quit swinging that leg in front of my face,' she added, taking a swipe at it.

'I'm not hurting you, and you should show more respect for your superior.' Jason grinned, clearly enjoying needling Izzy.

'Superior. What a laugh!' the girl spat.

'Could you two quit it? You're giving me a headache.' Lee raised his voice to be heard over the bickering.

Before a full-scale argument erupted, potentially bringing in the guards, Bruno sent, *Time to go, guys.*

Lee swung himself off the bed and moved to the bars before whispering, 'Man, am I pleased to see you.'

Jason pulled his leg up, leaned over the edge of his bunk and stared at Bruno. 'What do you mean "go"? The others are still with the Town Council. We must stay together—after all, we're supposed to be assisting with the Captain's mission.'

Theta—sorry, Thea—can catch us up if she wishes to, Bruno said. *But we have to go now. We may not get another opportunity to escape.*

'*We* are not going anywhere,' Jason said, his superior tones almost sounding commanding. 'If we are not supporting the Captain and Corporal Rodgers, we're acting alone, which is a big no-no.' His jaw set in a stubborn line, which on anyone else would make them appear stern, but it turned Jason into a petulant child.

There's no time to explain the details, Bruno said, *but we're not acting alone. Someone was already coming to rescue you, and I am helping them out.*

'And what then? Our assignment is to help the Captain return the escapee to Portsdown.'

I'm suggesting we help someone else from this time period—the key player in all of this, Bruno said. *Now let's get going.*

'Have you spoken to someone in charge? Are these new orders?' Jason said at the same time Lee asked, 'Have you spoken to Allan?'

Bruno chose to ignore Jason and answer Lee. *I spoke with him, and he wants to leave here too. I have agreed we will help him go back to Portsdown to complete his mission.*

'Are you sure that's a good idea?' Izzy asked. 'I mean, what will that do to the timeline?'

Bruno swallowed his own guilt at going against his mentor's wishes and said, *My latest news was the timeline might already have changed. But that is not why I am doing this. In my gut, it feels wrong to be supporting strangers when one of our own needs our help.*

Izzy nodded. 'I know what you mean.'

Lee grinned, 'I'm in.'

'No,' Jason said stubbornly. 'We are staying here until the others return.'

'Speak for yourself,' Izzy said, joining Lee by the bars.

Are you ready to go? Bruno asked.

'Yes, but how are you going to do this?' Lee asked.

As you suggested, I'm going to magic the lock.

'Isolde....'

'No, Jason, I'm going with Bruno and Lee.' Izzy placed her hands on her hips and glared Jason into silence.

Bruno quickly explained the escape plan, then blocked out the room around himself and drew every piece of magic from the air. He concentrated on moving the lock mechanisms, and after a few moments it clicked and the door released. Lee pushed it open.

Last chance Jason, Bruno said.

'I'm staying.' He crossed his arms and rolled away, turning his back to them.

'Have it your own way,' Izzy said, shutting the gate.

Bruno made sure Izzy and Lee were out of sight by the door before he stepped outside and moved back into position beside Colin. The boy was still trying to argue his way in, but when Bruno joined him, he said, 'Well, if that is the way you're going to be, I guess—'

Bruno jumped up, placed his front paws on the shoulder of the guard closest to him, and began licking his face.

'What the...!'

'Bruno, get down.' Colin made a half-hearted attempt to pull the dog off. The other guard joined him, yelling at Bruno to let go.

'Hey, leave my dog alone!' Colin began swinging punches at the second guard, who defended himself against the boy's ineffectual blows.

From the corner of his eye in the midst of the melee, Bruno caught Lee and Izzy running to the closest building. Once they had ducked in behind it, he dropped down and sat calmly beside Colin, who had a wide grin plastered across his face.

'Sorry about that, boys,' Colin said. 'He forgets he's so big and scary. He's a big softie, really.'

'Be off with you. You've caused enough problems,' said one of the guards, wiping Bruno's saliva off his face.

Dismissed, Colin and Bruno headed back the way they had come.

'That was fun,' Colin said, laughing as he walked. 'What's next?'

Can you show me where the stables are? We need to borrow a horse and cart.

CHAPTER TWELVE
GETTING AWAY

The idea was to borrow a horse and cart from the stables to transport Allan back to Portsdown. Everything else had gone to plan, so Bruno had no reason to think this phase would go any differently. As they entered the building, everything fell apart.

Sneaking in through a back door, they found a girl and boy talking heatedly by the only cart in sight.

'What are we going to do?' Colin looked down, waiting for him to take the lead.

Aren't they the kids from before? Bruno asked.

'Yep. Johan and his sister Basia.'

All right, I guess we'll wait until they're gone.

Bruno searched for a hiding place. The room fell silent. Bruno glanced up to find brother and sister had stopped talking and were staring at them.

'Hi, Colin,' the girl said. 'Who are you talking to?'

'My dog. This is Bruno.'

The girl laughed. 'Don't be silly, Colin. I haven't got time for games today. There is someone else here. I heard them speaking.'

'But it was him I was talking to,' Colin insisted, folding his arms across his chest.

'It can't be. We heard someone answer you,' Johan said. 'He suggested you hide until we leave.'

I should have shielded my speech, Bruno thought as the girl, Basia, searched the stalls for another person. I am getting sloppy.

Hi, my name is Bruno.

Johan's eyes widened. 'Either my mind is playing tricks on me, or that dog *is* talking.'

Colin perched on a hay bale, and Bruno flopped to the ground, resting his head on his front paws while they waited for Basia to finish.

'Basia, I think the dog really can talk. He just introduced himself.'

'Dogs don't talk, Johan.'

'Our dogs don't, but maybe dogs from the underground city do. The cities are more scientifically advanced now than in the pre-war world, so who's to say enhanced dogs aren't commonplace.'

I am not an enhanced animal, Bruno protested. *I use the magic around us to communicate.*

Basia spluttered. 'Now I know you're kidding. Magic is for fairytales.'

Bruno sat up and tried to look as commanding as he could. *You're wrong. Magic is merely another form of science.*

But I have not got the time to debate this. I'm a Guardian, a Time Guardian in fact, and I'm here to help Allan.

'Skipping over the magic and Time Guardian thing—which are too weird to contemplate—if you're here to help Allan, how do you propose to do that?' Basia asked, staring intently at Bruno, almost like she was boring inside his head in an attempt to read his intentions.

What do you think would help him? Bruno countered.

The brother and sister looked at each other, and finally Johan nodded.

Basia said, 'When Mother and Father were called away from lunch, we came here to think about what we could do to help him. We think the Council will hand Allan over to the soldiers.'

'It is their only option if they want to protect the community,' Johan added.

'And Allan wants to go home so he can tell everyone what it is like out here now.'

Won't the soldiers take him back? Bruno asked, wanting to check they were all on the same page.

'Of course, but we believe when they get there, the best case scenario is that he will be locked up for the rest of his life. Worst case.... Well, I don't even want to think what that might look like,' Basia said.

'So, Basia thought we should take him home ourselves,' Johan finished up.

Bruno cocked his head to the side and contemplated Johan and Basia. Up close, he had the familiar feeling he got when meeting with souls he had encountered before, and these two were very familiar. He had first met them as Barabal and John, and they had a history of resolving historical anomalies with him. Was this the universe trying to tell him something? Were they destined to save humanity together?

They obviously had no idea who he was, so he would have to tread carefully if he was to ensure they worked together.

Sounds like you have a plan, Bruno encouraged.

'Sort of, but there are only two of us, and Basia hasn't much experience outside of the community. And we only have this for protection.' Johan patted the revolver at his side. 'We can't take father's rifle—

'We—'

'No, Basia. He and Mum will need it to protect themselves on the way home.'

'We can take Jasmine with us. She can be pretty fierce,' Basia added.

Bruno was about to object to their taking the dog guarding Allan with them as the animal clearly did not like him, but Johan and Basia continued talking as if he and Colin were not there.

'Yes, but Allan's injured. He won't be able to walk far,' Johan pointed out.

'We can take the cart. I am sure Mum and Dad won't miss it for a few days,' Basia said, then laughed. 'And when we return, having taken the horse and cart will be the least of our worries.'

Finally, they fell silent. Basia stared at Johan, and eventually he nodded.

Well, it seems we are in agreement, Bruno said. *We take the horse and cart, pick up Allan, then meet up with a couple of my friends who also want to help Allan go back to the city.*

'Sorry?' Johan turned to look at Bruno. 'You're coming with us? And what other people?'

Bruno drew himself up even taller and said authoritatively, *Of course I am coming with you. I pledged my assistance to Allan, along with two friends who are waiting to join us. They are able to provide additional protection.*

Johan's eyes narrowed as he contemplated Bruno.

'He's a good guy,' Colin piped in. 'So are his friends. I can vouch for them.'

With his lips curling into a smile at Colin's words, Johan said, 'All right, I guess you can come along.'

'So, we're going to do this?' Basia asked.

Johan nodded. 'Mum and Dad are with the Council and some of the soldiers now,' he said. 'We need to act fast if we're going to put some distance between us and them before they realise we're gone.'

Bruno didn't need to be told twice. *Right, here's the plan. You two hitch up the horse and head to the single men's quarters. I'll help Allan down the stairs and meet you at the bottom.*

He turned to Colin. *Can you go and find Lee and Izzy and meet us round the bend from the barricades? And if you can find some sort of weapons for them to bring, that would be great.*

'There is a small armoury as you go into the men's quarters,' Johan said. 'I guess we can borrow an extra couple of rifles from inside. We have to bring them back though—arms are precious out here.'

Right. Everybody has their job, Bruno said.

'Wait a minute,' Basia interrupted. 'They're not just

going to let us take Allan out of here. We'll need to hide him—unless you want to fight your way out, that is?'

'You can take some hay and some of the old sacks from over there. Make a nest for him to hide in,' Colin said, blushing as he earned a smile from Basia.

'Perfect,' she said. 'Let's get moving.'

Bruno was patting himself on the back as he made his way to the building where Allan was. He wasn't usually this positive about his plans. Then again, this was the first time in a while he had been able to operate without constant scrutiny and direction from Beta.

Being in a magically barren time meant it would be difficult for the Guardians to monitor his every move. That meant he was able to rely on his own intuition, and it was liberating. Then his bubble burst.

After this was over, he was going to have to answer to the Time Guardian Council, just as Basia and Johan would answer to their parents. It was likely they would not be happy with his decision to support Allan in his quest to return to Portsdown. Leaving Thea behind would not go down well either.

He pushed his concerns aside. He would worry about all that later. For now, he believed the course they were on was their best chance for saving humanity. Not least because what they were doing before had not changed anything. Mostly, though, it was because Allan was the person at the centre of the anomaly, so he was the most likely catalyst for changing the fate of the world.

The Council may not see that now, but once he explained it after they saved the timelines, he was sure they would understand. And if they did not save humanity, then they would all be stranded here or worse, and facing the Council would be the least of their worries.

There was nobody on the street outside the building when he arrived. Bruno nosed open the door and darted up the stairs. Fortunately, no one was around up here either; no one except for Jasmine. Allan was asleep in the same bed with the dog stoically guarding him.

Bruno approached and the dog growled her warning. As Bruno moved closer, the noise grew louder.

Please be quiet, Bruno sent. *I don't want anyone to know I'm here.*

His efforts were in vain. Jasmine stood and began barking, ready to defend her charge at all costs. Fortunately, the noise woke Allan, and he leaned over to pat the dog.

'What is it, girl?'

Allan, time to go, Bruno said.

The boy's hand withdrew and he rubbed the sleep out of his eyes.

Please, if you want to leave Lyndhurst, we must go now, Bruno said, a little louder this time.

Finally, Allan got the message and levered himself off the bed. As he sat on the edge, he winched and turned a pasty white colour.

Bruno's dog eyebrows drew together and he put his head to the side as he considered the boy, wondering if he had overestimated his capacity to walk unaided. *Are you going to be able to make it downstairs by yourself?*

Allan stood, swayed, then righted himself before surveying his path to the door.

'I can lean on each of the bed ends until I make it to the door. Did you happen to notice if there was a handrail on the stairs?' Allan asked as Jasmine nudged his leg, as if she were directing him back to bed.

The boy ran his fingers through the fur on her head and said, 'It's all right, girl, just a little change of plan. You stay here and wait for Simon and Tanya.'

Bruno was sure Jasmine understood Allan's words, but, instead of obeying, she walked beside him as he shuffled his way to the door. It was as if she were helping him stay upright.

Bruno wandered ahead and checked the stairs. *We're in luck,* he sent. *There is a rail. Hold on. Wait by the door a moment. There are a couple of people in the dining room.*

Bruno dropped to the floor, hoping to make himself smaller so the men downstairs couldn't see him. He heard Allan close the door, and he turned his head to see the boy lean against the wall and take a breath. Jasmine stood beside him, and Bruno could sense her concern.

Through the glass in the front door, the outline of a horse appeared. Dampening his impatience, he humphed, dropped to the floor, and waited for the men to leave. When the two men headed down the corridor beside the stairs, he allowed himself a sigh of relief.

The front door opened and Basia popped her head in. Seeing the way was clear, she ran upstairs to help Allan down. Johan followed behind and tried the door opposite the dining room.

'Damnation. It's locked. It isn't usually,' he said as he tried the handle.

Bruno descended the stairs, sat down, and studied the lock. Relieved to find it was a simple padlock, he worked his magic and it fell open. Johan stared at him, amazement written on his face.

Bruno couldn't resist saying, *See, I told you magic was real.*

Shaking his head, Johan entered the room, returning with two rifles and a box of ammunition.

As he resecured the door, he said, 'I reckon we've only got about an hour before people start looking for us, and we want to be well on our way by then. We need to move faster.'

I couldn't have said it better myself, Bruno thought.

They exited to find Basia had helped Allan into the back of the cart and was arranging hay-filled sacks to make a comfortable bed and to hide him from view. Johan helped, and soon the escapee was hidden so well he could not be seen unless someone was looking down into the back.

'Jasmine, go.' Johan pointed back inside. The dog ignored him and jumped up into the cart, arranging herself so she was beside Allan.

Johan sighed. 'Well, I guess you're coming too.'

Bruno was congratulating himself for a plan well executed when he saw a rather rotund, flush-looking man rushing up the street heading towards them. Praying he would pass them by, he was out of luck. The man saw Basia and made a beeline towards them. Bruno slunk behind the cart, keeping out of sight.

'What a happy coincidence I should bump into you

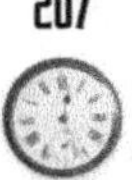

alone.' The man smiled at Basia.

'She's not alone,' Johan said. 'I'm with her. Is there something I can help you with?' The boy insinuated himself between the man and his sister.

The man glanced around, a little flustered, then moved to the side so Basia was in his sights again. 'I didn't realise you were doing quite so much stocking up while you were in town,' he said, moving towards the cart and avoiding Johan.

Bruno held his breath. Any close scrutiny would reveal Allan hiding in the back. As the man drew closer, Jasmine stood, placed her paws on the edge of the cart, and growled.

Taking a step back, the man blustered, 'Great guard dog you have there.' He frowned. 'I thought the animal was guarding the boy from Portsdown.'

'Basia and I are heading home. Dad asked us to take Jasmine with us,' Johan said, trying to draw the man's attention.

'We only came to pick her up and say goodbye to Allan,' Basia added. Although her voice was calm, Bruno sensed the girl's unease around the man, and his hackles rose.

'Well, my dear, I shall be sorry to see you go. I had hoped we might spend some more time together. Perhaps get to know each other a little better.' The man's voice was oily and ingratiating.

From his hiding place under the cart, Bruno could tell Basia was holding herself very still and very stiff, as if she were willing herself not to show how uncomfortable this man made her.

Her voice carried no trace of her unease as she said,

'I'm afraid not this time, Councillor. We must be on our way as soon as possible.'

'Um, well....' The man made no move to leave. 'Hmm, I think I might invite your parents over for a meal soon. You too, Basia. Time we put our relationship on a more formal footing.'

Over my dead body, Bruno heard Basia think.

As if e knew his sister would not be able to respond to this without giving something away, Johan said, 'We need to be heading home, and shouldn't you be at a Council meeting? Surely they must be waiting for you.'

'Um, well, yes, I was on my way there. See you soon, my dear.' The Councillor's voice was even more oily, if that was even possible, and Bruno felt nothing but sympathy for Basia. He fervently hoped for her sake this man was not going to play a big part in her future.

As the man walked off with a new spring in his step, Johan secured everything and started the horse moving. 'If he tells Mum and Dad he saw us, we have even less time than I thought.'

Bruno prepared to jump up onto the cart as it passed him, but Jasmine's growl assured him he would not be welcome. Running along behind, he soon caught up with Johan and Basia as they joined the Old Southampton Road.

The dilapidated buildings cast a long shadow over the high street as they walked towards the outskirts of town. Basia

stayed ahead of the cart, steering a course that kept them away from anyone who might take note of their passing. She need not have worried. The streets were almost empty and the people they did pass were too busy with their own thoughts to take much notice of the group. Even so, it was a very long ten minutes to the barriers. At any moment she expected someone to call for them to halt.

Also disconcerting was listening to Johan muttering under his breath. 'I've taken arms from the armoury, and Mum and Dad's horse and cart. My future is down the toilet.'

Dropping back to walk beside him, Basia said, '*We* are doing this, brother; *we* both bear responsibility.'

'But I am the oldest, and the male. You know what they're like. They'll blame me regardless of your role.' Johan's head dropped.

Basia hated seeing him like this. Her brother had always followed the rules, and this must be eating him up. 'You can still change your mind once we are through the gate,' she said. 'The dog said he has friends who will help. I will be all right without you and Jasmine once we find them.'

There was only one thing Johan took more seriously than following the rules, and that was doing what he believed to be the right thing. As she gave her brother a way out of this, Basia hoped he would choose to continue with her.

'This is what Allan wants, so I believe it is the right thing to do. We will only be gone a couple of days—three at the most,' Johan reasoned, talking himself back into coming along. 'Besides, none of you will get far without me.' He laughed and she joined him, relieved he was back on board.

Bruno snorted. *We got here without you. Please don't stay on our account.*

'I am staying for my sister, dog,' Johan said.

I told you, my name's Bruno.

'Sorry, of course you did. Anyway, it will be quicker with me along, and we will all have more chance of surviving. Besides, I'm not going to let my sister head off with a bunch of strangers.'

Suit yourself. And for what it's worth, I'm pleased you're coming, Bruno told him. *I think our chances of succeeding will increase and I believe your cool head might be needed.*

The gate across the main road was fast approaching. The bar remained firmly down as guards patiently waited for the cart.

'This is not good,' Basia whispered. 'They don't normally stop people leaving.'

'Hi, Ben,' Johan said. 'What's with the hold up?'

'Our orders are to question anything unusual, even slightly unusual... what with the soldiers in custody and all.'

'We've left like this a hundred times before. What do you think is strange about us?' Johan asked.

'The dog, Johan,' Ben said.

'Jasmine?' Basia laughed.

'No, the other one,' the other guard said.

Johan looked down at Bruno in puzzlement. 'This dog? What's odd about this mangey mutt?'

Bruno bared his teeth at Johan's comment.

Ben moved around beside Bruno. 'He was with the

soldiers? We left him at Ma Wilson's place this morning. Now he's here.'

Johan's face froze. 'You're kidding me.... With the soldiers? You're sure he's the same one?' Johan's voice wavered slightly, and Basia hoped Ben would not hear.

'Yep, I was at the farm when we captured them,' Ben confirmed.

I can explain, but we need to be on our way first, Bruno interrupted.

Basia looked around, wondering why the guards did not react to the dog speaking.

I have shielded my voice so only you can hear, he told her as if he could hear her thoughts.

Trying not to react, Basia watched Johan struggling with the fact that this dog was indeed from the underground city.

'And you're sure this is the exact same dog? And that he was with the soldiers looking for the escapee?' Johan asked again.

Bruno hung his head, and Basia's stomach clenched. What would Johan do? Was the dog double-crossing them? Did it matter who the dog was with? They just needed to get Allan out of here. Everything else could be worked out later. The dog looked as though he was preparing to run. She had to do something, and now.

'Honestly, Ben, we had no idea about the dog,' Basia said. 'He isn't actually with us. He started following along a couple of minutes ago. We think he's taken a shine to Jasmine. Nothing we say puts him off.'

Really? This is what you're going with? Bruno looked pained, and Jasmine glared at Basia. *Honestly, can all dogs understand everything?* she wondered.

Ben laughed. 'I don't think Jasmine is too interested. I've never seen her ride on the back of the cart like that before. I think she's putting as much distance between her and him as she can.'

'We can't shake him, so he must be keen.' At last Johan played along, and Bruno groaned in her head.

'Well, if you decide to breed them, it will be a nice litter of puppies. Don't forget me when they're ready to be weaned.'

Not happening, ever, Bruno sent as Ben returned to his companion and the barrier was raised.

'Do you want me to keep him here with us?' Ben asked as they walked through.

Basia stifled a grin as Bruno bared his teeth, causing Ben to back away. 'No, I'm sure he'll tire soon and head back to his friends,' she said.

Basia did not relax until she heard the barrier clip behind them. Beside her, Johan actually expelled a breath, he was so relieved to pass the first hurdle. Then the worst happened.

'Hold on, wait up,' the second guard called out.

Basia's stomach clenched so much she almost threw up. They must have caught sight of Allan in the back.

Try and stay calm, Bruno sent. *It might be nothing.*

Johan's fingers holding the lead rein were trembling. She shoved her own shaking hands into the pockets of her jeans, and sent a prayer to whatever gods might still be around to keep them safe. Johan took a calming breath, halted Nellie, and turned to face the man running towards them.

'Sorry to hold you up, guys. Ben forgot to ask if you could join the patrol tomorrow. We're a little shorthanded, what with needing to guard the prisoners.'

'I'd love to, but unfortunately, my mother's found out about my patrols, and to say she's not happy would be an understatement. So I'm going to have to beg off for a while until she calms down,' Johan said.

The man chuckled. 'Bad luck mate. I don't want you to end up on the wrong side of your mother. We'll find someone else.'

'Hey,' Johan called as the man turned to head back to the barrier. 'Put me back on the duty roster next week, though. Hopefully it will all blow over by then.'

'Okay, be seeing you.' He raised his hand in farewell.

Basia watched the guard retreat and made sure he was on the other side of the gate before she followed after the slow-moving cart.

'This is quite exciting,' she said as she caught Johan up.

'You're joking, right?' he said. 'My heart is beating so fast I think I'm going to have a heart attack.'

'So, you can go out hunting overnight with goodness knows what in the woods around you, and that's fine. We help one boy escape and suddenly you're a mess,' she teased him, trying to lighten the atmosphere.

Johan chuckled. 'What can I say, a life of crime doesn't suit me.'

As the road bent around towards Southampton, Bruno began to range ahead, searching for something. When he didn't find it, he asked them to slow down.

I thought my friends would be here by now, he said.

If it was possible for an animal to sound worried,

Bruno did.

'Can you contact them like you talk to us?' she asked.

I'm trying, but there's no response, he told her.

'We can't wait for them,' Johan muttered. 'They'll be after us soon, and besides, I'm not sure I want to wait for underground soldiers.'

They're on Allan's side, I promise, Bruno said.

Basia placed a hand on Johan's arm. 'It will be fine. Colin vouched for them. I am sure they will be here in a moment and you can see for yourself.' She glared pointedly at Bruno.

I'll keep trying. I'm sure they'll be here soon. The dog did not sound confident, and she wondered briefly if their venture was doomed to failure before it had even begun.

Lee ducked into the shell of a building, pulling Izzy behind him. Pressing his back against the wall, Izzy followed suit. Colin was not quick enough to join them and they listened as he greeted the Lyndhurst patrol they had spied moments earlier.

'Say, aren't you one of Ma Wilson's strays?' a male voice asked.

'What if I am?' Colin responded in his usual cheeky tone.

The man ignored his comment. 'Have you seen anything unusual out here?'

'Apart from you guys, you mean?' Colin quipped.

'Watch it, lad, or you'll get a clip around the ear,'

another one of the men said, and Lee sensed the mood change with those words. 'There are soldiers in our jail and these men are risking their lives to protect our community. The least you can do is show them some respect when they ask you a question.'

'Please don't push it,' Lee muttered under his breath, willing Colin to let it go so they could leave.

'What do ya think you'll find out here? More soldiers?' Colin laughed. 'It's just me and my mates, and some old buildings.'

'You guys know you aren't meant to be out here, don't you. We don't normally patrol this far out. Anyone could be hiding in these buildings,' the first voice said.

'Good point,' the second voice interrupted. 'What are you doing out here?'

Lee's stomach sank. Already nervous that they would miss their rendezvous, the close proximity of the guardsmen was not helping it settle down. Now their ability to successfully escape capture depended on a boy who seem intent on baiting their captors.

'Nothing much,' Colin said. 'Looking for an escaped dog. I was supposed to be taking care of him, but he ran away.'

Lad's smarter than I thought, Izzy sent.

'Well, don't let us hold you up,' the first guard said.

Frustrated at not being able to see what was going on, Lee listened. Some rocks fell nearby, and he suspected Colin was heading away. A few minutes later, the second guard said, 'Okay, lads, let's finish sweeping the area. I want to be back in time for dinner.'

About five minutes later, Izzy whispered, 'I think they're gone.' Moments after that Colin's head appeared

through a crack in the crumbling wall opposite.

'Couldn't you have been a little more polite?' Lee admonished. 'What if they had captured us—again?'

'You're kidding. If I didn't be me, they would have been suspicious.' Colin appeared unfazed by the criticism.

'He's got a point,' Izzy told him.

Before Lee could think of a suitable response, Bruno's voice broke into his mind. *Lee, Izzy, where are you?*

On our way, Lee sent.

About ten minutes later, the group broke through the undergrowth and onto a road. Bruno let out a bark of greeting.

'Got you here,' Colin said, a smirk plastered on his face.

As they approached the people Bruno was travelling with, the girl placed her hands on her hips in a gesture so familiar Lee could not help but feel homesick. Even the tone of her voice when she said, 'Okay, Bruno, time to convince us these guys are on our side,' reminded him of his sister.

'Yes, Bruno. How come the very soldiers Allan was running from now want to help him get back on his own terms? How do we know it isn't some sort of trick?' the boy asked.

He also seemed familiar, but Lee could not immediately place him. Then Izzy went googly-eyed, and he thought, *Jo, he is Jo—different body, same soul.*

You said we were running out of time. We can't stand around here while we sort this out. We need to go, Bruno said.

When no one moved, he continued, *Thanks for all your help, Colin. We couldn't have done this without you.*

'That is why I'm coming with you,' the boy said, his tone resigned.

'I'm not sure that's the best idea,' the Bebe-like girl said. 'Ma Wilson will miss you, and she'll skin us alive for letting you come along. If you leave now, you'll be home in time for dinner.'

Colin folded his arms, not budging. Izzy turned to Lee and nodded encouragingly.

What do you want me to do? he asked, careful to direct his thought to Izzy only, as Colin could clearly hear mindspeak.

Talk him into going home, she said.

He didn't know what to say. He hadn't much experience dealing with kids. Finally, he came up with, 'Colin, what we are doing is dangerous. People could get hurt, and maybe even killed.'

Great, Lee. Give him a gold-plated invite, why don't you, Izzy said.

He shook his head. What was she talking about? *What?*

'I'm not a baby, you know,' Colin said.

The stubborn set to his jaw told Lee Izzy was right: he had totally gotten this wrong. He changed tactics. What he needed was something for Colin to do that they could not.

'You're right. We do need your help. We just didn't want to ask. If you're not too scared....' Lee threw out the line and waited.

'I'm not scared of anything,' boasted Colin.

Now to gently reel him in. 'Then you're just the man I need,' Lee said. 'Colin, we need to delay anyone who might follow us to give us a chance to get a bit further ahead.'

Colin nodded his head. 'Of course. You don't want them catching you up before you reach the city.'

Lee smiled. 'Right.'

'And I can help you with that?' the boy asked, eyes round with excitement.

'I have an idea,' Lee said, trying to build the suspense. 'I was wondering if, when they realise Izzy and I escaped, you can do a big song and dance about looking for your dog Bruno. It might distract or annoy them. Do you think you're up for that?'

'Just ask Bruno. I'm good at this sort of thing,' Colin said.

'You might be late home for dinner,' Izzy told him.

'I don't mind,' Colin insisted. 'But will you be okay without me? You don't know much about life around here. Perhaps I really should come along.'

'They've got me with them,' Jo-boy said. 'I think I can do almost as well as you can. Besides, I want to ask you a special favour. When things quieten down, would you tell our parents Basia and I are fine and will be back as soon as we can? I want them to understand we will only be away a few days.'

Colin stood tall and said with a voice bursting with pride, 'I can do that. You can trust me.'

'Excellent. Can you sneak back in without being seen?' Lee asked.

'There's no one better at sneaking around than me,' Colin said as he happily trotted off. 'I'll see you all later.'

'I believe he thinks he is going to come back and catch us up,' Bebe-girl said.

'That is why I thought about the message for Mum and

Dad. They won't let him skip off that easily,' Jo-boy laughed.

Once Colin had disappeared into the trees, Bruno said, *Come on, let's move. They'll be after us sooner than we think.*

'Before we do, you owe us an explanation,' the boy who looked like Jo said, glaring pointedly at him and Izzy.

'We can walk while we talk,' Lee offered, sensing Bruno's impatience. 'If you don't like what we say, we can part ways.' As he said the words, he hoped they were not prophetic.

The other boy thought for a moment, nodded curtly, and said, 'You're right, we can. Let's go.'

He clicked as tongue and the horse began moving. Lee walked beside the Bebe look-alike and Izzy slotted in between her and the other boy. Although he didn't know their new companions, something about this felt right.

Let me finish the introductions, Bruno said. *Lee and Izzy, this is Johan and Basia. Their family looked after Allan, and they are going to help us take him back to Portsdown.*

'I thought it was *you* helping *us*,' said Johan.

Yes, indeed. That is what we are doing, said Bruno.

'Where is Allan?' Lee asked.

'Hiding in the cart,' Izzy snorted, not taking her eyes off Johan.

You only left Jo a few days ago, Lee said.

He is Jo, you moron, Izzy sneered.

'While it is nice to have names, it doesn't shed any light on why we should trust these guys,' Johan pressed.

'We've had a change of heart,' Lee explained. 'We don't

like what's going to happen to Allan when he is returned to the underground city, so we decided to help sneak him back in.'

Johan snorted. 'Really? You expect us to believe that?'

'Why wouldn't you?' Lee asked.

'Isn't it obvious? You're soldiers. Soldiers follow orders. They don't change their minds mid mission,' Johan snorted.

'What he said. So, what's the real story?' Basia asked. 'Why are you here?'

'I hate this bit,' Izzy said. 'Either we lie and try make up something relatively believable, or we tell them the truth and they never believe us anyway.'

'Why don't you try the truth? We're not complete yokels,' Basia said.

'What do you know about things that are beyond your wider world?' Lee asked, thinking his own sister would never believe the truth of what was going on.

'Are you going to start talking about things like magic?' Johan said. 'Because I watched Bruno use it to open a lock today with his mind, and I'm a believer. So, you tell me other strange things are going on—I'm listening.'

Long story short, we were sent here to stop something bad from happening. We became soldiers to do that, Bruno started.

'Soon we began to believe getting Allan back to where he belongs in one piece might be the best way to achieve that,' Izzy finished.

'See, no changing of side involved. We simply redefined our mission,' Lee added.

'You actually expect us to believe that?' Basia asked.

Bruno sighed, *I'm running out of energy, and part of*

me doesn't care what you believe. Trust us. Don't trust us. It is up to you. Either way, we all want to help this boy reach Portsdown. The only real question is: are we going to work together to do it?

'I thought we agreed you were helping us,' Basia laughed and Lee joined in.

He felt comfortable with this girl who was his sister, but not his sister. He wondered if Basia and Johan also sensed some sort of bond. His question was answered when Basia spoke again.

'It sounds odd, but I think we're meant to do this together,' she said to her brother.

'I don't think it is odd at all,' he said. 'I feel the same way, though I can't for the life of me say why.' He paused, then added. 'I am travelling with you, but let me make it clear: I don't actually trust any of you. Double-cross us or put my sister in danger, and I'll shoot you without a second thought.'

Johan's statement hung heavy about them until Izzy said, 'So, we're all good then?'

They laughed.

Izzy placed her hand on Johan's arm. 'You're doing the right thing helping us take Allan home. What you're finding difficult to reconcile is that you are doing something wrong to achieve that.'

Johan looked down at Izzy with wonder in his eyes. 'How did you know that? Do you have some form of telepathy as well as the ability to mindspeak?'

Izzy laughed. 'Let's just say I'm close to someone very like you.'

CHAPTER THIRTEEN
A SUCCESSFUL ESCAPE

Silence fell for a while as they pushed hard to put as much distance between them and Lyndhurst as they could. As they drew further away from the settlement, Lee noticed the lack of vehicles on the road.

‘When we came out of Portsdown Hill, old cars and trucks littered the motorway. What happened here?’ he asked.

‘Trade happened,’ Basia said. ‘Over the years we’ve built up a bit of a commercial relationship with the Southampton Protectorate. With carts moving backwards and forwards all the time, it made sense to spend time clearing the road. It made trips quicker, and trade became more frequent.’

There was only one cart the stables, Bruno said.

‘When a market is arranged, carts and tractors with

trailers make the trip into Southampton and return with what we need: food for the city and items that are hard to come by for us—machinery parts, clothing, books and things.'

'And you should be pleased we went to all that effort,' Johan said. 'It means we've got a straight through trip to the edge of Southampton, and we should be close to Portsdown Hill by early tomorrow afternoon.'

'Where are we stopping tonight?' Basia asked.

'There is a safe house along this road. Our patrols use it all the time. We should reach it just before sundown,' Johan said.

'Are you sure stopping at a safe house is such a good idea?' Lee asked.

'Why wouldn't it be?' Basia's tone was defensive.

'For starters, that is the first place people following us are going to look,' Lee said.

'We need to stop somewhere,' Basia insisted. 'The night is owned by the homeless and those who have nothing left to lose. Only those who are desperate themselves would be out with them. Besides, we will travel better if Allan is rested.'

Johan chewed his lip. 'It does make sense to keep going. If the guard expect us to stop overnight, they won't be in such a hurry to catch us up.'

Izzy looked up at him. 'What do you do when you're on overnight hunting trips or patrols and there is no shelter nearby?'

Johan frowned. 'How do you know we even do that? Do you guys in the city spy on us?'

Izzy winked. 'You wish! Anyway, we're not actually

from the city, remember.'

Johan's gaze didn't waiver.

'All right, I overheard some of the guards talking on the way into town about the best places to hunt when they are out on patrol. Some of them are too far away to be reached in a single day,' Izzy admitted.

He grinned down at her. 'We stick to open spaces and keep moving, weapons drawn. When we sleep, we do so in the open, or in an easily defensible position, taking turns to keep watch.'

'So, we can keep moving all night if we need to?' Lee said.

'Yes,' Johan admitted. 'Although we will need to rest and water the horse at some stage.'

So, if you led us through the night, how would we do this? Bruno had moved up beside them and looked up at Johan, tongue lolling out of his mouth.

Johan nudged Izzy. 'That dog of yours—is he just for show or can he help defend us?'

I'm not their dog, Bruno said, pulling in his tongue and trying to look less doglike. *Still, I am more than capable of using all the skills this body possesses—including the attack functions.*

Johann looked each of them over as if assessing their capabilities. 'It might be doable,' he said, 'but I'm taking a big leap of faith. I put a couple of spare rifles in the back you can have, if indeed you are able to handle one.'

'Why would you think we wouldn't be able to?' Izzy asked.

Johan's head tilted to the side as if he was assessing her as he responded. 'Because you told me you aren't soldiers. And if you're not soldiers, it is possible you have never shot a rifle before.'

'We needed some skills to pass as soldiers,' Izzy said. 'I've had some military training, and I'm pretty sure Lee has had a bit more.'

'I can hit what I aim at,' Lee confirmed. 'Without blowing off my foot,' he muttered under his breath and was rewarded with a chuckle from Basia.

'We also have knives if the fighting gets up close and personal,' Izzy said.

Johan raised his eyebrows. 'Once again—'

'Yes, I can use them. Knife fighting is a speciality of mine.' Izzy grinned.

'I can hold my own,' Lee added, hating to be outdone by Izzy.

They walked on a little longer, allowing Johan time to think. Finally, he said, 'Okay, here's the plan. We carry on along this road until sunset and perhaps a little beyond. Then we look for somewhere with running water and a defensible area where we can rest for a couple of hours.'

All right, Bruno said.

'Once the horse is good to go, we keep on until we hit the old M25. We don't start along there until daybreak because we're going to need light.'

'Why?' Lee asked.

'There are too many places along the road for the night people to set up an ambush,' Johan told them.

Remembering their experience leaving Portsdown, Lee agreed he would rather navigate the car graveyard in full light, and he was pleased Johan had thought of it.

'What about Allan?' Lee asked, worrying about a boy

he had yet to set eyes on.

Johan said, 'We might be able to keep the cart for a while, but on the motorway it will be a hinderance. We will put Allan on horseback when we reach the M25.' Johan turned to Basia. 'Will he be able to ride, do you think?'

'He can ride with me and I will support him.'

This is odd, Lee sent to Izzy. *It's like being with Bebe and Jo but different.*

You get used to being with different incarnations of the same people, Izzy said. *Besides, do you think they would have trusted us so easily without our past selves knowing each other?*

Lee looked down at Bruno. *Is this plan going to work? Is this going to make a difference? Or are we putting ourselves in harm's way only to make things worse?*

We won't find out the outcome of today's activities unless I contact Beta tonight, which I don't want to do because he will expect an explanation of all this.

But surely you and Izzy have some idea... a gut feeling? Lee pressed.

Bruno glanced up. *I could tell you it will all be okay and nothing we did will make the world end any sooner. Would you prefer me to lie like that?*

Maybe.... They walked a little further in silence before Lee said, *Bruno, are we ever getting out of here?*

The dog paused for a moment, then started walking again. *There are pockets of magic all around. I believe I could open a portal to return you home if things turn hairy.*

Lee was surprised at the wording. *Just me?*

You are our first priority, was all Bruno said.

'The sun will be going down soon, so we may as well

form up,' Johan said, walking round the back of the cart to retrieve the rifles.

'Allan's still asleep,' he said when he returned.

Basia nodded. 'He was in a lot of pain after going down the stairs. I gave him a strong painkiller to knock him out for a while.'

'I hope it wears off before we need to put him on the horse,' Johan said, a furrow creasing his brow.

Basia laughed. 'He'll be awake well before then.'

'Where do you want us positioned?' Lee asked as he took a rifle offered to him and checked it was loaded. Johan handed him a couple of spare cartridges, which he placed in an easily accessible pocket.

'Basia, you lead the horse. If anyone attacks us, it is your job to keep her calm and stop her from bolting.'

'Yes, sir.' Basia smirked.

Ignoring his sister, the older boy continued. 'Jasmine can stay on top of the cart and defend Allan. She's been doing that anyway, and can be quite fierce when she's protecting someone.'

I know, Bruno sent.

'Ah, yes, Bruno. Can you track?'

The dog nodded.

'Excellent. You can walk ahead and warn us if anything comes from the front. Izzy, Lee and I will work the back and the sides in rotation, keeping a look out for anything that might attack us. Out here we shoot first, ask questions later,' Johan finished off.

'What about radiation? Isn't it stronger at night, so we're more at risk, aren't we?' Izzy asked.

'The winds are blowing the wrong way to bring radiation

over at the moment. We are safe to be out for the next few days,' Basia assured her.

'Any more questions?' Johan asked. 'No? Let's pick up the pace. We have a lot of ground to cover if we want to be at the M25 by tomorrow morning.'

The sun was just beginning to set when Bruno felt the tingling. He opened his mind just a little, enough to sense who was trying to contact him.

Sigma? Bruno? I know you can hear me. Tell me where you are.

I can't, Thea. Before I give away our location you need to tell me where you stand.

Here we go again, Bruno. My allegiances lie where they always have—with the Council. They gave us a mission and I will follow it through to the end. Tell us where you are and let us come and collect you.

No. Although Bruno had suspected this would be the likely outcome of leaving Thea behind, he had hoped this time would be different. It never was. Now he felt the same loss he had when he realised the love of his life had chosen the Time Guardians over him. She would always choose them, but in his heart he still waited for the day when she would put him first.

This is such a waste of time, Bruno. Even though there is very little magic here, it's only a matter of time before the monitors figure out where you are and tell me.

Of course, but by the time they do, we will be so far ahead of you, you will not be able to catch us. Are you still locked up?

Oh Bruno, you still care.

I do, and that is the problem, Bruno thought, but said nothing.

When he didn't respond, Thea said, *The Council kept us with them all afternoon. They went to take food in to you guys about half an hour ago and found out you had escaped. Jason is being interrogated.*

Well, at least something good has come from this, Bruno chuckled, and Thea laughed with him.

He's swearing blind you let the others out. The guards think he is winding them up.

I bet that's going down well. Bruno enjoyed the thought of what they were putting the Time Fixer through.

No, and he's too stupid to see they think he is disrespecting them. Thea's tone was disdainful. *Did you truly not see this would happen when you encouraged the others to go along with you?*

Sighing, not believing he had to explain this, Bruno said, *I didn't incite them into rebellion. They could both see what we were doing was wrong—and I think you can too.*

That is not the point, Bruno. The Council gave us a job to do. We have to trust they know what is best, she said.

The mission is wrong, Bruno told her. *Alpha is wrong to force us to go through with it.*

Not our call to make, Bruno.

This was an argument they had had many times before.

After a long silence, Theta said, *I assume you realise*

you might be making things worse?

Yes, Bruno admitted, *but I don't believe we are.*

But you cannot say for certain....

This was another variation on the same old argument, and it always led nowhere. Bruno changed the subject. *What have the Lyndhurst Protectorate decided about the boy?*

Nothing yet. The guards left a few moments ago to collect him. I think they're going to let him make his own decision.... That is certainly what Simon and Tanya are pushing for now.... Bruno? You didn't do what I think you have?

Bruno didn't feel the need to answer that question, and Thea didn't speak for a few minutes, then said, *Something is happening, I've got to go. Don't do anything else stupid. We should be able to catch you up in a day or so.*

Not if I can help it, Bruno thought as Thea winked out of his head.

After an uneventful night, the group wearily walked towards the outskirts of Southampton. Johan led them along Hunters Hill, where they picked up the old A836 to follow all the way to the M25. Izzy, having spent a lot of her life in and around the New Forest, was proving useful as a guide, and Johan appeared confident in leading them along the route they plotted together. Lee relaxed back into doing as he was told.

'Strictly, this is militia-controlled territory,' Johan said, 'but I'm sure they won't mind us being here so long as we stick to the far side of the road.'

'Why take the risk if we could go a different way?' Basia asked.

'Because it is quicker and safer,' Johan told her.

Lee simply didn't care. They had rested for a couple of hours last night, but when the horse was ready, Johan had roused them.

'You wanted to do this,' he said when they complained and begged an extra hour.

'Allan rests better when the cart isn't moving, and we want him at his best when we have to put him on the horse,' Basia countered.

Bruno, can you find out from Thea if anyone is tracking us yet? Lee asked. *We might be able to rest a little longer if they are not close by.*

When I spoke to her at sundown, they had only just learned of our escape.

Can you talk to her again? Lee asked.

It is best not to. The more I contact her, the more likely it is we can be traced.

'Johan's right,' Allan said from his bed in the cart. 'The longer we stay here, the more likely it is we will get caught up.'

'It's all right for him,' Lee grumbled. 'He can go back to sleep.'

Not that he begrudged Allan his rest. The boy's appearance had shocked him. He was wan and pale, and his skin tone could only be described as grey. He needed all the rest he could get. Lee's grumbles were all for his own benefit. The only decent night's sleep he had had since arriving was the night in Ma Wilson's barn.

For the next couple of hours, Lee concentrated on placing one foot after the other. Every now and then he scanned the woods around them for signs anyone was following or preparing to attack them.

He and Johan had not long taken the rear guard when Bruno barked a warning from up front. The cart stopped moving and adrenaline kicked in, wiping away any thoughts of sleep. He scanned the area around him, but seeing nothing amiss, he looked to Johan.

'Stay back here. Izzy come with me and we'll go find out what is happening. Jasmine, guard,' Johan said as he walked past the cart. The dog rose, instantly alert.

It was an age before Izzy returned to tell him what was happening up ahead.

'Bruno ran into some of the Southampton militia out on patrol. They were about to send us packing until Johan appeared. Apparently, he's been on some scouting missions with one of their leaders. Now they're taking us on a shortcut along Spicers Hill. Their barracks is at a Tesco's superstore along the way.'

Lee perked up. 'I'm all for that. Anything that involves less walking,' he said.

'Even better, from the barracks they're going to take us to the M25. They'll store Johan's cart there while we drop Allan off. Couldn't have turned out better if we had planned it.'

Lee was impressed. 'They like Johan that much that they'll do all that for us?'

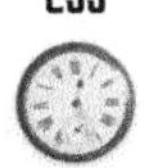

'No, silly. When they found out we are running from soldiers from the underground city, they were more than happy to help. Their leader said something along the lines of, "Anything to stick it to those bastards".'

'Weren't they concerned *we* are soldiers from Portsdown?'

'Johan convinced them we only dressed like this to help Allan escape.' Izzy smiled.

'Man, they must hate people from Portsdown,' Lee said as the cart began moving again.

'Of course they do.' Izzy said. 'The people out here are the ones the world left to die when the bombs dropped—the people they sacrificed for their own well-being.'

'I guess that would make you angry,' Lee admitted, thinking he would not be too happy at being told he was not good enough to be included in the elite club.

Izzy carried on. 'Through their own tenacity, these people survived, built their own societies, and have started trading with each other. Now that they are stronger, they're only too happy to deal some payback to those who sentenced them to death.'

'Well, when you put it that way, it sounds almost reasonable.' Lee laughed.

Even though the route was shorter, it still involved quite a bit of walking. Tired as he was, Lee was fascinated as they walked the outskirts of Southampton, through suburbs that he had driven in during another time only a week ago.

If he had been designing a set for a post-apocalyptic film, this would be what it would look like. Crumbling buildings, overgrown with vegetation and the air made heavy by the eerie silence. In eighteen short years, nature had reclaimed much of what man had taken.

'It must be a nightmare policing all this,' Lee commented, gesturing to the urban forest.

'I suspect they focus on stopping people from getting into the main residential areas, and leave all of this alone, much like Lyndhurst. And, as Johan said, any who slip through the gaps are pretty much shot on sight,' Izzy told him.

Lee blanched. 'That sounds barbaric.'

'It is, rather, but small settlements have been controlling large areas in this way throughout history.' Izzy's tone was matter-of-fact.

Lee had never been so pleased to see a supermarket in all his life when the cart finally rolled into the Tesco's carpark. Although not exactly invited inside and welcomed with open arms, they were led to some park benches outside the building, and were brought hot tea and porridge.

'This is luxury,' Lee groaned as he took a sip of real English Breakfast tea.

'Yep, almost like a home away from home,' Izzy laughed, but Lee could tell she was also enjoying the break and the little piece of normalcy.

The sun was fully up when a cart pulled up in front of them.

'Hop in,' the driver ordered.

Lee hauled his weary body up on to the tray in the back, then leaned down to help Izzy.

'I can do it myself,' she said.

'I know you can, but I thought it would be a nice gesture,' Lee said, trying not to feel hurt.

A puzzled look crossed Izzy's face, but she reached up and grabbed his hand. Once they were seated, Johan and a militia man lifted Allan up. He was made comfortable before Johan, Basia, and the two dogs joined them, Bruno making sure there was plenty of space between him and Jasmine. Another militia man tied Nellie to the back of the cart, and they were off.

Lee wouldn't say it was the most enjoyable ride he had been on, but it was a thousand times better than walking. They also had a chance to close their eyes for a few minutes and doze. All too soon, though, the wagon rolled to a stop and they were told they had arrived.

Lee and Izzy surveyed their surroundings. They were on one side of a barbwire barrier across an intersection by a roundabout. It took him a moment to work out they were on a slip road for the M25.

'Portsmouth's that way.' Their driver pointed.

'Thanks,' Lee said. 'We appreciate the help, and the break from walking.'

'No problem. If you come back this way, ask for Patrick. The militia is always happy to take on deserters from the city.'

'I'm not a—' Lee started.

'You guys never are.' Patrick smiled. 'But you make good militiamen anyway.'

Shaking his head, Lee joined the others. Allan was standing for the first time since he had met him, and Lee was shocked at how much the boy looked like Alain. A little thinner, and there was a fire in his eyes that Alain had not had, but their similarities far outweighed their differences.

Allan leaned against the cart and smiled at them as

they walked over. 'I would like to thank you for helping me,' he said by way of a greeting.

'We are only doing our job... and what is right,' Izzy said.

Allan's face clouded over. 'In my experience soldiers follow their orders, no matter the right or wrongness of it.'

'Well... um ....' Izzy was saved from fumbling for an answer by the arrival of Nellie with Basia on her back.

Allan was helped back up onto the wagon, and then onto the horse in front of the girl. By the time he was in place, he was as white as a sheet.

'Are you going to be all right to ride?' Lee asked. 'I mean, is your wound hurting?'

Allan shuffled closer to Basia and wrapped his arms around her. 'It's not that. It is just....'

Izzy laughed. 'I don't think he's ever ridden a horse before. The world looks quite a bit different from up there, doesn't it?'

'I'll be fine.' Allan sat a little straighter and pursed his lips, ready to endure anything to make it back home.

'Thanks, mate,' Johan said to their driver. 'I owe you guys one. I'll remember you when the strawberries come in this next year.'

'Our pleasure,' Patrick said as he drove away.

With Johan leading the horse, Izzy and Jasmin on one side and Lee and Bruno on the other, the strange group continued their journey.

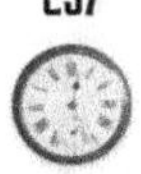

The M25, or the car graveyard as Lee like to call it, was exactly as he remembered: littered with abandoned vehicles that had either been stripped for parts, rusted away, or overgrown with vegetation. It was heartbreaking to see such sleek machines reduced to this.

As he walked he saw a number of things that could be salvaged from the vehicles which, if modified correctly, would improve the lives of people like Colin and his family. With the wealth of stuff for repurposing, why weren't more people harvesting it and making their lives better?

A movement caught his eye and he readied his rifle, preparing for potential danger.

'Basia, Allan, did you see anything behind that green car?' he asked.

Allan leaned forward. 'No. Wait a minute.... Wow, that is amazing.'

'What is it?' Lee asked, raising his rifle.

'A fox,' Basia said. 'Nothing amazing about that.'

'There is if this is the first one you have seen outside of a book,' Allan said, and Lee grinned at the look of wonder on the boy's face.

Relaxing, they carried on. Not long after, Allan asked, 'Lee, why are you a soldier?'

Lee's immediate reaction was to say he wasn't one, but he stopped himself. When he returned home, he would be joining the army, and he and been a military cadet ever since he started high school. So, in many ways, he was a soldier.

'I guess because my father was one,' he finally said.

Allan raised his eyebrows. 'Really?'

'Yes, and I wanted to be like him,' Lee said, defending

his decision.

'What, you mean someone who follows orders?' Allan's voice was incredulous.

'Not exactly, although it can be quite comforting knowing exactly what to do and when to do it,' Lee answered, but the words sounded weak to his own ears.

'What was it about your father you wanted to be like?' Allan prompted.

'Allan, stop badgering the guy. You only met him today and you want him to tell you his life story,' Basia said.

'I think I deserve to know if I can trust him. After all, he was hunting me yesterday and now he's not,' Allan told her.

'No, it's okay, Basia. I will tell you, Allan, if you'll tell me why you want to go back to Portsdown, even though it is likely you will end up in prison.'

'Deal. At first it was because I wanted to tell everyone about the world out here. I wanted to hit back at what I believe is a corrupt system in Portsdown. Now....'

Lee waited for Allan to continue. When he didn't, he prompted him. 'And now?'

'It is difficult to put into words. I've seen a little more and had time to think. Everyone is doing their best to survive after the war. I can't help thinking that if we all worked together, pooled resources and ideas, we would all have a better chance of surviving and developing and building a better world.' Allan blushed. 'That sounds trite, doesn't it?'

Lee smiled at how much Allan sounded like Alain. 'No, I think it is commendable.'

'I'm in no position to force our communities to work

together. What I can do is provide the people in Portsdown with information so they can make up their own minds,' Allan finished.

'Fair enough. And in answer to your question, what I admired about my father was how he protected people. How he always tried to help them. I wanted to do that too.' Lee looked defiantly up at Allan. 'And I thought joining the army would allow me to do that.'

Allan grinned. 'I knew there was more to you than a black uniform. Tell me, did you find what you were looking for with the army?'

Shrugging, Lee said, 'No, not really. Our mission did not allow much time for helping others, and I think I've found I'm not so great at following orders.'

Allan laughed. 'Not so surprising you're here with us then. What about you, Izzy. You don't strike me as a rule follower either.'

'Cheeky. I'll have you know I used to be just that. Before I found out that the people who make the rules always make sure the odds are stacked in their favour. After I learnt that, I decided to look for ways to change the rules.'

'In the Portsdown Army?' Allan asked.

'We weren't actually part of the army,' Izzy laughed. 'Didn't Bruno tell you? We've been sent here to stop something bad from happening—the soldier thing was just a cover.'

'Bruno? The dog?' Allan looked incredulous.

'He's the one who helped you escape,' Basia said.

And this is all the thanks I get, Bruno added.

'I am sure Allan appreciates it,' Basia told him.

'Hold on. You can hear the dog talk too?' Allan blushed. 'I thought I was hallucinating when he spoke to me in the barracks.'

'He's for real,' Izzy said. 'And for better or worse, he's committed to escorting you home.'

'I guess the joke's on me,' Allan chuckled.

Or on me, Lee thought. The previous conversation had been too close to the bone for him. Inside his head his own war was raging. His whole life he had planned to be a soldier, and now weeks away from achieving that goal, he was having second thoughts.

'Lee, if you could not be a soldier, what would you be?' Allan asked, and again Basia poked him in the ribs.

'These guys are helping you. The least you could do is show them some respect,' she told Allan.

Watching the two of them on the horse, Lee had an epiphany. Why hadn't he seen it before? Bebe and Alain, Basia and Allan—they belonged together.

'Come on, Basia. I only want to find out what makes Lee happy.'

It should be an easy question to answer—what makes you happy—but Lee had no idea. He loved his family. He enjoyed various activities and had a few friends he hung around with, but he couldn't remember the last time he was truly happy.

Actually, that wasn't strictly true. Pottering around in his aunt's shed pulling together a letterbox bomb with Alain had made him happy. Before that, it was hard to remember a time. Maybe when he was with his grandfather. Yes, definitely working in the shed with his granddad. It hadn't just been the company. Something about working with his hands made him happy.

'Lee, are you all right?' Allan asked. 'I didn't mean to stress you out.'

Lee wondered what he was talking about. He followed Allan's gaze down to his hands. He had twisted the rifle strap around and around his fingers and was working his worry out on the leather.

'Yes. No. Sort of. You made me realise I was so focused on the goals I set myself, I forgot to be happy.'

'Allan, can you say when you were last happy?' Basia tested her riding mate.

'Easy. When I walked out of the cave the other day and saw the sky. Not just because it was the first time I had seen it, but because it gave me hope for the future.'

'Oh,' Basia said, like the wind had been taken out of her sails.

Lee laughed, breaking the tension. 'You didn't expect that, did you?'

'No, Lee, I didn't. Izzy, how about you?'

'Mine's easy. A few days ago when I helped stop some people from hurting the planet.'

'Are you sure that made you truly happy?' Lee asked, remembering that Izzy had then said goodbye to her girlfriend, Jo, a previous incarnation of Johan.

'I was happy, just a different sort of happy. I fell in love with someone forbidden to me a long time ago. I can never be with them. But I'm happy enough.'

'Do you ever wonder what sort of life you would have lived if you stayed with your Jo?' Lee asked.

'All the time,' Izzy sighed.

Lee thought of asking the taciturn Johan what would

make him happy, but he didn't think the boy would answer. Instead, he asked his sister, and was surprised by her response.

'I am not sure I will ever be truly happy,' she responded in a voice so bleak Lee 's heart almost broke.

As if everyone else was feeling it too, the conversation petered out. Allan said something only Basia could hear and wrapped his arms more tightly around her. Not long after, the group bunched up as they came to a blockage in the road. Johan led the horse through a thin gap between some overgrown cars, and Lee waited with Izzy and Bruno for their turn to go through. While he waited, Lee pondered why finding his happiness was so difficult for him, and came to the realisation it was because he had spent much of his life living up to others' expectations.

Now it was their turn to go through, and just as he emerged through the gap, a ping against the car beside him caused him to dive to the ground.

'Take cover,' Johan ordered as he pulled Allan from the horse.

Basia jumped down after. Lee was busy trying to identify where the shot came from, but he couldn't get a clear view.

Bruno, can you see anything? he asked.

No. They're well hidden. All I can say for certain is there is more than one.

He listened, trying to work out what was going on.

Did you catch their scent? he asked the dog.

They must have approached from downwind.

Crawling for cover behind a car, Lee thought, *Great, this is where my life ends, on the M25, just as I am getting to know myself.*

Everything suddenly went quiet. Lee strained, listening for anything that would indicate what was happening.

Bruno? What's going on? Lee asked.

I think we're surrounded, so our best chance is to try and make it to the hills and regroup later. I will try and find you all.

Lee leaned forward and took a quick peek around the car, only to find himself face-to-face with the barrel of a gun.

'Drop it,' a rough voice commanded.

Lee did as he was told and raised his hands.

'And the knives.'

Reluctantly Lee complied, dropping the two knives concealed in his uniform beside the rifle.

'Now stand and walk that way.' The gun barrel indicated he should go right.

Standing, Lee realised he was not the only one being herded into a clearing between cars. All their group was banded together, even Nellie, Jasmine, and Bruno.

'I was certain we would catch you on the way back,' one of the men said, removing his helmet.

Great, Lee thought, the Portsmouth militia—again.

'Righto, move out.'

Basia refused to move. 'Allan has been injured. He can't walk very far.'

'Then I can shoot him now, or he can take his chances walking. His choice.'

The militia leader's voice was uncompromising. Basia looked mutinous, but Johan grabbed her arm and pulled her along. Lee moved beside Allan.

'Lean on me,' he said, taking some of the boy's weight.

It was a long, slow walk in the hot sun. The militia moved at their normal pace, and the weary group who had been walking most of the last twenty-four hours were expected to keep up. Supporting Allan made the journey doubly tiresome.

The passed the trail to Portsdown before moving past Cosham and into Portsmouth proper. If Southampton had appeared worse for wear, Portsmouth had been devastated. On the way into the Old Town, few buildings had been left standing.

'The naval base was a prime target for bombs,' Izzy commented.

A little while later, the Navy Yard came into view, and Lee smiled. 'Their targeting must have been off. Most of it is still standing.'

The smile disappeared when The Old Naval Shipyard Lee had promised himself he would visit one day came into view. It had been reduced to a pile of rubble. All that history, all those ships, the remains of the Mary Rose, the Warrior, boats of all types—all gone. That more than anything else brought home the devastation his world had experienced.

The militia halted them outside a barracks building that had been reinforced with bars over the windows and a sturdy metal door. It looked more like a jail than a place to sleep.

'Guess we're back in prison,' Izzy said as their escort led them inside.

The room was filled with bunk beds in two lines down either side, with a toilet block at the end.

'At least we'll get some sleep,' Lee answered. His legs were shaking with exhaustion and he barely made it to the bed after gently lowering Allan to the bunk beside him.

He tried his best to stay awake, not wanting to be vulnerable in a strange environment. Soon, though, his eyelids grew heavy and he gave in to sleep.

CHAPTER FOURTEEN
NEW ALLIES

'Hold the plane like this and you'll get a better finish.' His grandfather placed his hands over top of his as he demonstrated. When they were done Lee ran his fingers along the smooth wood—

'LEE!'

'Wh... what?'

'They're asking to speak with you.' Was that Johan?

Lee shook the dream from his head and opened his eyes to find Johan standing over his bunk looking fresh as a daisy. It was as if the almost sixty-kilometre hike they had done in less than twenty-four hours was nothing to him.

'Why do they want to speak with me?' Lee asked, a little confused. 'Izzy's more senior, and Bruno too. I mean, he's the one really in charge.'

Johan grinned. 'Bruno is a dog, so he can't go. And the militia here are not enlightened enough to believe a girl would be in charge. So you are the only one they will speak with. Come on. Allan and I are waiting.'

Lee tried to bring the door into focus. Eventually his eyes adjusted enough to see Allan standing and waiting for him with the assistance of one of the militia.

Propping himself up on his elbows, he asked, 'Is he all right? I mean, that walk was hard on him.'

'We took turns helping, which made it a little easier. And, while you were sleeping, a doctor came and checked him out. He gave him some more painkillers, and said the wound is essentially healed. Now he just needs to build up his stamina.'

'Good to hear,' Lee said, pushing himself to his feet and letting out a groan. 'I, on the other hand, am not so lucky. A sauna and a massage wouldn't go amiss.'

Everything ached. Lee concentrated on putting one foot in front of the other as he walked behind Johan. With every step he took, a new muscle twinged, and he couldn't wait to sit down. That was, until he was led into an office and plonked into one of the three chairs facing a large mahogany desk. Suddenly sitting seemed like too much of an effort, but the look on the armed militiaman's face discouraged any protests.

He groaned as he adjusted his position to get comfortable. Johan took the chair on the far side of him, and Allan was helped into the final seat. The chair behind the desk remained empty.

Lee fixed his gaze on the devastated dockyard through the window and took some calming breaths. His mind started to wander and his eyes had just begun to close when the door behind them opened and he started awake.

He resisted the urge to turn, and waited until a middle-aged man with greying military-cut hair pulled out a chair and sat down, resting his arms on the desk in front. A lean face with hawklike blue eyes surveyed the three of them. Lee shifted uncomfortably. This meeting was reminiscent of visiting the principal's office.

'So,' the man started, leaning back in his chair. 'You must be Johan from the Lyndhurst Protectorate. And you two are the people who escaped my men after trespassing a few days ago—Allan and Lee, is it?'

It was a statement, not a question, but Lee still felt the urge to correct him. Johan placed a hand on his arm, warning him to remain quiet.

'I am Commander Dunstan. Now that we have the formalities out of the way, what are you doing back in Portsmouth?' the man continued.

This was clearly a question, and it required an answer. Lee hesitated, trying to clear his head. Fortunately, Johan had nominated himself as spokesperson. Leaning forward, he said, 'We are all returning Allan to Portsdown. We were not aware your borders now stretched so far.'

Leaning his head to the side to better pin Johan down with his sharp gaze, the man responded, 'And you didn't think to request permission to come through?'

'To be honest we didn't think we had crossed into your lands yet—we were only just coming up into Fareham.'

The Commander's gaze swung upwards and focussed on their guard. 'Is that true, Roberts? Did you capture these people outside our boundaries?'

Behind him Lee could hear the man shifting position, and he bit back a smile. Maybe they would actually get out of this unscathed.

'Yes sir... just. We spotted the two soldiers and their mutt. They were wanted for a previous infraction, so we were within our rights.' The man's tone was defensive, and Lee could not help but smile at his unease.

A look of anger crossed the man's face and then disappeared as swiftly as it had surfaced. 'I'll deal with you later,' he said to Roberts. Turning back to Johan, he said, 'My apologies for the misstep. Our quarrel is not with you, or your sister. You are both free to go, with my apologies.'

'What about Lee, Izzy, and Allan?' Johan asked.

Commander Dunstan shook his head. 'As Roberts said, they are wanted for a previous infraction.'

'Maybe Lee, but not Allan,' Johan said. 'My father and I found him on a hunting trip a little ways back from where you found us.'

Nice, Lee thought, *We are getting out of this, one by one.* He blinked suddenly, realising that perhaps Izzy, Bruno, and he weren't. They had been in Portsmouth when they had run into the militia last time, and it seemed they didn't take too kindly to trespassers. As Johan had said to them, this place was a shoot first ask questions later type of environment.

The Commander clasped his hands, staring at Allan. 'So, you're an escapee rather than a soldier?'

'Yes, sir,' Allan answered.

'Were these soldiers returning you for interrogation and trial?' He nodded at Lee.

Allan smiled, 'No, sir. I was returning willingly and they are my escort.'

Commander Dunstan's eyebrow rose as if he was surprised. 'You were going back? Why on earth would you do that? You'd be signing your own death warrant.'

Allan blanched beside Lee. 'I wasn't planning on them capturing me, but I guess it is likely once I'm back inside. It doesn't matter anyway. I must return home.'

'Because?' The man encouraged Allan to continue.

Allan looked towards Johan, who nodded for him to go ahead.

'I came to find out if people were living a normal life above ground—if people from the underground could survive up here. I must report my findings.'

Sitting forward in his chair, the man now stared intently at Allan. 'I'm curious: what do you intend to say to them?'

Allan's hands twisted in his lap. 'That it's complicated.'

'Go on,' the Commander encouraged.

Allan took a deep breath and steadied his hands. 'Well, it is obvious people can live above ground, but I'm no longer sure thousands of people leaving the city is in anyone's best interests. It might make things worse for everyone, and I'm not sure we'd be welcomed. People from Portsdown tend to be vilified in your Protectorates.'

The Commander barked out a laugh. 'You're definitely not thought of in the best light, but we have absorbed some people from your community quite successfully, as has the Southampton Protectorate.'

Lee's head drew up in surprise. 'There are others like Allan?'

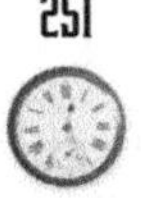

The man smiled. 'Of course, although they don't feel the need to risk their lives returning to tell others what it's like out here.'

Edging slightly forward on his chair, Allan asked, 'So, would you welcome more refugees?'

'That is a very broad question, and I'm not sure I can answer it. We certainly appreciate the skills people from the city bring with them—they're mostly workers and farmers—and we can always do with more farmers.'

'There is a "but", though,' Allan said.

'We cannot support the influx of a large number of refugees, and we certainly would not welcome any of your ruling class,' Commander Dunstan said.

The tension left Allan's body. 'I suspected as much.'

'Do you still wish to return, knowing this?' the man asked.

Lee shifted in his seat and watched a range of emotions pass over Allan's face as he considered the question. It settled on determined. 'If no one returns, how will people ever know there is an alternative? And if there is no alternative, how will the Representative Council ever change the way they treat the people? So, yes, I will still return.'

'It won't be easy for you to get in,' the Commander warned. 'Over the last week, patrols have tightened up. However, we may be able to help you.'

'Help me? Why?' Allan's tone was wary.

'Let's just say we share a common goal: a change of power inside Portsdown.' The man steepled his fingers as he spoke.

'How would that help you?' Lee asked before Allan

could get a word out, then blushed. This really did not have anything to do with him.

The Commander smiled. 'Well, young man, soldiers from the city patrol our protectorate like they own them. Although we speak with the military commanders and have come to an uneasy agreement on boundaries, our leaders would like to deal with Portsdown on an equal footing; we no longer want to be treated as second rate citizens. I, and others, believe this will only happen if there are changes on the Council.'

Lee nodded. This was a similar argument to the one he heard in Lyndhurst.

'So, do you want our help or not?' the Commander asked again.

There was silence while Allan considered the question. 'What would you want in return?' he eventually asked.

'That is easy: for you to talk with your group and tell them we would welcome skilled workers out here. Hopefully, it might encourage a few to leave, and maybe it will boost the resistance.'

'Sounds doable,' Allan said.

The Commander was not finished. 'The difficult bit is, I want you to set up regular communication lines, then return and tell me how we are to work together in the future.'

'That is a big ask,' Allan said. 'I am only a small cog in the resistance. How do you know I'm up to it?'

The Commander shrugged. 'I don't, but I am prepared to take the risk. And you also won't be going alone. I will send a small team in with you.'

Allan took a deep breath. 'All right, but only of Lee

and Izzy can come back with me. I won't leave them behind.'

The Commander frowned. 'Lee and... um... Izzy, is it, are from the underground city and they trespassed on our lands in violation of our accords. They and the other soldier must be punished to set an example to others.'

Allan shook his head. 'Before they left the city, they didn't even know about the militia or any agreement. They were only following orders. Besides, they are only here now to help me return to the city. It doesn't seem fair to punish them for any of that.'

Lee felt warm inside at Allan's words of support, and a little bit of hope at being set free began to grow.

The Commander frowned and rubbed his temples. 'I.... Although I have some sympathy, they are soldiers—symbols of the ruling elite—an elite who sentenced many of us to die. For me to show him leniency would cause an uproar in my own ranks, not to mention what my fellow Councillors would say.'

'You believe the world has changed in eighteen years, and you want more change, yet you won't even consider that some of the soldiers inside Portsdown might support that change. Besides, you are asking Lee here to pay for something that occurred before he was even born,' Allan argued.

You have no idea how wrong that is, Lee thought as he suppressed a smile.

'I understand, but—'

Allan did not allow the Commander to finish. 'And if we hang on to old grievances, how are we ever going to forge a new path together? How can we work with each other if we can't show tolerance and mercy?'

The Commander rubbed his brow again, 'You talk a good talk, son, and the future you outline is certainly one worth fighting for.' He took a deep breath. 'I really can't make that decision alone, but I guess it would be all right if we allowed Lee and the other soldier to accompany you back to the underground city to finish their mission. If they decide they don't want to remain there, then we can deal with their transgressions when they return.'

'I'm happy with that,' Allan said and turned to Lee.

Lee took a moment to respond. His mind was still whirling from Allan's words. For the first time since he had arrived in this crazy version of Hampshire, he felt like he was helping change the course of the world for the better.

'Lee? Lee!' Johan nudged him in the ribs.

'What? Sorry?'

'The Commander asked you a question,' Allan prompted.

'Oh, yes, I'm good with that, and I'm sure Izzy will be too.' He turned to Johan. 'What about you and Basia. Will you come too?'

'I think we will rest up before returning home, with your permission of course. Our parents will be worried about us.' Johan said. 'Although we will wait until you come back from your visit to Portsdown before leaving.'

'Please, make yourself at home in the meantime,' the Commander said.

With the threat of imprisonment, or worse, lifted, and a decision to return to the underground city made, Lee relaxed. Perhaps now he would be allowed to go back to sleep. When the Commander spoke his next words, he knew this was not to be.

'Now, young man, do you have a plan?' Commander Dunstan asked.

'I do,' Allan said. 'I used to work in the herbarium. I'll make my way back there and leave a message for my boss, as she'll be checking in daily. Then I will go hide in the cave entrance until they come and find me.'

The Commander again steepled his fingers, and Lee realised he did this when he was thinking. 'The first bit seems fine, but hiding in the cave you left through is out of the question. It will be guarded now.'

Lee watched the changes in Allan's expression as he processed the information. He went from hopeful to defeated in a matter of seconds.

'We didn't think this through,' he finally admitted. 'We assumed I would sneak out unnoticed.'

'No, son, you didn't. Then again, you and your friends aren't soldiers. You are regular people trying to make a difference,' the Commander said.

Allan shrugged. 'Knowing that doesn't help much.'

'We might be able to find a solution if we work together,' the Commander said. 'How many people work in the herbarium and how many of them are sympathetic to your cause?'

'Rosie, my boss, she's one of the leaders of the movement. She recruited me. Her assistant, Janet, is also part of the group. The two of them are only ones who attend meetings and actively fight for change,' Allan said.

'Out of how many workers?'

'There are six of us altogether,' Allan answered the Commander.

Lee's eyes began to drop as the Commander's questions began to mount. He shuffled in his seat to find a more comfortable position, then raised his head to find the Commander watching him.

'Not much longer now, son,' he said before returning his gaze to Allan. 'Out of the other three, how many of them would turn you in if they found you in the herbarium?'

Allan thought for a minute before answering. 'I don't think any would, but I can't be certain. Everyone who works there is loyal to Rosie; they would do anything for her. Whether this would extend to their turning a blind eye to my return, I couldn't say.'

The Commander turned and gazed out the window before swivelling back around and pushing himself out of the chair. He paced around the room, paused, and turned to Allan. 'How big is the herbarium? I mean, how many people can you hide in there?'

'It is the size of a big room— about three times the size of this office. There isn't anywhere to hide. But... you could hide... I guess... about ten people in the equipment sheds. The large machinery is hardly ever used, and a small group could stay there for days without being found.'

'But no one in the herbarium itself?' the Commander asked.

'Why is it important for someone to be there?' Lee asked.

'Allan needs to pass his message to someone high up in the movement, agree on lines of communication, then

get out. His best chance of doing that is talking to this Rosie person, and the only place we know she will definitely be is the herbarium.'

Lee nodded, and Allan sat forward on his chair. 'If we arrived for the early morning start, we wouldn't need to hide. Rosie and Janet are normally the two rostered on that shift. Sunrise is the best time to pick medicinal herbs, and the three of us are the only ones trained in that speciality. Otherwise, one, maybe two people could hide without being seen for a short period.'

The Commander retook his seat. 'Right, we have a plan. We found a back entrance a few months ago. We use it when we need to enter the city unseen. If you go in at night, deliver a message to Rosie, hide in the equipment sheds for the day, then leave the following evening, this could work. Are you up for that, young man?'

'I guess,' Allan said.

'Fine, we're done here then. Roberts will see you're all kitted out for your respective journeys. You're dismissed... and good luck.'

The three boys stood. Roberts opened the door. As they were leaving, the Commander said, 'Roberts, after you've taken them to the commissary and made sure they have everything they need, go pick a small team to go with you into the city.'

'But—'

'Or do you want to stay and talk about how you left our lands to pick this group up?' Commander Dunstan's voice had taken on a threatening tone.

'No, sir.'

SOLDIER

Roberts stomped down the stairs ahead of them, and didn't speak another word until he dropped them back at the prison, when he told them to be ready to leave at three in the morning. The only sign of their changed status was his taking the guard with him when he departed.

As they dropped their new packs inside the door, Allan turned pale and swayed. Basia rushed to his side and helped him to a bed.

'You should be resting,' she scolded, and Allan didn't object.

What happened? Bruno asked as Lee and Johan sat on a bunk, watching Basia fuss over Allan.

Izzy rifled through the packs. Looking up from her investigations, she asked, 'Are we going somewhere?'

'Yes. You, Bruno, and I are to join an escort taking Allan into the city so he can complete his mission.'

'What about Johan and me?' Basia asked, standing to face them.

From the tone of Basia's voice, Lee guessed she would not be happy with the answer, so he left Johan to respond.

'We've done our bit. We're heading home. We can wait until they return before leaving, if you want to make sure they are safe.' Johan braced himself.

Basia placed her hands on her hips. '*You* might be leaving, but I'm going with the others.'

'Basia, we are going home.' Johan's voice was low and commanding.

'No, Johan. This is my decision. I believe in what Allan is trying to do, and I want to help.'

'But—'

Izzy moved over and placed a hand on Johan's arm. 'She's old enough to know her own mind. Besides, we'll be with her.'

'Are you sure this isn't simply you wanting to see inside the underground city? I mean, you have been dreaming about it for years,' Johan asked.

Basia smiled. She had won even if Johan had not yet realised it. 'I can't deny there is a bit of curiosity involved. Mostly though, I want to help. If Allan is prepared to risk returning to the city, I want to do what I can to support him.'

'But....' Johan sighed. 'All right. I'm still staying here until you are all back safely.'

'Don't you want to come with us? I mean, for Basia's sake,' Izzy asked.

Johan shook his head. 'Sometimes too many people can place the mission at risk. Besides, if something happens someone needs to tell our parents and to be....'

Izzy nodded and squeezed Johan's arm. 'I understand.' Turning to the others, she said, 'There's a change of clothes in each of the packs. I bag first shower. I hope the water's hot!'

By the time Lee had taken the last shower in lukewarm water, food had arrived—accompanied by another pot of real tea. Appetite satiated, Lee lay down to try and get some rest before their early morning start. He had barely settled when he felt a cold nose touch his hand.

Lee, something must have changed in the timeline. Beta has been trying to contact me for the last hour or so, the dog sent.

That is good, isn't it? I mean, we wanted this, didn't we? Should we tell the others?

We did, and no, not yet. Bruno paused, laying his head on the bed beside Lee. *The Council might be able to tell us whether we have made things better or worse. Only, I don't want to talk with them in case they tell us to stop what we're doing, or worse, tell Thea where we are.*

Lee rolled over and stared into the dog's liquid brown eyes. *Is that wise, Bruno? We need to find out what is happening. Don't we need to know if our actions have sped up the end of humanity's time on earth?*

The dog flopped to the floor. *The problem with only being able to influence people from within the current timeline is that sometimes you set things in motion, and although you can control them for a time, after a while you realise they have taken on a momentum of their own. Once that happens, your ability to influence change is lost.*

I'm not quite sure what you mean, Lee said.

Do you think there is any way you can stop Allan from returning to Portsdown?

Lee thought for a moment. *Perhaps if he knew his actions would cause the end of time....*

But that happens anyway, regardless of what Allan does, Bruno pointed out.

Then no, I think there is no way we could stop him.

Bruno's head tipped to the side. *That is why I believe we have lost our ability to control what happens from now on.*

Lee nodded. *And so, knowing whether the changes are good or bad won't alter anything.*

Bruno sat and his ears pricked. He closed his eyes, then they opened in shock. *Thea and the others are close by. They must have been let go.*

Lee's stomach clenched. *Do they know exactly where we are?*

No, just that we are here. I overheard a snippet of conversation. They may be going for a bigger force to try and extract Allan.

As the full impact of Bruno's words hit Lee, he sat bolt upright. *If they realise we are working with the Portsmouth Militia then... Well, if the Portsdown Representatives get wind of it—*

And with Portsdown maybe having nuclear warheads, Bruno added.

Lee tensed. *Why are you telling me this now?*

If Portsdown took exception to the militia interfering in their affairs, they could potentially take it upon themselves to make sure they never interfere again. And that could be how the end of the world starts. Bruno's voice was flat as he spoke the doom laden words.

Suddenly I am not feeling so positive, Lee said.

There isn't much we can do except get some sleep and follow through with what we have started, Bruno told him.

I guess so. Lee rolled over and pulled the woollen blanket tightly around himself, no longer feeling sleepy.

CHAPTER FIFTEEN
PORTSDOWN

Moonlight threw the forest into a series of shadows, but still Basia could barely contain her excitement— she couldn't believe she was finally going to visit the underground city. All right, so it was more creeping in through the back door rather than turning up as a fully-fledged visitor— but the thought still thrilled her.

Mindful of the danger they were in, she tamped down her feelings and concentrated on moving quietly up the hill. She was out to show everyone she was more than just the tag-along Johan believed her to be.

Not only had she made it this far, but it was doubtful whether or not Allan would be here without her medical skills. Her father trained her to fight, so no one would need to look after her if anyone attacked them. She was ready to make a difference and she would not be left

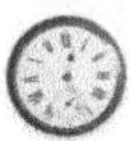

behind again.

The jeans and knitted top she had changed into back at the barracks were as black as the shadows, and she made use of them by avoiding the strips of moonlight. Taking a sip from her water bottle as she moved, she placed it back in the side pocket of her pack, which was heavy with basic medical supplies.

Ahead of her, Izzy and Lee walked companionably together. Behind, one of the four Portsmouth militiamen protected their rear. Beside her walked the huge German Shepherd called Bruno, who could speak to them, but would not talk to any of the militia. She was still getting comfortable with the idea he was a sentient being, which was something being kept secret from their companions.

Roberts, the militia leader, had been keen on leaving the dog behind, saying he would be a liability once they reached the city. Lee insisted on his coming, and Allan agreed, which killed any further discussion. Allan explained later they might need Bruno's ability to facilitate talking without speaking, but Basia knew the dog's skills extended beyond mere talking—he knew things no one else did.

Johan's decision not to come disappointed her. Not only was his presence reassuring, his tracking skills were second to none and, by all accounts, he was pretty handy in a fight too. He wanted to make sure one of them was able to return home to reassure their parents they were all right. He could be pretty stubborn when he made up his mind.

The long silent uphill walk to the cave entrance left Basia exhausted again; adrenaline and fear were the only things keeping her going.

Pausing outside the cave entrance, they put on head

torches. Roberts moved between them, reminding them all to keep silent as they walk through the caves. 'Voices echo and carry. Night patrols are not as regular, but we do not want to risk them finding us.'

Winding through the caverns, Basia stuck close to the others, sure that if she lost sight of them, she would be lost underground forever. A cold nose touched her hand. Bruno's gesture reassured her and calmed her nerves. Finally, they reached an internal door, and Roberts whispered for them to turn off and stow their torches.

In the gloomy half-light, the white corridors shone luminously. All her life she had dreamed of the underground city and the wonders it held, only to be disappointed by her first glimpse. She shook it off. The girl who dreamed of an easy life underground had gone. Basia was here to help change the world.

Allan led them through another maze, this time one of hallways with doors spaced at regular intervals on either side. As they walked, Basia counted up the door numbers, measuring their progress. 1-72, 1-74, 1-76. She guessed they worked like the old street address system she had seen in Lyndhurst.

Eventually they came to a stairwell. The group descended one flight, and Allan opened the door to another corridor. The label on the door opposite Basia read 0-263.

The lighting was dimmer. Allan explained that they had left the living quarters and were now traversing the industrial and agricultural level. It was still a little too early for people on the first working shift to be around, and their footsteps echoed in the empty hallways.

They stopped in front of a door numbered 0-000. Allan

placed his hand on a grey panel about chest height, and the door swung open. From the look of shock on his face, Basia realised he had not expected to be granted entry.

Trailing through after the others, her eyes opened wide as she surveyed the farm. Many stories high, a domed ceiling through which she could see the night sky crowned the structure. Looking closely, she did a double take. The stars were too bright and were arranged in a pattern that had long since passed at this time of year—the sky was fake.

She dropped her gaze and studied the mass of garden beds in front of her. Fields of grains and vegetables covered the floor. Around the edges were fruit trees and berry bushes. To her left she found a section dedicated to different types of nuts. Hanging from beams across the roof were vine plants. She spotted tomatoes and grapes and some foods she could not put a name to.

The produce was lush, the plants healthy, and the garden beds well tended. What she would not give for a garden such as this at home. In the distance large sheets of opaque plastic hung, rustling as the door closed behind them.

'The fallow fields are at the back,' Allan said from close by.

She turned her head to find him watching her, an amused smile on his lips.

'This is amazing,' Basia said, not wanting to be impressed by the underground garden, but unable to stop herself.

Their eyes met, sending a warm rush through her. She felt the heat rise to her cheeks, and broke the connection.

Taking her hand, Allan said, 'If you're impressed with this, wait until you see my favourite place—the herbarium.'

SOLDIER

Lee followed the others into the specialist herb growing area Allan called the herbarium. The room was smaller, and crammed full with all manner of herbs, along with other strange plants Lee was unable to identify. Allan's description had been accurate. The only place a person might hide was the space behind the sole workbench.

Like Lee, Roberts was surveying the room. 'Right, Allan. You hide yourself away and the rest of us will head to the equipment store,' he said, then added, 'You can join us after you've made contact and set up the lines of communication.'

Beside Allan, Basia folded her arms. 'I'm not going anywhere. I didn't come all this way to spend an entire day in the equipment shed.'

Lee also shook his head. 'Bruno and I are staying too. If anyone unexpected arrives, Allan may need support.'

'And me,' Izzy added. 'If there is fighting, Lee will need all the help he can get.'

Lee started to object, but Izzy winked at him, sending a terse, *We are in this together now.*

Roberts stared at them, shaking his head. 'I can't order you guys, so stay, go, do what you want. Remember though, I won't be sending any rescue parties for you. Allan is the only one I have been charged with bringing home safely.'

He jerked his head sideways. 'Come on, you lot, let's

go hide ourselves and catch some sleep; we won't be needed again until this evening.'

As the militia departed, Lee and Izzy took up positions either side of the door, hidden enough not to be seen from outside the room.

'Give us a nod if whomever arrives is not who you expected,' Lee said. 'Although I'm sure we'll be able to figure it out by their reaction to you.'

'Where do you want me?' Basia asked.

Lee said, 'I think we are counting on you to move Allan out of the road so we can deal with any threats.'

Izzy nodded.

'Hey, I can look after myself,' Allan protested.

'Under normal circumstances, sure. But your injuries aren't completely healed, and we've had an arduous journey. Let Basia help you out,' Lee said.

I could be good at this being in charge thing, he thought, followed by, *Is being good at something really a reason to do it?* Shaking his head, he pushed all concerns about his future to the back of his mind and focussed on the situation at hand.

So great and wise leader, what do you want me to do? Lee looked down at Bruno. He had totally forgotten about the dog. Perhaps he was not such good leadership material after all.

Stay behind me and keep yourself out of sight if you can. We might need you, even if only to frighten someone.

Leaning against the door frame, Lee relaxed a little while they waited for the day shift to arrive. Allan wandered round the herbarium showing Basia the gardens, explaining the uses of some of the more obscure plants.

'Most of these ones are medicinal,' Allan said, pointing to a group of herbs. 'If we had more time together, I could show you how to use them.'

Lee was so engrossed in their conversation he almost missed the entrance of the morning gardening crew. Only Izzy's hand signal alerted him to their presence, giving him time to ready himself for action.

'Allan, my dear boy, you made it back.' The cry came from a short, rotund woman with the wildest hair Lee had ever seen. A mass of black curls threaded with grey seemed to explode from the woman's head. She beamed as she rushed to Allan, wrapping him in a hug—quite a feat given she barely came up to the boy's chest. 'Are you okay?'

Lee became aware her companion still hung back, not saying a word. Allan had not described Janet, but Lee had no doubt the person in front of him was not her. A tall lanky man stood in the doorway, the scowl on his face sounding alarm bells in Lee's head.

Slipping in behind the man blocking his exit, Izzy's curt nod told him she was ready to act. The man's eyes were riveted on Rosie and Allan, and he appeared not to have noticed his new companions.

'I'm fine, Rosie. I promise you my wound is small, and I'm almost recovered.'

'The vid reports said you were mortally wounded,' Rosie said, worry lining her face.

'You know better than to listen to those.' Allan laughed. 'They like to blow things out of proportion to keep viewers switched on.'

'Still....'

'Rosie, this is Basia. She and her family found me

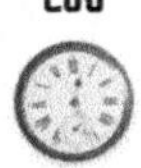

and tended to my health.'

'Hello, Basia,' Rosie said. 'Are you from around old Portsmouth?'

Basia smiled tentatively at the woman. 'No, ma'am. We have a farm in the New Forest.'

Rosie bustled Allan out of the way, now more interested in Basia than him. 'You mean people are farming there? That far away? I knew it!'

'We are farmers,' Basia confirmed. 'But we don't have half the range of food you have in your gardens. Compared to this, we are mere subsistence farmers.'

The grin did not leave Rosie's face. 'But still, this is marvellous—absolutely marvellous. You have no idea how pleased I am to find the world is repairing itself, and people can actually live outside of this cave.'

Lee's eyebrows rose in surprise as Rosie actually clapped her hands in glee.

'Rosie, he's a fugitive. We have to hand them over to the authorities.' The lanky man stepped forward as he spoke.

'Come on, Joshua, this is Allan. Yes, the soldiers are looking for him, but what has he actually done wrong? Gone for a walk outside?'

'I am happy to hand myself over—after I finish telling everyone what I found out there,' Allan reassured the man.

'I'm not a part of your fantasy group,' Joshua said and almost sneered. 'I keep telling you we're better off where we are, and always have been.'

Rosie turned, her hands outstretched as if pleading with the man. 'Joshua, there are a lot of naysayers and I know you're one of them, but humans are not made to live underground.'

'How can you say that? We have a roof over our heads and plenty to eat,' the man said.

'The air doesn't feel right, the lack of sun doesn't feel right, and the food definitely isn't right. It can't be, because we have to take a daily cocktail of multivitamins to stay healthy. It is past time we reconnected with Mother Earth,' Rosie lectured her co-worker.

Joshua's hands rose to his hips, and he took a stance blocking the doorway. 'I am aware of your beliefs, Rosie, and I wouldn't hurt you for the world. But what is important to me is not losing my position over something I don't want to be a part of. And I certainly don't want to be caught harbouring a fugitive.'

'Then go home. Forget you ever saw this. I'll record it that I did this shift alone,' Rosie pleaded.

'Too late. I'm on camera. My handprint opened the door.' Joshua took another step forward as if to grab hold of Allan.

Lee reacted, blocking the man's path, hand on the weapon at his hip. 'I'm sorry, that won't be happening. Allan will be leaving here with us. Someone will come set you free once we are gone. Then you can tell whoever you like whatever you like.'

Joshua started, then his gaze fixated on Lee's weapon. This hesitation allowed Izzy time to pull handcuffs from her pocket and snap it around a wrist. Joshua's shoulders slumped for a moment, then a blaze of defiance burned in his eyes. He turned as if to run, and almost bowled Izzy over as she grabbed the other end of the cuffs. Catching sight of Bruno beside her, he flung himself backwards, and the only thing that stopped him from falling over was Lee's grip on his upper arm.

'We can't have you going off alone,' Lee informed him. 'Izzy, could you do the honours?'

Deftly the girl pushed Joshua towards the worktable, aided by a growling Bruno. Pushing the man to the ground, she passed the handcuffs behind a table leg, then snapped it closed on Joshua's other wrist.

As she stood, she said, 'If you can promise to be on your best behaviour, I won't gag you.'

His mutinous gaze told her all she needed to know. From another pocket she pulled out a black gag and tied it in place. He struggled, but his actions were futile. Izzy had clearly done this before.

With the threat neutralised, Lee turned his attention back to Rosie and Allan, who were quietly discussing the information he had gathered, and what should be done with it.

'Rosie, we have to tell people what I have seen. Not just our group, but as many people as possible,' Allan was saying.

'I'm not sure—'

'I came back to do this, Rosie. I want to tell everybody about the outside. Force them to question what the Representative Council is doing, what they have been telling us—force a change.'

Rosie studied Allan carefully. Taking his hand, she said, 'If you are intent on doing this, the best way is to make a public declaration. And you'll need to do it soon because we can't hide you down here for long.'

Allan thought for a moment, then shook his head. 'The Council will never call a public meeting for this, and I doubt very much the vid network will allow me to speak, given everything they broadcast is pre-approved.'

'Then we'll have to do it the old-fashioned way.' Rosie's eyes glittered, with excitement.

'The old way?' Lee asked.

'Back before the war, when somebody wanted to talk about something, they set up a soapbox and made a speech. In fact, Speakers Corner in Hyde Park, London provided a specific place for such activities.'

'We could do it now. Go to the grand concourse, stand up on the dais, and tell everybody about how fantastic it is above ground,' Allan said, clearly infected with Rosie's enthusiasm.

Grinning, Rosie said, 'Perfect. It will be at its busiest now, and I'm sure we will persuade a few people there is life outside before the guards catch us.'

'We?' Allan asked.

'I'm coming with you. I wouldn't miss this for the world,' Rosie said.

And me,' Basia added.

Allan shook his head. 'No, Basia. This will be dangerous. Once I begin speaking, the guards will have no option but to lock me up. It may even mean a death sentence.'

'I'm done with others telling me what to do. I'm coming.' Basia's mouth set in a stubborn line Lee knew well from his sister.

'You may as well give up now, mate,' Lee told Allan. 'Her mind is made up.'

The boy took one look at the set of Basia's jaw and admitted defeat. Lee chuckled.

'If we're going to go, we better go now,' Rosie said.

Lee held up his hands. 'Hold on a minute. We should really tell Roberts.'

'You can update him when you join the militia in the equipment sheds,' Allan said as he made to move around him.

Lee grabbed his arm. 'We're coming too.'

Izzy and Bruno drew up beside Lee. 'We're your protection detail,' Izzy added.

Sighing, Allan said, 'Please listen to me. I don't want anyone getting hurt on my account.'

Lee and Izzy exchanged a glance before she said, 'We believe in what you are doing, and we will support you any way we can.'

'And all the while pray that humanity does not end because of it,' Lee added under his breath, earning a frown from Izzy.

'I can't talk you out of it?' Allan asked.

They shook their heads.

Allan sighed. 'Okay, let's do this.'

'What about Roberts?' Lee asked.

Allan shrugged. 'Either we'll be back in time for him to escort us back to Portsmouth, or we'll be somewhere where even he won't be able to help us.'

As the group made their way to the grand concourse, they received some strange looks, mainly because of the huge Alsatian accompanying them. Rosie greeted everyone as if walking through the corridors with a fierce-looking dog was something she did every day, which dispelled some of the tension. Lee's stomach clenched when they passed some patrolling soldiers. Surely, they would notice the dog? None of them did.

Lee frowned and looked down at Bruno. *How come they didn't stop us?*

There is enough magic for me to do an occasional "don't see me" spell, Bruno explained.

That's a thing? he asked.

Bruno nodded, as if not only was it a thing, but it was perfectly normal for him to do it.

How come you did not use it when we fought the eco-warriors? Lee asked.

Bruno chuckled. *I did, but I can only do it for a short time.*

As the flow of people around them increased, Lee realised they were in the equivalent of rush hour traffic. Everyone stayed to the left, creating two opposing flows of human traffic.

Allan led them into an octagonal space with eight corridors spoking off at even intervals. Traffic was guided through the central area by a roundabout, which stood about knee height. For four flights above, the spoke pattern was duplicated, only the central hub was smaller and the spokes were walkways, allowing a clear view up to the ceiling between each spoke.

Allan and Rosie were making their way to the central platform, with Izzy and Basia moving in their wake. By the time Lee had managed to catch them up, Allan was standing in the middle of the dais, clearing his throat.

Lee joined the others, arms outstretched, trying to make a bit of space around the roundabout to protect Allan from the crowd. Bruno slipped in between them, lying at Allan's feet, ready to jump into action should he be needed.

Allan's polite "Fellow citizens" was swallowed up by the noise. Bruno rose to his feet and used his voice to attract people's attention. Bruno barked for almost a minute before people stopped to find out what was going on. Lee gazed up to find people were also leaning over the railings of the upper levels.

'Most of you won't know me. My name is Allan Gordon, and I'm a gardener. I didn't want to be a gardener, but I was forced to do it to help humanity survive underground.'

People shuffled nervously, and some started to move away.

'Get to the point before you lose them,' Rosie said.

'But what if we didn't have to stay here? What if our lives didn't depend on everybody following the rules?' Allan carried on as if this was his plan all long.

People stopped moving, and the noise slowly died down.

'Where else would we go?' someone yelled out.

'The world is dead. We have no choice but to live here,' another responded.

'You're wrong. I just spent a few days above ground.' Allan's voice now rang out loud and clear.

There was a collective gasp and people drew back, horror on every face. It took a moment for Lee to realise they were behaving like him when he first arrived, fearful of radiation and what it might do to them. So fearful in fact, they instinctively avoided any hint of contamination even though it couldn't be passed person to person.

Ignoring this, Allan carried on speaking. 'I saw things out there you're probably not going to believe. There are communities of people living and, if not quite thriving, they're growing food, keeping livestock, and getting on with their lives.'

'Zombies and the dying,' a man yelled.

'You won't ever convince me the air is safe out there,' a woman close to Lee said.

A burly man pushed his way forward and challenged Allan. 'I bet they're riddled with radiation and die young. Probably not even able to have kids.'

'You are wrong,' Allan responded. 'There are some people with radiation sickness—' The crowd murmured, and Allan held both hands out as if to stop another tide of remarks. '—but most people are perfectly healthy. They face different challenges to us, but they live out a normal lifespan, and they're building a new world.'

'Prove it!' the man said. 'Prove you're not just telling us a story to stir up trouble.'

Allen mumbled, 'What now?'

Lee wondered if he'd lost the battle to change the tide of opinion. Then Basia placed a hand on his shoulder and pushed herself up on the dais.

'I am all the proof you need,' she said. 'I was born and grew up outside. Do I look radiation riddled to you? Do I look unhealthy? Do I look any different to any of you?'

'Her skin's a funny colour,' a young girl in front of Lee said, and at that moment he realised everyone around him, save the people with black skin, were pale and white, almost translucent.

Behind him Basia laughed. 'That is because I live

outside. Sunlight changes skin colour. It would happen to you if you decided to leave here.'

'I'm not sure I want to look all dark like that,' the girl muttered, and earned a glare from the black woman beside her.

'I'm not saying our life is easy, and few of the luxuries you are used to down here are available to us. But I do see the sky every day. I feel the wind on my face, the ground beneath my feet, and each year the earth gets a little better, and life gets a little easier,' Basia finished.

Allan stepped forward. 'Basia and I wanted you to know we can choose where—'

A strange crackling noise filled the air, and everyone ducked. Lee searched the crowd and found Captain Kiandra. Beside her stood Corporal Rodgers, his blaster raised. The Captain moved to prevent the Corporal from firing again, but was too slow to stop him. Lee half turned and saw Allan crumple to the ground.

Time slowed down around Lee. 'You dirty traitor!' Rodgers yelled.

'Grab Allan and let's get out of here.' Izzy's voice galvanised him into action.

Basia was shaking, but she took one of Allan's arms, and Rosie the other. Lee and Izzy grabbed his legs. The four of them carried Allan towards the corridor opposite the soldiers, a growling Bruno clearing a path for them.

Allan was a dead weight, and he slipped from their grasp. 'Drop your packs, then it'll be easier to carry him,' Lee instructed.

They followed his order, and Lee hauled one of Allan's arms over his shoulder. Izzy took the other. They moved more quickly now, and it appeared people were parting for them, then closing in behind. Were they trying to slow the soldiers down so they could get away?

They made it to the corridor, and stopped for a moment to catch their breaths.

'What now?' Basia asked.

Lee looked at Allan's white face, and wondered how long they could carry him. Not very long, he surmised, but he was damned if he would leave him behind.

'We have no option but to keep going,' he said, hauling Allan up again. He and Izzy moved more slowly under the burden, but they were putting a little distance between themselves and their pursuers.

'Rosie, can we escape this way?' he asked.

'Not easily,' she responded. 'What we need to do is find somewhere to lay low... but....' She looked up to the camera at the junction further down the hall.

Someone shouted their names, and Lee pushed himself harder, though every muscle burned. How were they going to make it out of this alive?

Over Allan's head he caught Izzy's eye. *Any ideas?*

No. Bruno?

Lee looked around. Where was Bruno? He half turned at the sound of a bark in time to see the crowd part and Bruno dash through the gap, followed by Roberts and his men.

'What the—' Lee started.

'No time for explanations, lad. We need to find somewhere to—'

Roberts was cut short as the door opened beside them. 'Quick, in here,' a diminutive dark-skinned girl said.

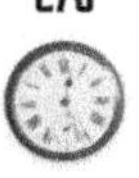

Looking around to make sure no one was paying attention to them, Roberts pushed the group through the door. 'Wait here. I'll be back.'

Lee found himself in the living room of an apartment which was reassuringly familiar in this strange new future. The door closed behind them, muffling the noise of the riot. He took a step forward, stumbled over a rug, and almost dropped Allan.

'Bring him in here,' the girl said, leading them to a bedroom.

Izzy and Lee placed Allan on the bed. Basia nudged them out of the way. 'My medical supplies were in my pack. Can you bring me some hot water and towels, and perhaps some painkillers?' she asked their host.

The girl nodded solemnly. 'Give me a moment.'

'All of you, out,' Basia commanded. 'I need space to work.'

It was only when he joined the others in the living room that Lee realised Bruno was not with them. Sinking into a sofa, he dropped his head into his hands, exhausted. How had everything gotten out of hand so quickly?

They had had a plan, one that moved everyone toward change in a controlled way. Now the underground city was rioting and there was.... He paused for a moment, trying to form the thought.... There was a kind of electricity in the air. Change was coming whether they were ready for it or not.

CHAPTER SIXTEEN
THE PATH TO WAR

Following the Portsmouth militia down the corridor, Bruno took time to glance back over his shoulder to check the progress of the riot. He padded to catch up with Roberts, determined to help the militiamen lead the chase away from his friends.

Sigma? Bruno? You're here somewhere. Answer me, dammit.

Thea, you're with Captain Kiandra? Bruno asked.

Yes, Jason and I are here. Give yourselves up. They only want Allan. I should be able to buy us enough time to take you three out of here.

Come on, Thea. You don't even know if we can gather enough magic for us to leave. Who knows what will happen to us.

Captain Kiandra and I will protect you, Thea said.

They shot him, Thea!

No, Roberts shot him, Bruno. He's gone off reservation. Our orders were to capture him and bring him in.

Bruno sighed. No matter how much he wanted to, he could not just give up. *We helped start this. We cannot just walk away.*

Bruno, do you know what you have done? History is in flux. The timeline has split into so many branches it is in total chaos. Please, stop this foolishness now, for everyone's sake.

Thea sounded scared, which worried Bruno. Thea was never scared.

I'm not sure even I could gather enough magic to portal you all out of here if all hell breaks loose, Thea added.

Bruno said nothing, thinking about his next moves as he padded after the militia, making sure the camera was able to track him heading down the left-hand corridor. The team moved a little way further down, then halted.

'Anton and Dries, you carry on,' Roberts ordered. 'Make sure the cameras catch you on the way out. Once you're out, head back to Portsmouth and let the Commander know what has happened. Henry, you come back with me. I think Allan could use your medical skills.'

Bruno sat and waited beside Roberts until his men disappeared from sight. The man took something out of his pack and pointed it at the screen. A few people trickled past them towards the riot, but Roberts made no attempt to move.

Bruno? You still there? This feels wrong. Something bad is happening.

I know, Thea. Sorry, I must go. I must make sure Lee

gets out of here safely, and he won't leave Allan. I'll keep in touch.

All right. Thea's voice was resigned. *But please, can you speak with Beta? He is beside himself with worry.*

'Henry, a big group is heading this way. Big enough for us to blend in,' Roberts said as Thea left Bruno's head.

Packing his device away, Roberts and Henry removed their packs and joined the group running down the corridor towards the hub.

'Come on, guys,' the leader yelled. 'If we don't hurry, we'll miss it—our one chance to show the soldiers we're not going to take their crap anymore.'

Others shouted encouragement as people rushed ahead, pulling hoodies up as they reached the area covered by surveillance camera. Bruno made sure to stay hidden on the far side of the group. Still, he incanted a "don't see me" spell just in case.

The corridors were filling up. Roberts and Henry linked arms to form a protective zone around Bruno, and began steadily working their way through the crowd. Moments later the three of them stood before the apartment door, ready to retrieve their friends. A quick knock and they were soon pulled inside, away from the chaos of the riots.

Soon after the guards left, Lee found himself with nothing to do. 'Won't you be missed at work?' he asked Jane, the girl who had let them into her apartment.

She pointed to the scenes of riots being shown on the room's television screen. 'I don't think anyone is going to miss me for a while. More so because I was supposed to be working the representatives loop today, and I think they are going to have their hands full for some time.'

He and Izzy continued watching the screen, making themselves comfortable on the sofa. Jane took supplies in to Basia, then she and Rosie moved to the door, talking quietly and keeping an eye out for Robert's return.

Lee allowed himself to switch off until a rather regal looking woman in her fifties appeared on the screen. With her red hair pulled into a severe bun and the equally severe lines of her military uniform, she immediately drew his attention.

Jane turned the sound up. 'She is the head of the Civil Guard,' she explained.

'I repeat: everyone is to return to their quarters immediately. We are suspending all work details and declaring a curfew until those who infiltrated our city are behind bars. Anyone who does not comply with the emergency orders will be detained by the guards and questioned carefully.'

'Held without recourse to legal help,' Rosie said under her breath,

'That's just great,' Izzy said. 'We're never gonna get out of here now.'

Rosie checked the peephole in the door before saying, 'I think it will be a while before things quieten down. We need to get you out of here before they do, because once everything is clear, the house-to-house searches will start.'

'Of course they will,' Lee said, feeling despondent. It

would be hard enough moving an injured Allan—why not make it even more difficult? He placed his elbows on his knees and rested his chin in the palms of his hands, getting more and more depressed as each minute passed.

He jerked to attention moments later when the door opened and Roberts entered, followed by Bruno and one of his men. Roberts opened the door to the bedroom to check on Allan. Seeing that Basia was struggling to deal with his wounds, he instructed Henry to do what he could to patch Allan up so he could be moved.

Once the door was again closed, and the militiaman said, 'We've left a trail away from here, and that should buy us a little time. We still need an escape plan though.'

He ran his hands through his hair in agitation. 'If only you had stuck to the plan and not gone sneaking off.' He glared at Izzy and Lee.

Lee didn't want an argument, but he realised Roberts deserved an explanation. 'Allan came here to tell people about an alternative way of life. Once Rosie suggested the idea of a speech, he was going to do it whether we went with him or not. I thought it best to at least protect him.'

Roberts shrugged. 'Fair enough, but why didn't you come and get us?'

'We didn't think you would agree to let us go,' Izzy said.

Roberts paused, stroked his chin, and said, 'Fair point.'

'How did you know we were in trouble?' Lee asked.

'Luckily, the agri workers were talking about a commotion on the main concourse. We overheard them and realised only one group of people could cause that much mayhem.' Roberts grinned, taking some of the sting out of his words. 'Look, I guess Allan has done what we wanted him to do—caused unrest and set up some internal contacts—the least we can do now is get him out of here.'

Lee was glad Roberts had taken charge again. If you had told him a month ago that he would give up leadership so easily, he would have laughed. In truth, though, he was relieved to let someone else make the decisions. It wasn't that he wanted to blindly follow another person's orders. It was more that he didn't want to be responsible for the lives, or potential deaths, of the others.

Roberts walked to the bedroom door and opened it. 'How's he doing, Henry?'

Through the door, Lee caught a glimpse of Basia and Henry working on Allan, who was attached to a drip.

'A lot of blood loss, but no lasting damage. Basia managed to clean the wound. I cauterised it and patched him up. We've given him fluids, which should help. I had to knock him out completely, so he can't walk. Moving him is not optimal, but if we have to, we can make it work,' Henry informed them as Basia frowned behind him.

'Moving him could kill him,' she declared.

'If he stays here, he will definitely die,' Roberts said.

'You can't know that for certain.' Basia's chin jutted out defiantly.

'But we do, love,' Rose interrupted. 'The soldiers want him, and they'll want to make an example of him once this period of unrest is over. The best chance of saving him is to get him out of here, and Jane and I think we have a way you can do that.'

'I work in the laundries. Today I was supposed to be doing the upper floors. My trolley and uniform are in the

closet. You can put your boy in the trolly and one of you, well, the girl with you, can dress as me. There is an exit to outside near the laundries,' Jane told them.

'Jane and I contacted a few of the residents. They are on their way here and will swap clothes with you. They will draw any soldiers away from your route,' Rosie added.

'It will be dangerous for them,' Roberts said.

'They have been training for this. They know the risks and will take them happily.' Rosie sounded almost gleeful as she spoke.

Things happened fast after that. Less than twenty minutes later, the small apartment was crowded with people. Clothes had been exchanged. Allan was placed gently in the trolley, drip and all, and covered with dirty linen. Basia was ready to wheel him out. The main group was debating how to cause enough mayhem to draw the guards.

'How will she know where to go?' Lee asked as everyone gathered by the door.

Roberts handed Basia a handheld device. Pointing to the screen, he said, 'I marked the quickest way to the laundry. Just avoid these blue dots if you can. They indicate large groups of people. It also disrupts the cameras a little as you pass. Not enough to worry security, but the picture blurs or shows a bit of static until we pass by.'

The decoys left first. A couple of minutes later, Rosie stuck her head out, waited for a large group to pass, then indicated they should go.

'Look after my boy,' she ordered them as she shut the apartment door.

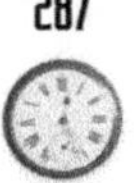

The corridors were crowded and noisy, and at first it was difficult to keep Basia in sight. As the crowd thinned, a new problem presented itself. With the order to return to quarters given, the army was out in full force, and they had to take quite a few detours to avoid them.

Lee's palms sweated, and he shoved his shaking hands into his pockets. Moving closer to Bruno for comfort, he wondered once again how things had fallen apart so quickly, and if he would ever see his family again.

Everything was going according to plan. Basia used the device to steer them away from soldiers and rioters alike, although they could hear confrontations happening all around them. Lee had almost started to believe they might escape unscathed when Basia halted, having just turned the corner to the laundry wing.

'What are you doing here?' a voice boomed.

Basia trembled, and Lee thought they were doomed. He waited out of sight, close enough to grab Basia and the trolley should he need to. The others ducked into doorways, out of sight.

It's all right, Lee, Bruno sent. *Soldiers love a bit of fear, and they would be surprised if she hadn't reacted that way.*

'I... I was working upstairs and I... I got sent home. I thought I would just drop the laundry off on the way. I don't want to get into trouble when it is not ready for tomorrow.'

A laugh echoed down the corridor. 'Love, no one is going to be worrying about their linens for a while yet.'

'Leave her alone, Peter. Can't you see she's scared. Come on, love. Do what you need to, then hurry home. You don't want to get caught up in all this fighting.'

'Th...thank you.'

Basia wheeled her cart forward. 'Um, my friend came with me to make sure I was all right. Can he come too?'

Basia waved Lee forward. The soldier in front of her gave him the once over before the nicer one said, 'Brave of you to escort her through this mayhem.'

Lee gave a nervous laugh as his stomach flip-flopped. 'She was determined to come. I couldn't let her go alone.'

'Good lad. Come on, Peter, we need to finish checking this section.'

The soldier moved past them and continued along the corridor. His mate followed, smirking. 'Don't stay too long. You don't want to get caught in a compromising position.' He sniggered.

Lee and Basia slowly walked forward. Behind them a radio crackled, and the first soldier responded. The second soldier's eyes bore into the small of Lee's back, right between his shoulder blades, raising the hair on the back of his neck.

In front of the door, Basia whispered, 'Oh no, they didn't give me a code for the lock.'

Bruno, there is a lock here. Can you magic it open? Lee asked.

No, the magic down here isn't strong enough for that, the Guardian sent back.

'Something wrong?' the second soldier called.

Lee thought he was going to throw up. Instead, he turned and said, 'She's scared, and forgot the code for a moment."

'Peter, go help them. We need to clear this area.'

'It is my first time being sent upstairs... then the lockdown...,' Basia said breathlessly as the guard reached over her shoulder and keyed in a number.

'Okay, unload your stuff and get out of here as quickly as possible,' he grumbled.

As Basia went inside, Lee watched the soldier return to his friend.

'What now?' Basia whispered.

'I don't... hold on....'

The first soldier put his hand to his ear, listened, then said, 'Insurgents are overrunning the green sector.' Looking down the corridor towards Lee, he yelled, 'Can I trust you both to go straight to your quarters after your friend is done?'

'Yes,' Lee answered to the soldier's retreating back.

Much to Lee's relief, he was soon joined by the rest of the team. Basia removed the drip from Allan's arm, and Lee helped her take him out of the basket. Meanwhile Henry fashioned a hammock out of the sheets.

'Wait here,' Roberts ordered. Retuning a few minutes later, he said, 'The exit is around the corner. One camera covering the door, no guards. We need to go through two at a time so we can disrupt the feed. I'll go first. Henry, you send the others through in twos at two-minute intervals after. The code is A256.'

They made it to the door without further mishap and waited just out of view of the camera. Lee's heart was pounding and his arms ached as Allan shifted in his makeshift stretcher.

He watched as Roberts keyed in the code and slipped through. The two-minute wait seemed like two hours. Then Henry was sending Basia and Bruno through.

Lee's palms were sweaty, and the sheet slipped.

'You need to carry him—fireman's lift style—otherwise we risk the cameras picking you up,' Henry said. 'Can you do that?'

Lee nodded.

He and Izzy placed Allan on the ground.

'Ready?' Henry asked.

'Yes.'

'Right, up.' Lee bent and scooped up Allan, still wrapped in the sheet hammock, staggered a bit, then righted his load. 'Go.'

Lee made it to the door as Izzy punched in the code. Then they were through and on their way up the flight of stairs behind.

After four flights Lee's knees were beginning to buckle. He was about to drop Allan when he felt the weight over his shoulder ease slightly.

'I can take him from here.'

With a sigh of relief, Allan handed over his bundle to Henry and made his way up to the cavern above.

Roberts waited for them at the top. 'Take a rest,' he ordered.

Henry placed Allan on the floor by Bruno and Basia. Lee stumbled over and joined the rest of the team. Roberts joined them, while Henry took his place by the external door.

'There are increased patrols,' Roberts said. 'I'm just trying to decide whether to make a run for it or hide for a while. The dogs aren't out yet, so I'm leaning towards hiding.'

'I don't like the idea of that,' Izzy said. 'I'll feel much better when we are all back and secure in the Portsmouth Protectorate. Roberts, your device can sense body heat, can't it?

'It can, but it is likely they would hear us coming before it picked up their heat signatures. Besides, they have similar technology to use against us.'

I can help with that, Izzy, Bruno said. *I think I can dampen our sound enough to not be heard unless someone is right beside us.*

Izzy smiled. *I can do that too. Between us we might be able to make this viable.*

'I can get us through the forest without making a sound,' Izzy said.

'What, you do magic or something?' Roberts scoffed.

'Don't knock it until you've seen it,' Basia said. 'Magic aside, we can't wait here forever. Allan needs medical help, and soon.'

Roberts frowned. 'You guys are strange, but I *am* tasked with getting Allan back alive.... So, what exactly are you proposing?'

Izzy said, 'I need Bruno to range ahead and check for patrol. Henry, Basia, and Lee can carry Allan. Roberts, you and I will take the rear and use your monitor to check for soldiers.'

Shrugging, Roberts said, 'This is the flakiest plan I have ever heard of.' He took a deep breath. 'I don't like having to move in the light, but I guess our options are limited. All right, if we are going to go, we may as well go now.'

They took a zig-zag path back to Portsmouth, avoiding tracks and moving through the bushes where they could. They had to backtrack a few times to avoid the alarming number of soldiers saturating the area.

The sky was just beginning to darken when Izzy called for a break. They hid under forest debris to wait for yet another patrol to pass. When Lee went to pick Allan up again, his arms shook and he suppressed a groan.

'I need a rest. I can't carry him anymore,' Lee whispered.

Roberts frowned. 'We are only about ten minutes away from the crossing. Let's make it to the edge of the bushland, then we can rest until the sun goes down. I don't want to be crossing the cleared defensive section in the light.'

Lee sighed. 'I think I can make it a little further.'

'Let me help you for a while,' Basia said, taking part of the sheet.

Just when Lee thought he couldn't take any more, Roberts led them to a bush. Pulling back the boughs, he revealed a herbaceous cave. They scrambled in and Lee immediately sunk to the ground, his limbs trembling with fatigue.

Basia unwound Allan from his bindings. He was grey, and a sheen of sweat had formed on his brow, but his breathing was regular.

Henry passed his water bottle around and shared some dried beef while Izzy took first watch. Lee curled up beside Bruno and tried to get some sleep.

He did not know how long he had been out for when he heard bushes rustling nearby. His eyes flew open to find Roberts staring down at him, finger to his lips. He froze as a large number of soldiers passed so close to their hiding place their feet shook the ground and their clothing brushed against the branches, revealing twinkling stars in the dusk sky.

'We're going to do some reconnaissance,' Roberts whispered once they were again alone. 'Henry is in charge until we return.'

Izzy stood to leave with Roberts.

Izzy? Lee said in alarm.

Don't worry, Lee. We won't get caught. She grinned at him. *And if we do, you and Bruno can rescue us.*

Take Bruno with you, he said.

The Time Fixer frowned. *What about you guys?*

We are safe here for the moment. Please, take him with you, Lee pleaded.

The boy is right. With the two of us, there is a better chance of all of us returning, Bruno said, rising to follow Izzy out.

Surveying the scene below, Bruno felt sick to his stomach. Spread out as far as the eye could see, a ring of Portsdown soldiers encircled Portsmouth. Facing them from inside the Portsmouth Protectorate's boundaries was the Portsmouth militia. Their ring consisted not just of soldiers, but of heavy artillery and mobile rocket launchers.

His first thought was, *What have we done?* His second

was to test the air for magic to decide if he could build a portal. Izzy looked down at him.

There isn't enough magic. Not here, anyway. And not for all of us, she said.

Her violet-blue eyes reflected his fear and worry. Beside him, Roberts shifted position and pulled something out from one of the pockets of his trousers—night vision goggles.

'Not a single gap in the band around Portsmouth,' he noted. 'I'm not sure whether they are here to keep us from getting back, or if they are here as retaliation for our entering the city.'

'Does it matter?' Izzy asked.

'Of course. If it is option one, we can give ourselves up and everyone backs down. Option two is more difficult... and your guess is as good as mine. Portsdown enjoys threatening to use their military might to wipe us out. Maybe this time it isn't a threat.'

'Can we make it across without being seen?' Izzy asked.

'No way. We are better to return and wait this out.'

About half an hour later, they were back in their hiding spot, and had broken the bad news to the others. Allan was awake, his head resting on Robert's pack. He had refused strong painkillers, wanting to keep his head clear.

'Will they stand down if I give myself up?' he asked.

Roberts shook his head. 'I don't think it's that simple. They might, but it is unlikely. Our situation would be so much better if we could communicate with base.'

Izzy looked at Bruno and he nodded. 'We might be able to help with that.'

Roberts chuckled. 'Magic again.'

Izzy smiled with not a hint of embarrassment. 'Yes.

And we may also be able to tell you what is going on in Portsdown as well.'

'Knock yourselves out,' he said as he stretched out on the ground. 'I'm going to get some shut-eye.'

'Bruno, you talk with Thea while I try and make a connection with Johan—after all, we do have a history, so it's our best bet for Portsmouth.'

Roberts chuckled. 'Now I know you're having me on. You're getting the dog to talk to our enemies.'

Basia glared at Izzy. 'What do you mean you and Johan have a past?'

Lee placed his hand over Basia's. 'I'll explain later, but for now we need to let these guys work.'

CHAPTER SEVENTEEN
THE DRUMS OF WAR

Izzy closed her eyes and concentrated on the pin pricks of magic on her skin. In her mind she pictured her one true love, Josephine—remembering her brown hair always neatly held back in a bun, her warm brown eyes, and the dimple in her left cheek when she smiled.

Love filled her heart as she allowed it to open just for this moment. Using that connection, she reached out for Johan.

Johan, can you hear me?

Mmm, what? Who? a sleepy voice answered.

Johan, it's me, Izzy.

She felt a jolt, like electricity, followed by confusion. Izzy hated using this type of mind link to communicate because emotions as well as words were exchanged. Trying to shield herself as much as possible from Johan's feelings, she spoke again.

Johan, we are trapped outside the perimeter, and we need to know what is going on before we decide what to do.

Fear and worry worked itself through the bond. *Basia? Is she all right?*

Yes, she's fine. She's with me now, Izzy said.

Relief almost overwhelmed her. *Good. I don't know what I would do if anything happened to her.... How would I explain it to—*

Johan, do you know what's happening?

Yes, a little bit. Mum and Dad arrived with a contingent of the Lyndhurst Guard early this morning, along with some of the Southampton militia.

What? Why are they all there? Izzy was not sure if the fear building in her stomach was her own, or was a result of her connection with Johan.

After the meeting at Lyndhurst, everyone was worried there would be a retaliation from Portsdown, and none of us can face it alone, Johan told her. *I was with Dad and the Commander trying to sort out accommodation when the call came through about your activities.*

What call? It was Izzy's turn to be confused.

From Portsdown, threatening war if Allan and all of the Portsmouth spies were not handed over for trial.

Izzy's heart sank. *Oh dear, that is not good at all. What did the Commander say?*

A Militia Council was called. Mum and Dad are in there, along with Representatives from Southampton. I believe, from rumours flying around, they are also looping in Protectorates as far away as Guildford and Chichester.

Still not sounding good. Izzy knew now the churning

in her stomach was all her own.

It isn't. They are talking about taking a final stand against Portsdown, saying they will never give in to the cities again.

Oh, no. Can anyone talk sense into them, Johan? They can't really mean to go to war.

Johan's voice was firm when he responded. *They won't back down and hand you over, if that is what you are worried about. My father is trying to convince them to consider peace talks to agree on an accord between our communities.*

How likely is that to happen? Izzy asked.

He has a little support, but your guess is as good as mine, Izzy.

The connection was growing fuzzy and she was just about to break it when a flow of worry overwhelmed her.

Izzy, bring Basia home... please.

I will do the best I can, she said. *It would be easier if there weren't so many soldiers between here and you.*

I will see what I can do about that, Johan said.

Izzy smiled and broke the link that was both so familiar and very foreign.

When she opened her eyes, she found three faces turned towards her, a triple mask of expectation. Henry and Roberts snored gently and Bruno was curled up by Allan, clearly not yet finished with whoever he was talking to.

It took a while for Bruno to gather enough magic to make a connection, then it took a few attempts to actually reach Thea. At first, he thought she was blocking him, then he remembered magical energy was limited underground, so he put a little more force behind his call.

Sigma?

Yes, it's me, Thea. I was just touching base to find out what was happening underground since Allan dropped his bombshell.

First, tell me, are you all safe?

Bruno was touched by her concern. *Yes. I won't tell you where we are, I don't want to compromise your position, but we are all right.*

Good. Now what is it you need?

Did you know Portsdown is holding Portsmouth to ransom for our return? Bruno asked.

Yes. Our regiment has been assigned to guard the Representative Council, and they have been in nonstop meetings since I spoke with you last.

Bruno felt a wave of relief that Thea was so close to the action. *Are they going to declare war?*

I believe they have given the Portsdown Protectorate twenty-four hours to produce you. Time runs out at two o'clock tomorrow afternoon.

They might find that difficult, Bruno chuckled. *They have no idea where we are.*

That is interesting, and exactly what they are saying. I will see if I can make it known they are telling the truth. It might buy us some time to sort this out.

Thea, how serious are they about going to war? Bruno asked.

They are divided. Most want to wipe Portsmouth off the face of the earth, but a small group want to work with the Protectorates to find a solution to end all these small attacks, Thea informed him.

What's stopping them from acting, then?

Thea laughed. *The little matter of a full-scale riot, which is taking longer to control because representatives sent the bulk of the army to encircle Portsmouth.*

Is there anything we can do to stop a full-scale war? Would turning ourselves in help?

Thea said something Bruno was unable to make out as the connection slipped. Reaching out a little further, Bruno gathered more magic and tried again.

What was that, Thea?

Oh, you're back. I said, it would help, if we could find a safe way for you to do it, maybe as part of peace talks.

That sounds ambitious. Bruno was skeptical. *Are you able to influence anyone to that end?*

I've managed to get myself attached to one of the more moderate Representatives, Thea told him.

Representatives? I guess you're using that term loosely, Bruno said.

Actually, no. He's one of the few original elected members and he will not retire until they stop passing seats down to their children and actually hold elections.

Bruno laughed. *That sounds novel.*

You'd be surprised. There are three or four Council members who agree with him, including two who inherited their seats. They believe agreeing to hold elections in Portsdown followed by peace talks with the Protectorates is the only way humanity will survive in this part of England.

Oh, Bruno said, wondering how such a small group could make a difference.

They are concerned putting down the riots with force will not extinguish the movement for change. Thea's tone was worried. *They see the big picture and believe Portsdown cannot withstand sustained attacks from within and without.*

Combine this with the Protectorates wanting to flex their muscles…, Bruno added

Look, Bruno, we are where we are. All we can do now is work with the moderates in both camps to prevent war. I will work on Tobias. Can you do the same on your side? Thea asked.

Um….

Bruno, just for once can we work together? Exasperation filled Bruno's head.

Thea, it's not that I don't want to help, it's more I don't know how much help I can be from where we are. But I will try. And I will talk to the group about giving ourselves up in return for peace talks happening.

Did you contact Beta yet? Thea asked out of nowhere.

If Bruno could have blushed, he would have. *No, I thought it best to leave him out of this. I don't want him to get into trouble for something that I decided to do on my own.*

If you need any help once we sort this out—

Thanks for the offer, but I know you didn't want any part of this, so I won't drag you into it, Bruno said.

Now that I've seen more of Portsdown, I think perhaps we should have done things differently from the outset. Portsdown was set up by good people trying their best to save humanity, but the ruling elite has become corrupt

and will do anything to protect their position. If Allan had been returned to them, it would only have bolstered their iron control of the Representative Council.

A small flicker of hope began to grow in Bruno's heart. *You mean you actually think I did the right thing?*

Don't be ridiculous. You disobeyed orders, Thea said, dashing Bruno's sliver of hope. *You should never have gone against the Council; that isn't our role.*

There she was, the same old Thea seeing everything in black-and-white. He changed the subject. *And Jason? Is he all right?*

He is with Rodgers. They are assigned to policing the riots. I think Captain Kiandra had had enough of the two of them and was more than happy to loan them to another regiment.

Bruno gasped. *I thought Corporal Rodgers would be behind bars after shooting Allan.*

Although Captain Kiandra demoted Rodgers to Private for his behaviour on our mission, he is now being hailed a hero and was promoted to Captain for his actions. Jason has become his lapdog and seems to relish the opportunity to enforce the anti-riot emergency acts. When we leave, I am not sure he will want to come with us.

However much he is enjoying himself, at some stage he will have to escape and find Izzy. Jason is not strong enough to magically portal out of here by himself, Bruno said.

If I had my way, I'd leave him behind, but I have promised to return him to his people if he can't find his partner.

There was little left to say, or perhaps there was so much but now wasn't the time—there was never a time to say all the unsaid words. Bruno sighed. *I had best go.*

Good luck with trying to sort things out from your end. Bruno cut communications.

He lay with his head resting on his paws for a while, enjoying the peace and quiet. Although he hated to admit it, his conversation with Thea had struck a chord. He no longer had confidence in the Time Guardian Council, and at some stage he would need to decide whether or not he had a future with them. He stretched. But not now—now he had to stop a war, then he had to find enough magic to return everyone home. When that was done, there would be time to worry about the future.

The tree hide was quiet when Bruno opened his eyes to look around. Izzy smiled at him as she met his gaze.

I told them all to get some sleep, and that you might be a while.

Izzy, I am wondering if we should contact someone at headquarters before we decide our next move.

If you contact Beta, you are braver than me. I have not contacted Cynthia since we left Lyndhurst.

Bruno bared his teeth, which seemed to be what dogs did when they wanted to smile. *I don't want to do it, but perhaps we should find out what is going on up there before we decide anything.*

Allan stirred beside him, snuggling into the warmth of his body. Lee snorted and rolled over. Bruno envied them their rest.

Okay. The sooner you do this, the sooner you can sleep. Izzy's tone was sympathetic, and he appreciated the support.

Reaching out with his senses, Bruno found a pocket of magic and drew it to himself. He searched for more and added it to his store. This would be a long conversation and he wanted to make sure he had enough magic to see it through.

Finally, he could put it off no longer. He called to his friend and mentor.

Beta.

Sigma, is that you? Finally! I've been trying to get hold of you for days.

Already on the defensive, Bruno humphed. *I only spoke to you two days ago. I don't know what all the fuss is about.*

Not long after we last talked, total chaos broke loose here. Alarms went off, and the World Fixers... what a stupid name that is... had something similar going on over there. I don't know what you are doing, but you have to stop it—now!

Bruno took a deep breath before answering. *Beta, we can only suggest things, and once I decided to help Colin break Lee and Izzy out of jail, things sort of snowballed into helping Basia and Johan free Allan. I'm afraid things took on a bit of a life of their own.*

We can go into the rights and wrongs of things after this is over. What we need you to do now is convince Allan to lay low for a while. Keep him quiet so he doesn't fan the flames of rebellion any further, Beta instructed.

I don't think he is going to be a problem for a while. He

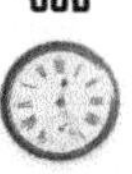

has been injured and can barely sit up, let alone stand to make any more speeches, Bruno said.

At least that is one less thing to worry about.

Beta!

I hate to be the harbinger of doom, Bruno, but it is chaos here. The timeline is split and monitors from the Time Guardians and Time Fixers are in agreement—war is imminent, and that war is likely to cause the end of mankind on earth.

We may be on the brink of war, Bruno agreed, *but I fail to see how that would result in humanity being exterminated.*

And that is why you should be listening to us and not branching out on your own, Beta admonished. *We have access to more information than you do.*

The rebuke churned Bruno's stomach. He was already afraid their actions had accelerated the very thing they had been sent to prevent.

Okay, I'll bite, Beta. How do they see this playing out?

The academics believe the world is in such a precarious balance that another couple of nuclear explosions will see the onset of nuclear storms even more violent than the ones after World War Three. It will push the environment over the edge and the earth will become a barren wasteland. It will only be a matter of time before all life dies out.

You can't seriously believe that? Bruno asked, his heart thumping, not wanting to believe what he was hearing.

It fits in with what we are seeing here, Beta said.

Bruno rested his head on his paws, feeling sick to the stomach. *We have to fix this, Beta. We have a plan.*

No, don't do anything. Find a pocket of magic and

return everyone home, Beta instructed.

Thea says the only way to prevent this war and save the world is for us to turn ourselves over to Portsdown, Bruno said.

Sigma, you could die in the nuclear explosion. And if you don't, then any magic in the area will be extinguished. None of you will be able to return home. If you leave now, you will have a front row seat to the future, and if you don't, you will be a footnote in history.

Bruno wanted to argue that of course they would stay and fix this, but he knew this was a major decision and he believed that each member of his team should make up their own minds.

I will ask the others and let you know what they say, he finally said.

Well, that is better than nothing, I guess.

Beta, what about Thea and Jason?

They are safe enough underground for the moment. She has asked to be allowed to stay until the point war is declared.

Bruno felt a small glow inside. Thea was staying to help.

Jason has gone off reservation. He told his handler if it was good enough for you to do whatever you wanted, then it was good enough for him, Beta said.

Bruno chuckled. That guy was a moron.

Bruno?

All right, give us until the end of the twenty-four-hour deadline to fix this. If we aren't able to, I will send all those who want to go home at two o'clock tomorrow, he confirmed.

Good. And you?

I don't know, Bruno admitted.

Bruno... we have to.... Beta sighed. *Good luck.*

Thanks, I'm going to need it.

Bruno felt strangely alone after the link was severed. In the past he had relied on Beta's guidance and had followed his lead blindly. It was odd to be taking this first step alone, and in such a critical situation.

Whatever happened, whatever everyone else decided, he knew he would not leave this world to a war he had had a hand in starting. Would the others agree with him?

This time when he opened his eyes, he found Allan staring at him.

'Will you stay and try and sort this out?' the boy asked him.

Bruno started, realising he had not shielded his conversation. *You heard that?*

'Some of it,' Allan admitted.

How much?

'From when Beta said he had been trying to reach you for days.'

So pretty much the whole thing.

'I guess so. Bruno, we have to do everything we can to stop this war. I won't be able to live with myself knowing I caused this to happen.'

This is not all you, not by a long shot... but I understand, and I feel the same. Let's wake the others and see what we can do.

CHAPTER EIGHTEEN
A GLIMMER OF HOPE

Bruno's cold, wet tongue swept across Lee's face, waking him instantly from his doze.

'Wha—'

Basia's hand slapped down over his mouth. 'Shh,' she whispered.

Groggily looking around, he remembered where they were—in their tree cave with thousands of soldiers from Portsdown roaming nearby. He nodded, and Basia took her hand away.

'What's going on?' he asked, scanning the faces around him.

'Time to talk turkey,' Izzy said. 'Bruno and I spoke with Portsmouth, Portsdown, and... well... someone with an overview of the whole situation.' She looked pointedly at Roberts and Henry, as if waiting for them to say something.

When they didn't, she continued. 'Things aren't looking good. There is a way we can help, but we must all decide whether we want to do what is asked of us.'

For a moment Lee stared at Izzy and Bruno blankly. How could things get any worse than they were now? As Izzy began to explain the situation they were in, he wished he hadn't asked.

When she had finished, leaving out a piece Lee could guess at, that humanity's survival hung in the balance, no one spoke. Lee's instinct was to say, 'Take me home now.' He didn't, though, as he was well aware some of his own actions had led them to where they were now.

Roberts laughed. 'You expect me to believe this is real?'

It was Henry who answered him. '*I* think it is. During the past few hours, strange voices have been floating in and out of my head. Maybe these people can mindspeak to each other. If they can do that, who's to say they can't talk to people further away.'

'I must be the only sane one here.' Roberts shook his head. 'But it doesn't matter. My orders are to take Allan back to Portsmouth, and I am going to do just that. The rest of you can do what you want.'

They all whispered frantic responses to this challenge, then all stopped at once as the sound of a twig snapping filled the air. While they waited for this new threat to pass, Lee peered at the faces of his travelling companions, trying to work out what each of them might decide to do.

When Bruno signalled it was all right to continue, he added, *One at a time. Allan, you go first.*

'I am going to give myself up, and I am hoping some of you will come with me, if only to help me get there,' he said.

'No, you're not,' Roberts responded. 'You are going back to Portsmouth.'

Allan's jaw set. 'I started this, and if there is even a small chance I can prevent thousands of people from dying, then I need to take it.'

'The Commander told me you are important as a symbol for change. He wants you back and I will be taking you,' Roberts argued.

'And that is the very reason he must go,' Henry said. 'With him on the loose, Portsdown will never bargain with us.'

Roberts frowned. 'You're on his side?'

'I am going to go with him to turn myself over, but only if that means there will be peace talks.' Henry confirmed his decision.

'What about the rest of you?' Roberts asked.

'Bruno told me he is going,' Izzy said. 'And if he goes, I must go too.'

'And you?' He looked at Basia, who was glaring at Allan.

Ignoring Roberts, she said to him. 'Soldiers shot you once, yet you stood up and spoke out for change, earning yourself another wound. Maybe it is time to sit back and let others place themselves in the line of fire.'

Allan took her hand. 'That is not who I am, Basia. I believe we must all fight for the changes we want, and I did that. Now things are out of control, and I can't just walk away and leave it to others to tidy up my mess. I must take responsibility for my actions.'

A sad smile drifted across her face. 'I know who you are, and I didn't think you would do it, but I had to ask.' Raising her head, she finally answered Roberts. 'I go where Allan goes.'

'That leaves you, Lee. Please tell me someone else here has some common sense,' Roberts pleaded with him.

Lee did not answer immediately. He had come here because he felt good about what he and the others had done in the New Forest, preventing the spread of a vicious disease. He had wanted to feel like that again. Instead, they had brought humanity to the brink of extinction. It would be so easy to leave, return home, and let the Time Guardians try and fix this another time.

Unfortunately, like Allan, he found it difficult to walk away from his mistakes. And to make matters worse, he believed in what Allan was trying to do. This world needed to change if humanity was to survive, and if there was a small chance he might be able to help make that happen, he had to try.

'Sorry, Roberts. You're on your own,' he said.

Having taken his stand, Lee's stomach decided to do somersaults, and it took all his willpower not to throw up. His life was on the line here. Not just because he might die, but also because of the even bigger risk that he would be imprisoned in the underground city, unable to return to his home because of the lack of magic.

'If you believe you must do this, then I will leave you here. Alone, I can sneak through the Portsdown lines and be back in Portsmouth within the hour. While I think you are all barking mad, I will do what I can to persuade people to set up the peace talks you all believe will prevent all-out war.' Roberts rummaged in his is pack as he spoke.

Pulling out his water bottle and rations, he passed them to Lee.

'Eat what you can, drink plenty of liquids, and rest until sunrise.'

Lee took a sip of water and passed the bottle around.

Roberts gave his handheld to Henry. 'We are not far from Cosham. Do what you can to get the talks held near the Marriot Hotel on the corner of the A3. It is close enough that you can be first to arrive. Also, no one holds the land, so it is neutral, and the area around it is relatively clear, eliminating chances of a double cross.'

'Thank you,' Allan said. 'We appreciate the advice.'

'And listen to Henry. He's sensible and knows the area like the back of his hand. That is all I can offer. I hope it goes well for you.'

They said their goodbyes, and Roberts slipped quietly through the branches.

'Bruno and I need to make some plans. You guys get some rest,' Izzy said.

'I'll take first watch,' Henry said.

'Can I help with anything?' Lee asked.

Izzy thought for a moment. 'Can you still sense magic in the air, Lee?'

He concentrated and expanded his senses until he felt pinpricks on his skin. He smiled. 'I can.'

'I will get you to join with me while I contact Johan. You can boost my power and make it easier for me to concentrate on the conversation.'

Reaching for Lee's hand, she said, 'Okay, let's get busy.'

Izzy's hand was warm, and her grip firm. She exuded a calm that helped slow Lee's racing heart.

Johan, can you speak?

The response was immediate. *Izzy, I have been waiting for you. I have my father here too in case we need him, and we have some good news.*

Beside him Izzy relaxed. *I hope you are going to tell me you arranged some sort of peace talks.*

No, but I believe we have the next best thing. My father and the Commander have agreed to meet with two representatives from Portsdown to discuss a cease-fire.

One of the knots in Lee's stomach loosened.

There is only one problem, Johan said. *You all have to be there. They will not meet under any other circumstances.*

His stomach clenched again. He should have known it was too easy. Izzy did not respond immediately, and the silence hung heavy in Lee's head.

Johan, Lee here. How can we be sure this isn't a ploy to draw us out?

Short answer is, we don't, completely. The only reason we are considering it is because one of your troop was there with a man called Tobias.

That would be Thea, Lee said.

Correct, Johan confirmed. *She said to tell you she did her bit, now you must do yours. We took that to mean you had been working with her to bring this about.*

We have, Izzy acknowledged. *We have spoken about it and agreed we will face the consequences of our actions, but we want to choose the place.*

This time Johan was slow to answer. *We can agree to that, within reason. Portsdown gave us a list of sites they*

believe to be suitable. We are to pick one. The deal is each side will send a troop in at 09:30 to secure the area. The meeting will begin at 10:00 sharp.

Roberts suggested the old Marriott hotel in Cosham. Is that on the list?

Johan confirmed it was, and Lee began to believe this plan might just work.

Your way there should be pretty clear, as we have agreed no further troop movements, Johan informed them.

Roberts should be back with you soon, and he will update you on our position in person. I need to go now, Izzy said.

Wait! Did you say Roberts is no longer with you? Johan asked, sending panic down the link. *Damn. We agreed Basia and the Portsmouth militia would not be included in the exchange. Henry was to guide you to look after Allan, and Rodgers was to bring Basia back to Portsmouth.*

Lee was overwhelmed with Izzy's sense of fury and betrayal.

So, you are happy to sacrifice strangers to save yourselves, she spat.

Sorry, Izzy, that was not our intention. We thought the city was only interested in having their own returned, Johan said.

Apart from Allan, we no more belong to them than we do to you. I thought you understood that. Fortunately, your sister has more integrity than the lot of you put together. She and Henry decided they would give themselves up along with us if it meant stopping a war, Izzy said.

Izzy, I'm sorry. I tried to do my best, but no one would listen to me. Please, can we talk about this when you get back?

Lee sensed Johan's confusion and regret, and he was sure Izzy was able to as well.

I think it is unlikely we will be seeing each other again, Johan.

But....

Thank you for all you have done. You can leave the rest up to us now.

The connection was abruptly terminated. Lee turned to find tears streaming down Izzy's cheeks. She wiped them away furiously. 'I cannot believe Jo was happy to hand me over like that,' she said.

Lee squeezed her hand. 'It wasn't Jo, or Josephine, it was Johan, and he probably had no say in the matter.'

She smiled tremulously at him. 'Thank you for trying to make it better. My head understands that, but it doesn't lessen the wound to my heart.'

A wet nose nuzzled its way under his hand, and Lee patted the dog's head. *She will be all right.*

'I will be fine,' Izzy confirmed. 'Okay, everyone, everything is in place. Cease-fire talks are being held at Cosham and we need to be there before the others arrive at 9:30 tomorrow. Henry, can we make it there in time?'

Henry narrowed his eyes and looked at the handheld device Roberts had left for them. 'We will need to leave about 06:00 to arrive in time. That gives us time for three hours sleep before we need to leave.'

'I am not going to be able to walk very fast, so perhaps we should leave at 05:00?' Allan smiled wanly.

'You guys catch some rest. Bruno still needs to talk to Thea. I will keep him company and keep watch,' Lee said.

As the others settled down, bodies close together to

preserve heat, he and Bruno moved to the outer edge of the group. The dog lay beside him, and Lee curled his hands in his warm fur.

Do you want me to help you like I helped Izzy? Lee asked.

Please. Mindspeak in a magical limited world is taking a lot out of me.

Lee drew some magic to himself, then concentrated on feeling the warmth of Bruno's body beneath his hand.

Thank you, that is perfect, Bruno told him.

Bruno, perfect timing. I was about to reach out to you. Thea's voice rushed into Lee's head. *Hello, Lee, nice of you to join us.*

Just a quick one this time, Thea. We only wanted to let you know it is on. We will be at the cease-fire negotiations, Bruno informed her.

I knew you would be. Allan is not going to do anything foolish to screw this up, is he?

We are all aware of the consequences of our previous actions. We don't want to place these talks in jeopardy, if indeed they are genuine, Bruno said.

They are genuine, Thea confirmed. *Rioters control much of the underground city, and Portsdown cannot fight a war on two fronts. Tobias will attend representing the moderates, and one of the Generals will be going with him to ensure any agreement will be supported by the Representative Council.*

Good.

See you tomorrow, Thea sent.

Today, Bruno corrected.

Thea winked away. Lee let go of his magic, and leaned back against the branches. He closed his eyes, willing

sleep to come, but he was too keyed up. Opening his eyes, he found Allan watching him.

Allan propped himself up on an elbow, wincing in pain as he did, and whispered. 'I can't sleep.'

Basia rolled over and sat up. When she was comfortable, she moved to help Allan into a semi-sitting position where he was able to talk without straining too much.

'Why can't you sleep?' Allan asked as he rested against Basia.

'We may be on the verge of all-out war, and the only thing that will stop it is us turning ourselves over to the enemy,' Lee answered, and they laughed. 'It doesn't do much for my stomach... or my anxiety.'

'I mean to negotiate with them. I hope they will agree to take me, on my own,' Allan said.

Basia tensed, as if she was about to object. Then she shook her head. 'I want to tell you not to be so noble, convince you that we all had a hand in this. But you won't listen.'

Allan smiled and took her hand. 'I would listen to you, but it wouldn't change anything. I believe they will settle for me. Once I give myself up, I will probably not see the light of day again, so I need people to carry on fighting for a better world, for a united Hampshire. I want you to promise me you will do that, Basia.'

Basia caught her lip between her teeth and worried it for a moment. 'I want to make a grand declaration that I will carry on the fight. Not just for you, but because I believe in what you tried to do, but I am just me. I am not sure I can do it.'

Allan turned slightly so he could face Basia. 'I know

you, Basia, and I believe you can do this. I am not sure how I can say that after such a short time together; maybe we are soul mates who keep finding each other through time.'

You have no idea how true that is, Lee thought. 'I hope they will let us *all* go, but if they don't, I will help you, Basia. Whatever it takes. I will be there for you.'

Lee, Bruno warned. *You should not make promises you can't keep.*

He ignored the Guardian. 'If we are all awake, why don't we head out. Perhaps if we move now, we can sleep a little before the others arrive.'

Basia frowned. 'Allan should rest a little more.'

'I don't think one hour more is going to make a difference to Allan either way,' Henry said. 'There are painkillers in my pack that should block out the pain but leave him able to walk. They only last for four hours, and I only have two doses.'

He reached into his pack, extracted the medicine, then passed the pills and some water to Allan. 'They are pretty quick acting, so by the time we're packed and ready to go, they should be taking effect.'

As they got ready, Basia kept glancing at Allan, almost as though she couldn't believe she was helping him walk towards capture and imprisonment. When they were ready to leave, she schooled her face into a bright smile and offered her arm to Allan. Lee's heart almost broke at the gesture.

'I don't think Allan believes he will live through this,' Lee said quietly so no one would hear him, a tear slipping down his cheek.

After their escape through the bush the evening before, their journey to the Marriott in Cosham was a breeze. Henry kept them within the tree line, but far enough away from the Portsdown circle of soldiers that they did not need to worry about being spotted. They made better time than expected, and reached the road in front of the hotel just after six.

There they hit a pinch point. They did not want to give themselves up until they were sure the peace talks were happening, which meant they needed to break through the ring and run across the open ground to the hotel carpark.

As they crouched in the bushes, Henry shook his head. 'I can't see a way through without being seen. Perhaps if we go further round back.'

'By then it will be light and they will spot us for sure,' Lee argued.

'If we can make it to that outcrop, the open ground is only about fifty yards across. Bruno and I could try a "don't see me spell",' Izzy said.

It would be tricky to do it for this many, for that long, Bruno said.

Henry frowned. 'What if you had a distraction? Could you do it then?'

'You're not thinking of doing anything that would result in your capture, are you?' Izzy asked in a way that clearly transmitted she would not agree to any such thing.

Grinning, Henry said, 'I'm not a martyr. No, I thought I would light a little fire to take their attention from the road. I promise to hide well so they won't catch me, and I will try and meet you in the hotel if I can make it through.'

'Perfect,' Izzy said.

Without another word, Henry passed something to Basia, then melted back into the forest. The rest of the group headed towards the cover Izzy had pointed out.

'Right, gather as much magic as you can—you too, Lee. We will need to stay physically connected as we cast the spell for this to work. Basia, can you help Allan across?'

Basia nodded, and they all readied themselves, waiting for a smoke plume to appear to tell them it was time to go. Lee's palms were sweaty. The sky was just starting to lighten. If they waited much longer, this would not work.

A shout rang out into the night, and the forest behind them became a hive of activity.

'Now,' Izzy said, and they moved from their cover.

Lee grinned. It was working. There were no yelling voices indicating they had been seen. No footsteps rushing after them. They were going to make it. Just as they reached the edge of the clearing, Basia tripped and stumbled, almost dropping Allan. Lee rushed forward to stop him from hitting the ground.

'Damn,' Izzy said. 'Spell's gone. Everyone run.'

Lee practically dragged Allan the last few metres, his heart pounding, expecting to be shot at any moment. Fortunately, Henry's fire distraction worked as planned, perhaps even better, as they made it to cover unscathed.

Huddled in the shadows of an overgrown garden, scanning for sounds that would indicate they had been seen, they caught their breaths.

They waited a at least ten minutes before Izzy said, 'I think we are okay to move.'

I agree. And if we don't go now the sun will be up, and we will be easier to spot, Bruno added.

Surveying the building, Lee wondered how they would get inside to hide. A functional motel like many others in the pre-holocaust world, it appeared to still be structurally sound, although the windows were boarded up, and it looked desolate and abandoned.

The weary team made their way through the gardens. Round the back of the building, they found a loose board covering a window. Izzy and Lee prised it off while Bruno kept watch.

Lee climbed inside first, and waited while Izzy and Basia propped the board against the wall and helped Allan and Bruno through the opening. Once the girls had joined him, Lee leaned out and hauled the board up, wincing as it scraped up the crumbling brickwork, then pulled it back in place, hiding their entry point as best he could.

They made their way through a darkened corridor to what was once the lobby of the hotel. There were still a few random chairs, and the carpet, although a little mouldy in places, was not too bad.

'This is cleaner than expected—too clean to have been completely abandoned for almost twenty years,' Basia said as she made Allan comfortable on the floor. 'There may still be running water in the kitchens. I'm going to see what I can find.' She walked back the way they came, with Bruno padding behind.

The morning dawned purple-red through a gap in the wooden boards over the doors. Lee peeked through, keeping watch as Izzy took up a position at an uncovered window to the side, able to see through the foliage that had grown over the building.

Basia returned with a jug of water, two white mugs, and a bowl. She put some water in the bowl on the ground and Bruno moved over to drink from it. She handed a cup of water to Allan, and Izzy walked over to drink from the other one while Lee remained on watch. 'You'll never guess what else I found,' she said, winking as she left the room.

She came back a few minutes later with bowls of steaming liquid. 'There was still gas in one of the stoves, and I found some tinned soup. It should be okay to eat.' She grinned and Lee could not help but join her.

He was starving, and he was sure that although the food was probably well past its use by date, it wouldn't harm them. The warm tomatoey liquid filled his stomach and he almost groaned in pleasure. *What a great last meal*, he thought darkly as he returned to his post.

Over the next few hours, they changed positions, taking turns at watching. Boredom began to set in. At around nine, Basia gave Allan the last of the medication for his pain, and he dozed for a while. Lee wished he could do the same, but he was still way too keyed up.

Lee? Bruno's voice popped into his mind. *Something is happening.*

Staring through the gap between the boards, he could

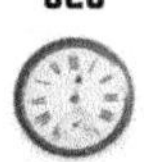

just make out a large group of soldiers wearing Portsdown colours enter the carpark. He smiled when he recognised Captain Kiandra and Sergeant Thea as they ordered the troop to form up about twenty metres from the doors.

Moments later a similarly sized contingent wearing mismatched military gear joined them. Roberts ordered them to stand at attention, and went over to talk with Captain Kiandra.

'I think this is the real deal,' Lee informed the others as Basia and Izzy rushed to the window and looked out. 'Roberts and Captain Kiandra are in charge of security, and I would trust both of them with my life,' he added.

What are they doing now? Bruno asked, pacing behind Lee, frustration tinging his words.

'They are pairing up and checking the area. Oh, that's unexpected. An electric car has just pulled up and they are erecting a gazebo and putting tables and chairs inside.' Lee chuckled. 'I wonder if this is what peace negotiations looked like in medieval times? Tents set in the middle of the battlefield, and all that. All we need are brightly coloured pennants and we will be set.'

'I think you have a romanticised notion of medieval battles,' Izzy responded dryly.

'Has anyone thought about how we are going to leave when it is time?' Allan asked from behind them. 'I mean, we can hardly break through the doors, given they are boarded up.'

'Since you ask,' Lee smiled. 'These doors are boarded up from the inside and held on with nails. I think I can use my knife to quietly prise enough of them out to be able to remove a panel when we are ready to leave.'

Izzy joined him and inspected the door.

'What, don't you trust me?' Lee asked.

'It is not that—well, yes it is that, sort of. It's just this is too important to stuff up our entrance.'

'Thanks for the vote of confidence,' Lee said dryly.

'You are right though. You start working on the nails and I will keep an eye on what's going on outside.'

Lee pulled out his knife and set to work removing every second nail. It was tough, slow work, especially as he had to keep the noise down, and he wished he had started sooner.

'Something is happening,' Izzy said when he was almost done.

He stopped and joined Izzy by the window, leaning his forehead against the cool glass. Cars were pulling up outside, and the two sets of soldiers formed a corridor between them and the gazebo.

Captain Kiandra leaned down and opened the door of the first car. A broad well-muscled man exited. His military bearing told Lee he was probably the General Thea mentioned. He was followed by a slim dapper man, bent with age, who tidied his wispy white hair before following the General to the gazebo, where he took a place beside Captain Kiandra.

The door to the second car was opened by Roberts. The Commander was first to alight, and he was followed by a middle-aged man. If Basia's gasp of delight was anything to go by, this was most likely her father.

Once the formalities were completed, the delegates took their seats and Captain Kiandra and Roberts moved to order their troops to encircle the tent.

After the initial flurry of activity, nothing happened. No one spoke. No one moved.

'What are they waiting for?' Lee asked.

Bruno, if you're here, now would be a good time to show yourselves. Thea's voice entered Lee's head.

He laughed. 'Oh. They're waiting for us.'

Basia went to help Allan to his feet, while Izzy and Lee pulled at the door covering. In spite of all Lee's efforts, it wouldn't budge, no matter how hard they pulled.

'What now?' Lee asked, as the door shuddered. It shuddered again, and they moved out of the way just in time to avoid the wooden panel falling to the floor.

Wide-eyed, they were greeted by a grinning Roberts. 'Well, that could have gone better,' he said.

They all piled out, and a Portsdown soldier patted them down to make sure no weapons were taken into the pavilion. The group slowly walked over to the gathered officials. As they walked past Captain Kiandra, she actually smiled in welcome and said, 'Of course you'd be at the centre of this upheaval, Private Lee.'

Lee grinned back, but couldn't think of anything suitably cutting to say in response.

Just as they reached the gazebo, a shout rang out from where the cars were parked. Everyone turned as one to find out what was going on. Behind a wall of soldiers, Lee couldn't see a thing.

The Commander looked across at Tobias and asked, 'What is this? Some sort of double cross?'

'No, nothing like that. General Wilson, is this your doing?' the dapper man asked.

The general shook his head as the soldiers in front

reached for their weapons and moved into attack formation.

Lee's eyes widened in surprise. In front of him stood Jason, brandishing a weapon and yelling something about stopping the fall of civilisation.

'Jason?' Izzy said. 'What in the—'

A shot rang out, and Lee turned to see a red stain spread across Allan's shirt moments before his friend crumpled to the ground, almost in slow motion.

'No!' Basia wailed, dropping to her knees beside him.

Lee took a step to join her, but was pushed out of the way as soldiers moved to support the delegates. Then all hell broke loose.

More bodies pushed their way between Lee and Allan. He tried to break through, but each time he was pushed even further backwards. He turned his head, frantically searching for Izzy and Bruno. Where were they? Where they okay?

Bustled to the edge of the crowd, he was in time to see two Portsdown soldiers grab a figure by the side of the hotel. 'Corporal Rodgers,' Lee said in amazement.

Then the amazement turned to fury. He had shot his friend again. This maniac had to be stopped. He charged forwards, only to be hauled back into place by someone grabbing his arm.

'Stand down, Private,' a voice said, and he whirled around to break free only to find himself face to face with

Captain Kiandra.

'But he—'

'He will be taken care of, I assure you,' the Captain said. 'But if you rush in there now, it could be you joining your friend. We are one shot away from these talks collapsing.' The Captain's voice was firm, and her grip was even firmer. 'Don't do anything to undo what might be achieved here today,' she said in a voice meant only for him.

Over the shoulder of a Portsdown soldier, Lee saw Captain Rodgers brandishing his weapon and shouting obscenities at anyone who tried to approach him. Then he began babbling about Allan bringing about an end to civilisation.

As he watched the scene unfold, his anger towards Rodgers was replaced by fury at himself. Why hadn't he been more careful? Why hadn't he realised Jason was merely a diversion, and that Rodgers would be the real danger? Jason? Where was Jason now?

He looked all around and found that while everyone else's attention was turned towards the hotel and Corporal Rodgers, Thea had grabbed Jason by the arm and was physically hauling him towards the tree line. The Time Fixer was pulling back, yelling, 'You all got to choose who you supported in this bun-fight! I chose to support Rodgers.'

'You moron,' Thea snarled, reaching for her handcuffs. She snapped one end on her wrist, and the other around Jason's. Once he was secured, she stopped pulling and stood very still. Lee saw the air behind her shimmer. Jason, his attention still on Rodgers, obviously had no idea what was happening, because when Thea relaxed he did too, thinking he had won. As he did, Thea gave him one final tug and the two of them fell through the portal and disappeared.

As the portal snapped closed, Lee dragged his gaze back to the scene of chaos in front of him. Now both sides had their weapons pointed at each other and accusations were flying. *No,* Lee thought, *Captain. Kiandra is right. Everything has all fallen apart.*

On the ground, Basia cradled a very still Allan, tears streaming down her face. She raised her eyes and met Lee's gaze. She shook her head, and with that simple gesture Lee knew the truth. Third time was not lucky for Allan.

He stumbled and would have fallen except for the Captain's grasp. 'Stay strong,' she said. 'This is not over yet.'

Roberts stood beside Basia, making space for her father to get through. The man reached down and pulled Basia to her feet. He hugged her and said something into her ear. She struggled free of his grasp and turned to look at the soldiers around her, as if seeing them for the first time.

'No,' she shouted. 'No, don't do this. If you stop the talks now, he will have died for nothing. Don't let hatred and fear be his legacy. Show that madman he is wrong, that this is not the end of civilisation, but the beginnings of a new one.'

No one moved. Basia wrung her hands. *Come on,* Lee thought. *You can do this.* As if Basia heard his words, she turned to him. He nodded once, and she drew herself a little straighter.

'Please, we all need this cease-fire,' she pleaded. 'Finish the work you came here to do.'

'She's very compelling,' Captain Kiandra said.

'Will you support her?' Lee asked.

The Captain frowned. 'I will do what the General and Representative Tobias order me to do. Soldiers must follow orders or everything will crumble in to anarchy.' She looked pointedly over to where two soldiers were bundling Rodgers into a car.

'Will you kill us if they tell you to?' Lee asked.

'Let's hope it doesn't come to that,' the Captain said, her lips curling into a smile as she returned her gaze to the scene under the gazebo, waiting for her orders. 'But if it does, I will be sad about it. I commend what you're trying to do.'

With Rodgers removed from the scene, the carpark was eerily quiet. It was like the hundred or so people there were held captive on a knife's edge, trapped in a moment in time. Then Basia's father glanced at his daughter before walking to the table and sitting down. 'Well, gentlemen, shall we get on with what we came here to do?' he asked.

No one moved. Lee's heart thudded in his chest. This could still go either way. Representative Tobias surveyed the scene, then retook his seat, shooting a meaningful look at the General.

General Wilson locked eyes with the Commander and no one moved. Lee's stomach clenched.

'Show some faith, Lee. No soldier truly wants to go to war. We face death every day, and we will do almost anything to avoid all-out bloodshed among our comrades.'

Captain Kiandra's remark was more comforting than it had a right to be.

As if on some secret cue, the two military men turned and took their respective seats at the table. Crisis averted, soldiers began moving back into position. Roberts ordered two of his men to take Lee and Basia into the hotel. Izzy and Bruno suddenly appeared beside Lee.

Where were you? he asked, his worry making the words sound more tart than he intended.

Thea needed a little help making the portal, Bruno said.

'Where do you want us, Captain?' Izzy asked.

'Go inside with your friends. I don't think we will be needing you any more today.'

They didn't need to be told twice.

CHAPTER NINETEEN
AFTERMATH

Allan's body was laid under a sheet in one of the conference rooms off the main lobby. Basia followed the soldiers in, and stayed with Allan when they left.

Lee, Izzy, and Bruno sat in the corner where Allan had slept less than an hour ago. Exhausted and defeated, no one said anything. Lee dropped his head into his hands and let the tears flow. Izzy hugged him, and Bruno lay across his lap. When his tears ran out, they stayed like that, drawing comfort from each other.

'We brought a change of clothes and food for you. If one of you wants to come with me to the car,' Roberts said some time later.

Izzy rose to her feet and followed him outside while Allan's two escorts remained just inside the door. To protect them or to keep them in, Lee had no idea, and he was too tired and emotionally drained to care.

So, you opened a portal? Lee asked.

Bruno humphed and laid his head on his paws. Lee ran his hands through the Guardian's coat, somewhat soothed by the action. Bruno appeared to feel the same way as he relaxed against Lee.

Bruno, did we help, or did we just bring things to a head?

The Guardian did not answer immediately. When he did speak, his voice was uncertain, and this concerned Lee.

We had no history of what originally occurred here, and therefore no way of knowing if we made things better or worse, only that we created a number of options that weren't available before. We should find out more in a couple of days, but our role is over. I will be able to take you home and we can put all this behind us, Bruno said.

Lee started. Of course he would be going home soon—Thea had already portalled out. Only, he was not ready to leave. Allan had started something with his speech, and he wanted to be a part of it a while longer. Besides, he was not yet certain what he would be going back to. He glanced at the door they had taken Allan through. Could he leave Basia to do this alone? After all, he had promised her he would be there.

How do you decide when your job is done? Lee asked, buying some time to think.

Normally we leave when history is back on track, but we can't tell that here. I am guessing that when the timeline extends beyond what we could see before, we can consider our job done. What will you do when you go home? Bruno asked, as if he guessed the root of Lee's questions.

You know, I'm not sure. My life was all planned out. I

knew who I was and I knew where I was going. After recent events, I'm not sure I want to be a soldier anymore. Not least because I found I am not good at blindly following orders. I don't know how my father's been able to do it all his life.

Given your career path, I think you will end up doing more of the ordering and less of the following, Bruno said with a laugh.

But everyone starts at the bottom, even if they are an officer at the bottom.

You can still change your mind—I mean, you don't have to report for duty for another two months, Bruno said.

True. So many thoughts were running through Lee's mind, it was difficult to catch hold of a single one.

He had no real reason for wanting to rush home, and lots of reasons for staying here. But he wasn't sure if he was ready to make that decision. Yet he knew Bruno was on the brink of suggesting they would need to leave sooner rather than later.

Mixed up with all the worry about his future was a longing to get back to his family. His parents would arrive in England soon, hoping to celebrate Christmas with him and his sister. Ah, Bebe, his twin. He wanted to share this adventure with her so badly.

Bruno, you said when we came here you could take me back to almost exactly the same time that we left. Is that true no matter how long we stay? Lee asked.

Bruno shifted slightly in his lap. *It is not an exact science, but yes, I can get you back within a few hours of when we left, no matter when we leave.*

Are there any limits on that?

No limits in terms of time travel, Bruno said, *but you*

wouldn't want to leave it too long. I mean, a month or two is fine. After that, especially at your age, it becomes difficult to explain away the physical changes.

Physical changes? Lee was curious.

Well... you're still growing and... your facial hair is growing in thicker. And I've noticed your physique has become a little leaner, and you're a bit sunburnt, Bruno said. *That alone will be difficult to explain away in the middle of an English winter.*

Lee laughed, earning a strange look from the Portsmouth guards. *Oh, I see what you mean. Still, if we don't go back straight away, will that cause any other problems?*

Bruno tilted his head to the side, as if to get a better look at Lee. *I guess for me it would. I'm not supposed to stay too long in one place because it might alter history. Your staying would probably do the same.*

If that's your only worry, then I think we'd be okay. I mean, we came here because history and time were going to stop, so there really isn't anything more we can alter.

Lee could almost hear Bruno's mind ticking over as he worked out how big a problem staying on a little longer would be.

Finally, the Time Guardian said, *You know, I think you're right. An extended stay shouldn't make any difference whatsoever, or if I'm wrong and it does alter something, history will right itself anyway. I take it you're seriously considering not returning for a while?*

Lee did not answer immediately. He still has some doubts, but part of him knew it was the right thing to do, given the havoc they had caused here. *Yes. I promised Basia. And... and I believe I can do something more here.*

What about home? And your family? Don't you want to see them? Bruno asked.

Of course he did, but he could wait a few more weeks.

Let me think on it and talk with Izzy. I don't see why we must rush away and if we are in agreement it will be easier to deal with our Councils.

Unless of course we've got it all wrong and the world still ends in the next couple of days, in which case this conversation is moot, Lee said.

Bruno snorted, *Well, that's a lovely thought.* The Guardian rose to his feet. *I'm going to see how Basia is doing.*

Now that he had made his decision, it was like a weight had been lifted. Lee leaned back against the wall and closed his eyes.

The room was dark, and Bruno was pleased dogs were gifted with night vision. He found Basia sitting on an old wooden chair, head tucked into arms that leaned on the table soldiers had placed Allan's body on. He had been covered by a tarp, but Basia had reached underneath to clasp one of his hands in her own.

She didn't move as Bruno settled in beside her, placing his head on her lap.

'I suppose you all think I am mad, grieving so hard for someone I only met a few days ago.'

Not at all. I have met you and Allan in many lifetimes,

and in each one you found each other and formed a bond like no other, Bruno told her.

Basia's voice was barely above a whisper when she asked, 'In any of those times, did Allan and I ever end up together?'

Yes, but it was a very long time ago. You were a lady in the English court, and he was the King's apothecary.

A smile tugged at her lips. 'What was I like then?'

Much the same as you are now. You fought against the limited role you were born into, and tried to improve the lives of others. In fact, in many of your previous lifetimes you were known as a force for change.

'I am pleased I was once so strong. I don't believe women can actually make any difference in my time. Or maybe just not this woman.'

I don't believe that is true. I think you can do anything you put your mind to.

She turned her head and gazed into his eyes. 'I made this promise to Allan, and I don't think I can keep it. I am not a leader. I don't think I can stand up in front of others and inspire them to change.'

You did inside the city.

'I was able to do that because Allan was there,' she said

You will have Lee with you, Bruno told her.

She smiled a little. 'I will, but I am not sure that will be enough.'

I believe in you, Basia.

'Wish I did. Perhaps if I had other girls my age stand up and be counted, I might have more confidence....' Her voice trailed off.

Bruno had an idea. *I believe Izzy will be returning to her original timeline after this. Your incarnation is far away, in Australia, another country on the other side of the world. Would you like me to ask her to take you with her so you can see what women are really capable of?*

'You mean like you brought Lee here?' Basia's voice was uncertain.

Yes.

'But I promised Allan I would carry on his fight.'

As far as the people here are concerned, you would only disappear for a few hours. You can leave tonight, and Izzy will return you before everyone wakes up.

'If I did this, do you believe I would become a better leader?' Basia asked.

I can't promise that. What I can promise is that you will learn more about yourself and be better able to decide whether or not leadership is for you.

Basia let go of Allan's hand, and sat up straight. 'I can't go back to my old life, and I guess it won't hurt to learn more about myself so I can carry on Allan's work. I will go with Izzy, if she will take me.'

Back in the barracks in Portsmouth, Bruno saw Lee and Izzy settled. Basia was spending some time with her parents before her father returned to the peace talks in the morning. Jumping up on a bed, Bruno settled down. It was time to report.

His stomach churned. What would he say to Beta? He had let him down by going off on his own. And by

now Theta would have had a chance to convince everyone her story was the only one to be believed. Surely she would have painted him as the bad guy for not following orders and bringing the world to the brink of extinction.

He sighed. He could not put it off any longer, especially as he knew Izzy would be contacting her handler as soon as she had the energy to do so. They had made sure their stories were aligned, and they were best presented close together if their version was to be given credence.

Beta? It's Sigma ready to report.

Sigma, I have been waiting for you.

Hold on, this was not his mentor. The voice was female for a starter, and sort of familiar.

Gamma, where is Beta? Bruno asked.

I am afraid Beta was reassigned—

Because of me? He had nothing to do with anything I did here. Bruno could not live with himself if Beta had been reprimanded for something he had done.

Oh, we know that. No, Beta's work with the Time Fixers during this crisis was exemplary, and he was promoted to the new role of Time Guardian Ambassador. He took up his post this morning. We felt it better he move sooner rather than later, lest he be tainted any further by your actions.

Oh, that's good, I think, Bruno said, a little uncertain. With his ability to consider all sides in a conflict, Beta would make a great ambassador. Bruno only wished he had stayed around long enough to say good-bye to him.

I am to be your mentor now, and I want you to come home so we can sort out this mess you created, Gamma instructed.

I am not finished here—

The timelines remerged, history is stable, and the world

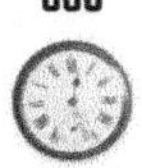

will go on for a good few more years yet. There is nothing more for you to do. In fact, I would say given recent events, the sooner we extract you from the situation the better.

Bruno tried again. *I want to at least stay for Allan's funeral.*

Oh yes, Allan. You know, we offered him a chance to ascend when he was at death's door. He told us given the constraints he saw you work under, he could do more if he was reincarnated. He turned us down. Can you believe it?

Bruno bared his teeth in a smile. Yes, he could well believe it. Events over the last week had him wondering what would have happened if he had made the same decision when he was asked to ascend all those years ago.

We had news he was reincarnated straight away, Gamma continued. *Born this morning to a family in Guildford. His five-year-old brother was overjoyed at the news. We believe his brother to be a reincarnation of Lee. History must love them for their souls to endure for so long.*

Hearing the news warmed Bruno's heart. With those two in the world, and Basia leading the reformers, there was real hope for the future.

So you will come right away.

What about taking Lee home? Bruno had to ask, as it was expected he would.

He was not going to explain to this dour soul that he had agreed to let Lee stay a while longer. Beta might have been persuaded, but he was sure she would not allow it.

The Time Fixers agreed Izzy can take him home before she returns.

Well, that sorted that problem. Now all he needed to do was decide if he cared enough about being a Time

Guardian to return and fight for his position.

Sigma?

All right. I will come. Just give me a couple of hours to say my good-byes and head back into the forest, he said.

Report to me immediately on your return!

The connection dropped.

Uncoiling himself from the bed, Bruno trotted over to Lee and gently snuffled by his ear. The boy reached out a hand to push him away. *This calls for something stronger,* Bruno thought as his tongue darted out and washed over Lee's face.

'Bruno. Yuck.'

Good, you're awake.

'I wasn't.'

Lee, I have been called back. I need to leave now.

'What? No! Bruno, you can't go! I thought you were staying too.'

So did I. But I have to go back and face the music. Do you still want to stay here if I am not around?

Lee screwed up his face, then rubbed his hands over it as if rubbing away the last vestiges of sleep. 'Are you heading to the forest, you know, to gather enough magic to make a portal?'

Yes, sort of.

Lee sat up and began pulling on his boots. 'I'll walk with you.'

As Lee sorted himself out, Bruno padded to the next bed. Izzy's eyes were already open, and she reached out a hand to scratch between his ears. It was disturbing how pleasant it felt.

'I heard. Don't worry, Bruno. I will take Basia with

me and look after her. And I will make sure I come back in time to pick up Lee if you don't get a chance.'

Thank you, Izzy. It has been a pleasure working with you. I hope we get a chance to do so again. Perhaps I will try to join you and Basia in Winchester.

'Back at you, Bruno-Trouble-Lala.' She laughed and gave him a final pat between the ears.

The cool breeze off the ocean ruffled Bruno's coat as he and Lee walked along the docks towards where the forest met the sea. They could not go out of the protectorate boundaries as the town was still circled by Portsdown soldiers, although there were fewer of them and they were less heavily armed.

Are you sure you don't want to go home? Bruno asked.

'I will be fine. Izzy told Basia they are going to leave tonight, and she will have her back before morning. If I change my mind, she will portal me back then. Otherwise, she will send someone to check on me once a week until I am ready to leave, just as you would have done.'

Sounds like you don't need me around anymore. Bruno hated sounding so sulky, but he was surprisingly hurt by how well everyone was doing without him.

'I don't need you, Bruno, but I wish you were able to stay. I thought we were going to make sure things stayed on the right path together. Can't you come back once you have had your telling off? I understand there is enough magic for you to be able to.'

Bruno sighed. *If I did that, the Council would find out you had stayed on, whereas if I don't return, then it will be a couple of months at least before they pick up a deviation in either timeline.*

'Doesn't that also apply to Izzy?'

Her people are a little more loose about these things, so she should be able to get away with leaving you here for a little longer, Bruno said.

'Oh. So this is really good-bye?' Lee's voice wavered.

I am afraid so, Bruno said, stopping at the boundary.

'I don't know what to say. I'm going to miss you, and thanks for bringing me,' Lee said, his words charged with emotion he could not articulate.

You're thanking me for almost getting you stranded or killed in an apocalyptic future? Bruno laughed.

'Life is never dull with you around. No, seriously. I will miss you. And good luck. I hope we get a chance to meet again. If not in this life, then in another.'

Bruno was swept into a hug, one he was strangely reluctant to leave.

Sigma, it's time.

I must go, Lee. I hope it goes well for you, both here and when you return home. I know whatever you choose to do, it will be the right thing for you, and for the world.

Bruno walked across the dock and down to the shore, not able to look back, tears streaming down his face. The water swirled around his feet and he leapt in.

Her hand could still feel the brush of Bruno's fur as she rolled onto her back and wiped the tears from her eyes. How had that dog managed to get under her skin? She had thought her shell strong enough to keep everyone out.

Izzy calmed her breathing and forced her sadness to the back of her mind. It would not do to speak with Cynthia when she was so emotionally charged. Just in case the Council denied her request to return to her original life so she could reconfirm her commitment to the Time Fixers, she wanted to have her thoughts and arguments marshalled.

Cynthia, hello?

Oh, Izzy, sorry, I wasn't expecting you quite so soon. Can you wait a moment?

The connection was muffled, and Izzy thought she heard her mentor saying, 'Sorry, Beta, I have to take this. Can you pop back later?'

Izzy?

Yes, I'm here, Izzy said.

I'm not sure whether to yell at you for your actions, or hug you for extending the timeline. Cynthia's voice sounded amused, so Izzy knew she was in the clear.

If I get to choose, I go for option number two.

Cynthia laughed. *Isolde, you are truly exasperating.*

There was a fondness in Cynthia's voice under all the scolding, bringing a smile to Izzy's face.

Is there even any point in getting you to report formally?

You mean, come back to headquarters? Izzy asked.

Yes.

Izzy grimaced. *I will if you ask me to, but you had sort of promised that after this mission....*

Cynthia's sigh was loud and heavy over the connection, transmitting the weight of her feelings. *They have agreed, Izzy. You can go. They have given you one month to extend your timeline from the point you decided in London to join us. You must return to London just before your death.*

It was all Izzy could do to stop herself from clapping her hands in glee.

Before then you must return Lee to his time, then you can return once you can gather enough magic to go back that far in the timeline, Cynthia instructed.

I will fulfil my promise to return Lee, Izzy confirmed, not feeling at all obliged to inform her mentor of the deal she had made with Bruno. That reminded her.

Cynthia, have you got something going with Bruno's mentor Beta?

Cheeky! Perhaps we should be following the "don't ask don't tell" rule here. Unless, of course, you want to go over some of your decisions over the last few days back here in headquarters.

Smiling, Izzy said, *Point taken.*

Off with you now. I have things to discuss with our new Ambassador. We will talk in about a month, although you can always contact me before then if you need to.

Bye, Cynthia.

Izzy was smiling as she swung her legs off the bed. Lee was coming back through the door as she pulled on her shoes.

'You ready to go?' he asked.

'Yep, I'm going home. Back to my dingy bedsit in London, to be precise.'

He wrinkled his nose. 'Couldn't you think of somewhere nicer to take Basia?'

Laughing, Izzy said, 'It's easier for boys, this time travel thing. How do you think Basia and I would do walking

around London in 1913 in these?' She swept her hand down, highlighting the combat trousers and shirt she wore.

'Oh, I guess not so well,' Lee said. 'You might gather some attention.'

'And not good attention as we will be right at the peak of the suffragette movement, when women who dressed like men were often brutally attacked.'

'I will miss you,' Lee said.

Izzy's heart melted a little more at his comment. She would miss him too. Dammit, what had happened to the shell of indifference she had built around herself? Impulsively she gathered Lee into a hug. 'I have to go. Stay safe. Basia and I will be back before you know it.'

She pushed him away, and Lee's lopsided smile was the last thing she saw as she rushed from the room.

Basia was waiting at the edge of the encampment where they had agreed to meet on the opposite side of the protectorate where Bruno had already made his portal. Izzy was pleased they had prepared for the worst when making their plans on the way back from Cosham.

Basia pulled her cardigan around herself. She looked nervous.

'Are you having second thoughts?' Izzy asked.

'Yes.' She shook her head. 'No. I'm just a little... scared.'

'That is perfectly normal. We all are, our first time.'

'Will it hurt?'

Smiling, Izzy took the girl's hand and led her into the forest. 'No, but it's not pleasant. I am told it helps if you hold your breath as you walk though.'

Quickly gathering her magic, Izzy swept her hand in a circle to create the portal. Without a backwards glance,

she pulled Basia close and stepped through before the girl could change her mind. As the portal closed behind her, all she could think was, *Wait for me Josephine, I'm coming home.*

Beta settled into the 1970s style sofa and accepted the drink Cynthia held out towards him.

'How are you settling in?' she asked.

He shifted slightly as she sat down, still not used to being in a true physical form.

'It is odd, but your people have made me welcome. Perhaps more so than Gerald will be finding back at Time Guardian headquarters.'

They laughed at the shared joke.

'So, Izzy has gone?'

'I believe so. We cut contact with our people taking the opportunity of recommitment. It allows them to fully emerge themselves in their old lives.'

'And I hear from Gamma that Sigma is back at headquarters, being hailed as a hero by all accounts.' Beta smiled, happy his protege was finally getting some recognition for his work.

'Alpha must be spitting tacks,' Cynthia laughed.

'Oh, he is, and that has made this whole adventure worthwhile—that, and... dare I say, meeting you.'

Cynthia's smile turned her face radiant. 'I feel the same.'

Taking his glass from his hand, she helped him to his

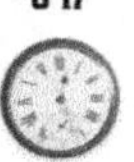

feet. 'Now we have a bit of time, I want to show you some of the highlights of my world.'

'You know, you don't need to convince me to stay. I am right where I want to be.'

'I know, Harold, but I can sweeten the deal for you.'

Hearing his name for the first time in hundreds of years brought a glow to Beta's heart, and where Cynthia led him next brought a blush to his cheeks. Yes, he was definitely right where he wanted to be.

ABOUT THE AUTHOR

Vivienne has been writing books since she was fifteen years old, but only friends and family were allowed to read them. Forced to give up work because of family commitments she was encouraged by friends and family to finally put some of her writing out there for others to read.

In the real world after leaving university with a BA in History and Politics she worked as a Personnel Officer, an Office Manager, a Project Manager, a DBA and IT Manager then as a Business and Data Analyst, adding an MSC in Information Systems along the way. In her world she continued to write.

Born in Invercargill (New Zealand), she has lived in; Dunedin (New Zealand), London (England), Petersfield (England) and currently lives with her husband and son, their dog Trouble and kitten Lola in Sydney (Australia).

For future releases and current news you can find Vivienne at **www.viviennelfraser.com.au** or on Facebook at **www.facebook.com/vivienneleefraser**

ACKNOWLEDGEMENTS

This book started in the bedroom of a fifteen your old girl in New Zealand, and finished in a converted bedroom during pandemic lockdown in Sydney Australia.

My first ever book, After the Holocaust, was only ever read by my sister and my best friend. My sister lost the story because of the poor spelling and grammar. Fortunately my friend said she enjoyed reading it.

Fast forward far too many years later and I was looking for a future plot line for my Time Guardian series, and I stumbled across my old book.

The old characters are still there, Alain, Barabel, Sigma, John Isolde, and of course Lee. I hope you enjoy their new incarnations and adventures.

As always, I had a lot of help brining this book together. My thanks go out to the team at Hot Tree editing. Honestly, without these people you would all be like my sister and become so frustrated you would not enjoy the story. Which leads me nicely into thank Sandy for catching all those last minute mistakes.

Thanks to Kim Last from Kila Designs has managed, once again, to produce an amazing cover. And many thanks to Jim and Sam who always support me by feeding me and keeping the house going so I can meet editing guidelines.

And thank you to you for reading my stories. I am always amazed and surprised when someone enjoys what I write.

www.ingramcontent.com/pod-product-compliance
Lightning Source LLC
Chambersburg PA
CBHW070047120726
47909CB00002B/309